DEADLY WEAPON

Adrianna was a very smart, very savvy woman. A cruder female might have thought of using a gun or a knife to dispose of Ruth's philandering, plagiarizing husband, Hal.

But Adrianna knew perfectly well what her most devastating weapon was.

Her sensational body, coupled with her sensual skill.

She was about to take that weapon out of its sheath to offer Hal an experience no cheating hubby could resist . . . or survive.

She only hoped the other wives could match the loving care with which she was living up to her part of

THE
AGREEMENT

THE
AGREEMENT

*Sarah L. McMurry
and Francesco P. Lualdi*

A SIGNET BOOK

NEW AMERICAN LIBRARY

PUBLISHER'S NOTE

This novel is a work of fiction. Names, characters, places, and incidents either are the product of the author's imagination or are used fictitiously, and any resemblance to actual persons, living or dead, events, or locales is entirely coincidental.

Copyright © 1986 by Sarah L. McMurry and Francesco P. Lualdi

SIGNET, SIGNET CLASSIC, MENTOR, ONYX, PLUME, MERIDIAN AND NAL BOOKS are published by New American Library, 1633 Broadway, New York, New York 10019

First Printing, September, 1986

1 2 3 4 5 6 7 8 9

PRINTED IN THE UNITED STATES OF AMERICA

For Jack, Jean, and Mike

—I—

1

John G. Farrelly, M.D., P.A., had no idea he would be dead within six minutes. He also had no idea his adored wife, Adrianna, had made the final arrangements.

Farrelly's single-engine Beechcraft Bonanza was slicing through the brittle night air at 170 knots. He'd just radioed the flight service station at Poughkeepsie and the controller advised him that the weather at Lake Placid was good, VFR, just a few scattered cumulus, unlimited visibility, and no precipitation.

A light snow had been falling when he'd hurriedly taken off from his private grass strip in Westchester County. But as he'd headed north over the state toward the Adirondack Mountains, the air had gradually cleared and the sky now glittered around him with cold, crisp stars. A classic night for flying, he thought. Too bad he wasn't in the mood to enjoy it.

Farrelly glanced impatiently at his watch. Only half an hour to go and he'd know what this was all about—why Adrianna had been so harshly insistent that he fly up to Lake Placid now, tonight. She'd phoned him at the hospital, interrupting his critical first session with a highly disturbed new patient, and asked that he come to see her right away. No, on second thought, he decided, she hadn't really asked him to come. She had demanded that he come. The stridency of her tone had left little doubt about that.

The doctor shook his head in bewilderment. Eight years married, they had been lovers for two years before that, and he still didn't understand his wife half the time. If he was going to be completely honest with himself, Farrelly acknowledged, he didn't understand Adrianna most of the time—a fine admission for a psychiatrist to make, and one his patients would hardly find comforting if they knew. Here he was, at sixty-five years of age, a respected doctor of psychiatry with enough degrees to fill a bowl of alphabet soup, and he couldn't figure out his own wife—his beautiful, charming, fascinating enigma of a wife.

Farrelly sighed so deeply it was almost a moan. He'd given Adrianna everything she wanted, or said she wanted. Didn't she live in an elegantly furnished Manhattan town house that was the envy of all her friends, spend her weekends entertaining at their lovely old renovated farmhouse in the country, drive an outrageously expensive white lacquered Jaguar XJ6, and carry a handbag full of credit cards that she exercised liberally in all the better shops? He'd never denied Adrianna anything. Including the sincerity and security of his single-minded devotion to her.

And if that weren't enough, Adrianna also shared his status as a prominent, successful Manhattan doctor from an old-line family, with a resultant social life that left him exhausted just to look at her complicated appointment calendar. Adrianna had certainly adjusted beautifully to his frequent and sometimes long absences from home, filling her time with lunches, teas, and committee meetings that occasionally lasted well into the late evening hours.

Yet there remained this persistent, nagging gap somewhere in their relationship, as though she wanted something else from him. Something Farrelly couldn't quite define, couldn't quite put his finger on. And obviously, couldn't supply. He'd given up years ago trying to figure out what that missing something was, but in moments such as this, when he was alone with nothing but his own thoughts for company, his mind invariably returned again and again to this elusive flaw in his marriage. Fifteen years ago when Norma died, leaving him a widower with an adolescent son, he'd thought the world had ended for him. Until he met Adrianna. Tall, beautiful, auburn-haired Adrianna. She'd twisted his heart into knots the first day he'd met her at the television station where she worked as an assistant producer, and she could still do so today. In fact, today she had.

Farrelly's eyes scanned the instrument panel: altitude 6,500 feet, oil pressure, fuel pressure all were in the green. This completely unexpected flight was going well, although he knew he should have taken time to do the preflight check properly. But he'd been in too much of a hurry to get off the ground before the weather closed in.

He was tired now. Very tired. He'd had a long day, made longer by that unnerving call from Adrianna. Of course she phoned him at the office occasionally, but never at the hospital and certainly never to demand in such strong terms that he cancel the remainder of his appointments and come to her immediately. Tomorrow would be too late, she insisted mysteriously. He had to come to Lake Placid now. Tonight. "You have your own plane," she had reminded him harshly when he started to object. "Use it!"

Adrianna told him twice—no, three times—that their whole future together depended on his caring enough to do as she requested without asking any more questions. She wouldn't, or couldn't, explain any further on the telephone.

Lake Placid—that was one of the things Farrelly found most difficult to understand about all of this. Why had Adrianna gone to Lake Placid in the first place? They'd visited the winter resort area together about five years ago and Adrianna had pronounced herself bored to tears. She didn't ski and she didn't ice-skate, which hadn't left a great deal to occupy her time except to sit in front of the hotel fireplace soaking up hot spiced wines while he explored the slopes. Two days of that and Adrianna was ready to pack her bags and go back to New York.

It wasn't that Farrelly begrudged Adrianna a short vacation alone from the city, but if she'd held off only two or three more weeks he might have been able to juggle his schedule around enough to accompany her. If not for an entire week, then at least for a long weekend. But Adrianna could be incredibly stubborn, that much he knew about his wife, and now her stubbornness apparently had gotten her into some kind of trouble. Apparently extremely serious trouble. All sorts of hideous possibilities churned through Farrelly's mind, from outright kidnapping for ransom to a tortuous revenge plotted by a former patient. Whatever the scenario, Adrianna was obviously in great danger.

All thoughts of Adrianna abruptly vanished as Farrelly felt the plane's engine skip a beat. Tensely he waited for the almost imperceptible roughness to come again, and when it didn't he decided it must have been his imagination. Flying over the mountains at night in a single-engine aircraft was something experienced pilots tried to avoid, and Farrelly was no exception. But Adrianna was his wife, his life, and he had to reach her, had to help her.

Without warning the engine missed again and again, the whole plane shaking and bucking in protest. A brief glance at the instruments showed that his air speed was dropping rapidly.

Then the engine quit altogether.

As he had been taught, Farrelly quickly trimmed the plane for best glide speed, and with deliberate thoroughness went through the engine-out procedure: master switch on, switch over to auxiliary fuel tanks, fuel pump on, full rich mixture on. Only then did he try to restart the engine.

Nothing.

He was at 4,500 feet now and losing altitude at 850 feet per minute. That, he calculated, gave him about five minutes to get the engine restarted and find a place to land. Below him Farrelly could see nothing but the black humps of mountains. No cities, no towns, no lights. Nothing but blackness. He switched his radio to the emergency frequency, 121.5 mhz, and made a concerted effort to keep the panic out of his voice. "Mayday, Mayday," Farrelly calmly called. "Bonanza 5530-Quebec, calling Mayday."

There was an instantaneous acknowledgment from the Albany controller.

As Farrelly pressed the microphone switch to report his position, the silent, powerless plane slammed into the side of White Face Mountain. The explosion was so great that a forest ranger twenty miles away saw the orange halo of flames, vivid against the black midnight sky.

And in Lake Placid, Adrianna Cummings Farrelly waited serenely in bed for the official announcement that she was now a thirty-nine-year-old widow. A very, very wealthy widow. Whether that would make any difference in the performance of the young and virile stranger asleep beside her interested her not in the slightest.

2

He never knew it, of course, but the eminent Dr. John Farrelly actually began dying on an overcast afternoon roughly six weeks earlier, the day Adrianna Farrelly returned home sooner than expected from a disappointing shopping expedition to Bloomingdale's and found John, two dark-suited lawyers, and the chancellor of the United Presbyterian Medical School encamped in her living room surrounded by untidy piles of legal-looking documents.

"You're a lucky woman to be married to such a fine man." Chancellor Conrad B. Williams III beamed at Adrianna as she neatly draped her coat and gloves across the delicate antique side chair near the door. "Imagine the honor, the prestige! You must be very, very proud of him, my dear."

Adrianna smiled politely at the flushed chancellor and glided across the thick, sculptured carpet to greet her husband, her slim, elegant figure outlined in clinging folds of russet wool crepe. She lightly brushed her lips across Farrelly's cheek, the touch of his skin on hers transmitting an undercurrent of suppressed excitement in her normally sedate and unflappable husband.

"What a lovely surprise—to be surrounded by so many charming gentlemen," Adrianna said, bestowing a personal smile on each of the other three men. "John, you really ought to have told me you were holding a meeting here today. Certainly we could have done more for our guests than this!" She indicated the large

14

silver tray on the sofa table bearing the remnants of sandwiches and an untouched plate of petits fours.

"I don't think anyone minded, darling. Actually we were going to lunch at the club, but I'd forgotten they were having some special affair there this afternoon, and this was the only quiet place I could think of on the spur of the moment. Too distracting at the office or the hospital, I'm afraid."

Adrianna idly picked up one of the long legal-size sheets of paper lying on the coffee table. "May I?" She glanced questioningly around the room. "This isn't one of those hush-hush medical cases wives aren't supposed to see, is it? About a patient?"

"No, no, nothing like that. Go ahead and read it if you like." Farrelly watched with happy impatience as she scanned the closely typed lines of the document. "I hope you can make sense of all that legal mishmash, darling. I certainly can't—but then, that's what these gentlemen are for. To explain it to me, in plain English."

Williams, she noticed with a vague sense of unease, was watching her almost as eagerly as Farrelly, while the two attorneys remained silent and inscrutable. Adrianna returned the paper to its place on the table with a helpless little shrug. "I'm afraid I can't make much of it either, although it looks a little like part of a trust agreement. Is it?"

"Not exactly, but you're close, darling. It was to be a surprise." Farrelly laughed gently. "A wonderful surprise. I'm only sorry you came home before we had a chance to finish going over all the details. I wanted to wait until everything was in final form and then show it to you as a completed package." Farrelly put his arm around her shoulder and squeezed. "I know you're going to be thrilled about this, darling, as much as I am."

Adrianna smiled indulgently at her husband and settled down on one of the antique white brocade love seats placed at right angles to the fireplace. "I'm sure I will, John. As soon as you tell me what this is about." She glanced again at the two lawyers standing stiffly by the bay window overlooking the rear garden. They seemed to be avoiding her eyes, waiting perhaps for her to graciously withdraw so they could get on with their business. If that was the case, Adrianna thought with a certain amount of satisfaction, they were in for a long wait. She had no intention of withdrawing until she knew precisely what John Farrelly was up to.

Farrelly moved in front of the massive hand-carved green marble mantelpiece, hands clasped loosely behind his back as he gazed fondly down at her. "Well, I guess the cat's out of the bag now, as they say. No point in not letting you in on it, is there?" He radiated benevolent good cheer as he beamed at the other three men in the room.

"I don't know when I've ever been so excited," the chancellor chirped, rubbing his palms together. "I mean, to be in on the ground floor of the John G. Farrelly Center for Psychiatric Research!"

"Now, Conrad, I wanted to tell Adrianna myself, and you've gone and spoiled the surprise."

Williams, suitably chastened, retreated to the bay window to stand with the lawyers. "Sorry, John, truly sorry. Of course you do."

"The John G. Farrelly Center for Psychiatric Research?" Adrianna asked, puzzled. "I never heard of this before." A slight shiver pricked the hair on the back of her neck, a premonition that she wasn't going to like what John was about to disclose.

Farrelly shuffled through a pile of papers on the coffee table until he found a rolled-up architectural sketch depicting the exterior of a building. "Here it is. Yes. Now, look at this, Adrianna, and tell me what you think. Outstanding, isn't it?"

Adrianna stared blankly at the drawing he'd handed her. "I agree, it's a very handsome building, John. But I'm afraid I still don't understand what this has to do with all these papers." She waved her hand toward the table, indicating the disorganized clutter that threatened to spill over onto the floor.

One of the lawyers coughed politely and stepped away from the group clustered at the window. "George Edmonds, Mrs. Farrelly, of Burke, Edmonds, and

Petrelli. Perhaps the good doctor would like me to fill you in?"

"Good idea, George," Farrelly boomed with relief. "Better coming from you, I think. Clearer, anyway. This legal claptrap gets so involved at times."

Adrianna automatically sized up George Edmonds' bedroom potential without consciously realizing she was doing it. Basic WASP background, enough money to buy into a decent law firm, a bit on the stuffy side. Probably had a wife and two-point-three children up in Connecticut, would never intentionally fool around with a female client but wasn't averse to an extramarital encounter or two, as long as it didn't interfere with business or the family. Edmonds was not particularly handsome, nor did he present much of a challenge, but as Adrianna acknowledged to herself, a casual night spent together sometime might come in handy as extra insurance if she ever needed him professionally.

"If you please, Mr. Edmonds. I would certainly appreciate an explanation from someone. This is all very confusing."

Edmonds planted himself next to Farrelly in front of the fireplace and waved an arm at the overflowing coffee table. "These papers, Mrs. Farrelly, represent the cornerstone of a great foundation. A very special foundation which your husband is setting up to endow a new and unique research center at United Presbyterian."

"I had planned on doing all this in my will," Farrelly broke in, "but George here convinced me that at sixty-five I'm still a young man with quite a few years left. And I do so want to see this research center set up and functioning properly. And the best way to accomplish that is to set up the foundation now while I'm still alive and kicking."

Adrianna shifted her gaze back to Edmonds, silently encouraging him to continue.

"Er, well, yes. As I was saying, the board of trustees estimates it will cost approximately twenty million dollars to build and equip the research center you see in that drawing. Your husband has generously offered to match any and all donations up to eight million dollars, with a further two million dollars earmarked for initial operating expenses."

"Ten million dollars?" Adrianna could feel the blood draining from her face. "You did mean ten million dollars in total, didn't you, Mr. Edmonds? Gracious, John, that's an enormous sum of money!"

"I told you she'd be surprised!" Farrelly laughed heartily. "Isn't this a wonderful idea, darling? It's been my dream, my goal, for years. And it's finally going to become a reality! I can hardly believe it."

"Neither can I," Adrianna echoed softly.

Adrianna had no precise knowledge of John's worth, and doubted that John did either, but even so, ten million dollars represented an extraordinary amount of money to give away merely to assuage the old fool's ego. Even without seeing a current balance sheet, Adrianna was keenly aware that the sum of ten million dollars had to constitute a very substantial portion of her husband's total estate. Adrianna felt herself growing increasingly furious at the revelation that John could blithely throw away so much of his money, with its inevitable reduction in her own eagerly anticipated inheritance, without so much as a word to her first about his intentions. He had to rely on strangers to break the news to her. Strangers who couldn't possibly imagine what it was like to endure eight years of marriage to a boring, depressing old fossil who was obviously beginning to go senile!

Adrianna was able to conceal her rising distress, however, and when she spoke again, her words conveyed a deceptive disinterest. "When will this research center be built, John?"

Williams trotted over to flank Farrelly on the other side. "If all goes smoothly with the legal end"—Williams blinked toward Edmonds—"we hope to break ground in the spring of next year. Perhaps around April. The college already owns the land, so it's simply a matter of clearing away the old building and putting up the new."

"I see."

"Of course it will take several months to set up the foundation, hire staff, and so on," Edmonds chimed in. "And there are a few administrative odds and ends we have to work out first—stock transfers, conversion of assets, that sort of thing—but I should think we ought to have the necessary papers in final form within eight to twelve weeks. Then John will have to draw up a new will and possibly revise some of his testamentary trusts—"

"Let's not bore Adrianna with all these trivial details," Farrelly interrupted cheerfully. "It's the big picture that matters, and I know she's just as happy about all this as I am, aren't you, darling?"

"Of course, John," she lied smoothly. "It sounds wonderful. Truly wonderful. You gentlemen must forgive me if my enthusiasm is somewhat muted, but I'm afraid you've completely overwhelmed me. A project as ambitious as this one will require some time to absorb."

Williams, Edmonds, and the still unintroduced junior lawyer departed shortly afterward, each shaking her hand solemnly and pronouncing John Farrelly one of the greatest humanitarian physicians since Albert Schweitzer. How fortunate she was, they told her over and over again, to be married to such a generous, philanthropic man.

"Fortunate," however, was hardly the word Adrianna would have chosen at that moment to describe her feelings about either John or his new project. "Betrayed" was more accurate, she thought as she quickly climbed the winding staircase to her third-floor bedroom to dress for dinner. Adrianna pushed open the door and viciously kicked off her shoes, giving brief vent to her shock and rage. Eight to twelve weeks wouldn't give her much time to avert this disaster. In order to do that, she'd have to remind herself constantly to remain calm and rational.

Fortunate. The word rang in Adrianna's ears as she restlessly prowled the bedroom so sensuously decorated in soft, silken hues of cream and apricot. Perhaps those men were right, she concluded. Perhaps she was fortunate in a way. After all, if she hadn't returned home early and walked in on that conference, she wouldn't have known about John's plans for the research center until it was much too late to stop them.

There was no question in Adrianna's mind that she would have to stop those plans from going any further. She simply could not allow John Farrelly to throw away such a large proportion of his estate on mental misfits. A million or two might have been marginally acceptable, but ten million dollars? Never! That money was the only reason she'd married the stuffy prig in the first place, and certainly the only reason she stayed married to him. And she'd given him good value for his money, hadn't she? Playing the devoted, attentive wife to perfection for eight long, soul-destroying years.

Adrianna unbuttoned the wool crepe dress and let it slide to the floor, where it settled into a reddish-brown stain against the soft cream of the thick carpeting. Yes, she had given John good value for his money, she decided emphatically, simply by graciously enduring eight years of the most tedious evenings imaginable surrounded by his boring cronies, none of them younger than sixty, feigning ecstasy on those increasingly rare occasions when he approached her for lovemaking, and listening with seemingly rapt attentiveness as he expounded ad nauseam on his views of life, philosophy, and, above all, psychiatry—psychiatry as envisioned by Sigmund Freud. Not a word, or a thought, ever crossed John Farrelly's lips about art, music, the theater, or anything else that might even remotely interest Adrianna.

Over the past eight years Adrianna calculated she'd heard more about Sigmund Freud and his theories than most doctoral candidates. As far as she was concerned, Freud was a fraud, particularly when it came to deducing the inner workings of the female mind. And so was John Farrelly for swallowing all that inane drivel which he then spouted as though he'd developed the theories himself during the course of his own professional experience.

And now John was going to devote the remainder of his life, and a sizable portion of his personal fortune, to perpetuating this idiocy? Not if Adrianna could help it, he wouldn't. That money was hers by right. She had earned every dollar of it, and she was going to keep it.

Adrianna sat down at the mirrored dressing table and stared at her flawless reflection. The only question was, how?

3

Adrianna was exhausted and more than a bit on edge when she walked into the crowded restaurant at lunchtime the following day. She'd been through a ghastly night, lying wide-awake in that huge bed listening to John Farrelly snore contentedly, at peace with himself and the world. There had been moments, during the bleakest hours of the early morning, when Adrianna had had to fight the irrational impulse to go down to the kitchen, find a butcher knife, and plunge it deep into her slumbering husband for the sheer satisfaction of watching him slowly bleed to death. Unfortunately, wives who did such things to their husbands usually wound up in jail. Or a padded cell. Neither alternative appealed to Adrianna.

"Your table is ready, Madame Farrelly."

"What? Oh yes, thank you, Bruno. Are the others here yet?"

"No, madame, you are the first. As usual."

Bruno pulled out the table so Adrianna could slide gracefully into the far corner of the banquette, her seat of preference from which she could watch the entrance without being in full view of the lunchtime clientele. Not that it mattered a great deal where she sat when she was lunching with her women friends, but certain habits, once formed, were difficult to break, and she always felt more comfortable secluded in a corner.

Leonardo's was one of the more popular restaurants in midtown Manhattan, particularly with the literary set on expense accounts. That ensured a reasonably good chance of spotting a slightly inebriated celebrity author or two holding forth at great length about the last book, or the book that was about to come out. These authors, however, were not the sole reason Adrianna and her friends returned to Leonardo's month after month, although they did provide interesting topics for speculation and gossip when their usual subjects began to bore. Leonardo's food was undeniably good if somewhat overpriced, the service attentive, and the decor tastefully comfortable. Of prime importance to the women, however, was Leonardo's powder room. It was absolutely immaculate.

"Would Madame care for something from the bar?"

Adrianna pulled a cigarette from the chased-silver case in her handbag and lit it casually, as though she were giving the question careful consideration. It was, in fact, a ritual of sorts they had established: Bruno would straighten the place settings while Adrianna lit the cigarette and scanned the room before rejecting the suggestion.

Bruno was turning away in anticipation of Adrianna's dismissal when she unexpectedly motioned him back. "I think I will have a drink, after all," she announced. "Something light, though—perhaps a daiquiri. A frozen daiquiri, if you please, Bruno. Not too sweet."

Daiquiris were terribly out of fashion, but Adrianna was never influenced by what others decreed to be in or out of fashion, and what she wanted now was the astringent freshness of something tart, something that would make the lining of her mouth pucker. Perhaps it was the cigarettes—the chain of cigarettes she'd smoked since John had unveiled his little "surprise" the previous afternoon. Naturally John was forever nagging at her to quit smoking, if not for her own health then at least for his professional image as a physician, but she enjoyed smoking, and no amount of harping about it was going to make her quit, image or no image.

"Adrianna! Sorry to keep you waiting again. Isn't Millie here yet?"

Ruth Larkin scooted swiftly into the banquette at Adrianna's left, shrugging off her coat as she moved along, bony arms scraping along the edge of the table. "I really don't know why that idiot coatroom girl won't take fur at lunch. Such a bother to have to sit with it, but it's too cold out there for my old cloth."

Adrianna edged over to allow Ruth more room on the seat for her coat. "You should have asked Bruno to take it for you," she pointed out. "The girl wouldn't dare not accept a coat from Bruno."

"I know, I know. All these years in New York and I still let people like that little twit intimidate me. Sometimes I wish I could be more outspoken—more forceful. More like you, Addy."

Adrianna flinched at the nickname. Ruth and Millie, who was yet to arrive, were the only two people who dared to use that despised diminutive to her face. Outside of her father, of course, but he was not among the scant handful of people she truly cared about.

"How many times have I told you that you're never going to get anywhere until you start asserting yourself, Ruthie?" she said harshly, and just a shade too loudly. "You cannot, I repeat cannot, go around letting coatroom girls, headwaiters, and cabdrivers walk all over you like a human doormat. It simply drives me up the wall when you allow people to take advantage of you! It always has, and always will!"

Adrianna stubbed out the cigarette in the minuscule ashtray while Ruth stared silently at the tabletop, fingers plucking at the hem of her napkin.

"Oh, honey, I'm sorry. I shouldn't have shouted at you like that." Adrianna reached over and lightly touched Ruth's arm. "It's not your fault I'm in an absolutely foul mood today. Forgive me?"

Ruth gazed at her thoughtfully. "There's nothing to forgive. You're quite right, I am a human doormat. That seems to be the way I'm made, whether I like it or not." She paused while she carefully refolded the napkin and placed it neatly beside the salad fork. "But really, Addy, raising your voice like that in a public restaurant, particularly over something as silly as a coatcheck girl? How very unlike you! Is something wrong?"

Adrianna flashed one of her most engaging smiles.

The smile, however, did not extend to her eyes. "Don't pay any attention to me, Ruthie. It's nothing I can't handle," she answered brightly. "Why don't we go ahead and order for Millie, since she's so late. We both know what she likes to have."

"For heaven's sake, Addy. This is me, remember? I knew you long before you ever married the great and famous Dr. John Farrelly and joined the international jet set." Ruth was still watching her friend closely, and caught Adrianna's almost imperceptible reaction to her husband's name. "It's John, isn't it?" she said simply, more as a statement than a question.

Adrianna sighed deeply and leaned back against the padded leather banquette. "That great and famous doctor as you call him—psychiatrist to some of the most important people in New York, Washington, and Hollywood, confidant to presidents, kings, and prime ministers—is nothing but a self-serving, sanctimonious son of a bitch."

Ruth started to laugh, but something in the expression on Adrianna's face stopped her cold. "I haven't seen you this angry with John in years. Not since he gave back the ruby necklace to that Saudi Arabian prince. What's he done this time? Given back an oil tanker?"

Millie Phillips flopped breathlessly into the seat at Adrianna's right, her tousled mop of blond hair glinting with half-melted snowflakes and her silk jacquard blouse slightly askew. "Missed the express train again," she panted by way of explanation. "Why the long faces on you two? Somebody fire Bruno?"

"Adrianna was about to tell me why she thinks John is a self-serving, sanctimonious son of a bitch."

"So why should John be any different from the rest of them?" Millie asked quizzically. "I haven't met a man yet who wasn't. Especially the two I had the misfortune to marry."

"Oh really, Millie. Sometimes you're impossible!"

"I mean it, Ruth. I can't name a single man I've ever known who wasn't totally self-absorbed and self-centered. When you cut through all the talk and get to the bottom line, men only want some obedient little drudge they can look down on and kick around. When they're not too busy screwing us, that is. Literally and figuratively."

"My God," Ruth said, genuinely shocked by Millie's vehemence. "I know you've had some rough times with the men in your life, but you sound as though you hate all men! You can't mean that."

"Who says I can't?" Millie asked flatly.

The women were silent as their waiter set down a carafe of house wine, deftly retrieved Adrianna's half-finished daiquiri from across the table, and quickly departed.

"Well, Millie," Adrianna said, indicating by her tone that the subject of men in general and John in particular was now closed, "what's going on with your lovely little girls? Are they still having trouble in school this semester?"

Millie tugged at the clump of curls cascading over her forehead, the bright red of her nail polish iridescent against the paleness of her skin.

"Millie?"

Mildred Wozackie Phillips raised her saucer blue eyes and arranged her features in a half-smile. "Sorry, my mind was wandering, Addy. You were asking about the girls? They're fine, just fine. Evie's full-blown into adolescence now. Since she turned thirteen last month she's spent every free minute locked in her room with the stereo going full blast. Sometimes I can't hear myself think in that house." Millie uttered a funny, hollow little laugh. "Thank goodness I have four more years of sanity left before Deedee reaches that stage! Evie claims the music helps her concentrate on her homework—although you certainly couldn't tell by looking at her grades. They're awful. Just awful."

"I bet Evelyn is turning into a little beauty. She was always such a pretty child," Ruth said with a touch of wistfulness. "Seems like ages since I've seen either one of them. At least a couple of years. I probably wouldn't recognize them anymore!"

"Evie is pretty enough, I suppose," Millie agreed,

"but the one I worry about is Deedee. I look at her sometimes and wonder how I could have produced something with so much promise of true beauty. Natural beauty. Not like me at all. Whatever I have going for me is the end product of fifteen cosmetic factories—and your help, Ruth. Lord, the money I spend now on night creams alone!"

Millie nodded at Adrianna. "Deedee reminds me of you, sometimes. You're a natural beauty too, Addy. You don't get that gorgeous hair color out of a bottle, or lie smothered in mud packs every week to keep the wrinkles at bay."

Adrianna laughed, a rich, melodious laugh of amusement. "If you only knew the half of it, Millie! It takes a lot of hard work and money to achieve this so-called 'natural' beauty. And it gets harder every year. Just ask my hairdresser!"

"None of us is getting any younger," Ruth pointed out matter-of-factly. "Maybe we should learn to accept entering our forties gracefully. We may as well—there's nothing we can do about it."

"Speak for yourself, old girl," Adrianna said, laughter still echoing in her voice. "I intend to stay young forever! When you two are old, senile, and bedridden, I'll be dancing through the days and making love through the nights!"

"I bet you will, too," Millie agreed. "Where's that waiter with our lunch? You did order for me, didn't you? If he doesn't come soon we're going to be late for the theater. And you know how I hate walking down that aisle with everyone staring and whispering about how rude it is to come in after the curtain's gone up."

The light dusting of snow that had feathered out over the city during the morning was gone by the time the three women emerged from Leonardo's, but the wind had picked up in short, sharp gasps that whipped at their clothes and blew soot in their eyes. It was early in the season yet for the sort of heavy snows that turned city side streets into long, unbroken blankets of white and snarled commuter traffic for days on end, but the leaden clouds hanging low overhead carried forbidding reminders of storms not so long past and of those soon to come.

The women scurried along the pavement, dodging afternoon shoppers and sightseers as they hugged the skimpy shelter afforded by the buildings. They agreed without exchanging a word that it would be next to a miracle to find a free cab in this kind of weather, particularly a cab with a driver willing to take them just the few short blocks over to Broadway.

"Are those picket signs?" Ruth groaned as they rounded the corner near the theater. "At our theater?"

Millie pushed away the ends of the head scarf flapping across her face and squinted through the wind and debris. "Looks like it from here. I wonder who's on strike? They wouldn't dare walk out on matinee day, would they?"

They would and they had, the picketers marching in a loose, ragged circle under the marquee, those carrying signs using them as shields against the wind. A small knot of people huddled around the box office, with an occasional angry voice rising above the wind and street noise.

Adrianna motioned to the other two women to find what shelter they could in the doorway while she edged her way into the group around the box office. They lost sight of her for a few minutes; then a shifting of bodies revealed a brief glimpse of her tall, elegant form pressed close to the glass as she spoke with the woman inside. After what seemed like an eternity to Ruth and Millie, Adrianna emerged from the crush.

"Canceled," she announced grimly. "All performances canceled until further notice. Apparently Equity called some sort of last-minute strike—I didn't get all the details."

"They can't cancel on us," Millie protested. "We've got tickets!"

"We had tickets," Adrianna corrected her. "What we have now are refunds."

"What are we going to do now?" Millie demanded, her voice rising in a tentative wail of disappointment. "I don't want to go home so soon. Everything's arranged for the girls to stay with friends after school, only Ed will be there, and—"

"None of us want to go home," Adrianna broke in soothingly, taking both women by the arm. "So we won't. We're not that far from the Algonquin—we'll run over there for Irish coffees, all right? It'll do us good to have a nice long chat."

Adrianna, however, was the only one who actually ordered an Irish coffee at the Algonquin. Millie, with her insatiable sweet tooth, settled for a sickly sweet plum brandy, while Ruth, who normally avoided anything stronger than wine, amazed them both by asking for a vodka martini—a double vodka martini.

They were sitting in a quiet corner of the lobby, letting the warmth soak back into their bodies, when a tall, angular woman dressed in sensible tweeds passed close to their table. Millie, who'd been quietly gazing off into space, suddenly sat up.

"Say, Ruthie, isn't that woman carrying a copy of *Twin Lives*?" she asked excitedly. "Look, there on the back. I can see your husband's picture!"

Ruth drained her glass and signaled for a refill.

"Aren't you even the tiniest bit excited to see some stranger carrying Hal's book around?" Millie demanded. "Good Lord, if Ed had written a book that made the *New York Times*'s bestseller list, I'd be out there peddling copies on the street corner!"

"No you wouldn't," Ruth slurred, her words fuzzy with vodka.

"Of course I would, if it helped boost sales and brought in more royalties," Millie insisted.

"No you wouldn't!" Ruth repeated, her voice rising sharply. "You don't understand anything, Millie, so why don't you just leave me the hell alone?"

Millie flushed a deep, angry crimson. "Don't you dare use that tone of voice to me, Ruth Ellen Larkin," she shot back.

"All right, you two," Adrianna intervened firmly. "Remember where you are, please."

Ruth sagged back in her chair, shoulders hunched as

she sobbed openly, loudly, black streaks of mascara furrowing her gaunt cheeks. "I hate that man. I hate him! Mother of God, how I wish I had the courage to kill him for what he did to me!"

Adrianna and Millie exchanged looks of baffled astonishment. These three women had been friends for nearly twenty years, since their time in college together. Although the days of sharing their most intimate secrets had long since passed, each thought she had a fairly good idea of what was happening in the others' lives. But neither Adrianna nor Millie was prepared for Ruth's impassioned outburst.

It occurred to Adrianna, as she and Millie anxiously sought to quiet Ruth, that perhaps the three of them had drifted farther apart than she had realized. These more or less regular monthly lunch-and-theater sessions were something they had kept separate from their normal day-to-day lives, separate from their own families. They hadn't done so intentionally, but had rather permitted the pattern to evolve naturally. The three of them were married to three very different types of men who would have found little in common with each other, and socializing as a group would have been awkward at best. In fact, Adrianna and Ruth had never even met Millie's second husband, Ed Phillips, although they'd been married nearly five years. Nor did Ruth and Millie have more than a vague, nodding acquaintance with John Farrelly.

As for Hal Larkin, the "new" author who was garnering so much literary attention with his first novel, *Twin Lives*, he was an acquaintance both Adrianna and Millie had agreed they would prefer not to renew. They'd met Ruth's husband once in the early years of their marriage, when she'd invited them to one of those supposedly chic little cocktail parties thrown by World Fashion Magazine Group, where Larkin was, at the time, a senior editor. Not only was the party a bore, but Hal Larkin turned out to be a first-class boor himself—one of those men who apparently believe women should feel honored to have him intimately fondle the most private portions of their anatomy in public.

The first time Adrianna had felt his hand slide farther down her back than was appropriate, she had simply moved away, putting the starry-eyed Ruth between Hal and herself. The second time it happened she did a graceful little sidestep, bringing the sharp point of her high heel down on the top of Larkin's foot, using the full force of her weight to nearly pierce the soft leather of his expensive shoe. Adrianna offered profuse apologies for her clumsiness, of course, but noted with satisfaction that Larkin hadn't tried to touch her again for the remainder of the party.

Adrianna never could understand what Ruth saw in that man, or by the same token, what Hal Larkin had seen in Ruth, at least enough to marry her. Ruth was no "natural" beauty according to Millie's definition, although she had learned how to choose the most flattering clothes and makeup during her stint at World Fashion Magazine Group, where she'd met and fallen in love with Hal. Ruth was of medium height, with a tendency toward slenderness that, at the moment, bordered on the skeletal. Her short-cropped dark hair, which had been flattering six months ago, now accentuated her fleshless face, giving it the startling starkness of a death mask.

Adrianna vaguely recalled that both she and Millie had commented several times in recent months on Ruth's steady weight loss, never dreaming that it was due to anything more than regular dieting to maintain a fashionably slim figure. But then, they hadn't really questioned her about it, had they? And Ruth hadn't volunteered any explanation, either. Until now.

4

The town house was still and quiet as the heavy door thudded closed behind Adrianna and Ruth, blocking out the sight and most of the sounds of the early-evening traffic churning through the thin slush less than twenty-five feet away. Entering the house after it had been left vacant for even a few hours made Adrianna uneasy, as though the narrow five-story building could somehow resent being abandoned, even temporarily, by its human occupants.

It was an odd notion, she knew, and one that John, no doubt, would tell her arose from some deeply repressed fear that she might be abandoned also. But then, John always had some pat explanation for everything she said, usually couched in Freudian psychological jargon that grated on her nerves. Adrianna often wondered why John could not accept even the most innocuous statement for what it was without trying to unearth some deeper, hidden meaning. She'd lost track of the times he'd driven her to total exasperation with the response, "What you really mean to say is . . ."

Fortunately, though, John had flown to Washington that morning and wasn't scheduled to be back until late the next evening. He never told her whom he was going to see on these frequent secretive consultations, but she could usually figure it out, based on a word dropped here, a phone conversation overheard there. This time, she gathered, the patient was the teenage daughter of someone very high up in the administration who had managed to scramble her brains with a combi-

nation of cocaine, Quaaludes, and alcohol. A not unusual situation, Adrianna had learned, for those who
walked in the shadowy corridors of power.

Adrianna helped Ruth off with her coat and hung it
up to dry on the ornate rack near the door. They'd left
the Algonquin shortly after Ruth lost all four of her
double vodka martinis in the ladies' room, and now she
leaned limp and ashen against the antique hand-painted
wallpaper in Adrianna's foyer.

The hesitant sprinkling of snow had returned while
they were still inside the hotel, so Adrianna had been
relieved when the doorman ushered the three women
directly into a cab that was discharging passengers at
the entrance. Even though it was out of the way, they
had dropped Millie off at the station to catch the train
back to White Plains before she and Ruth proceeded to
the town house. Adrianna briefly wondered during the
ride whether she was doing the right thing by taking
Ruth home with her for the night, but Ruth was obviously in no shape to be left on her own. Or worse, to be
left on her own with Hal Larkin. Whatever he'd done
must have been incredibly cruel to reduce Ruth to this
state.

The housekeeper, familiar with Adrianna's penchant
for coffee at all hours, had left a freshly brewed batch in
the coffee maker before she'd gone home for the night.
The bright red light winked cheerfully in the dusky
gloom of the large kitchen as Adrianna skillfully guided
Ruth into a chair and brought over a couple of cups.

"Could you manage a piece of toast? A cup of tea,
perhaps? Something to settle your stomach?"

"Please, no, Addy." Ruth shifted uncomfortably. "Just
coffee. I don't think I could keep anything else down."
A sheepish little smile tugged at the corners of her
bloodless lips. "I must have created quite a scene with
all those drinks. I wouldn't blame you and Millie for
being disgusted with me."

"No one's disgusted with you, Ruthie, just terribly
worried. Double vodka martinis are hardly your style,
are they?"

Adrianna switched on the overhead fluorescent lights

and was reassured to see that Ruth had gotten herself under control again. A tenuous control, perhaps, but certainly better than a short while ago.

"Are you ready to tell me what this is all about?"

Ruth sipped cautiously at the hot coffee, then put the cup down carefully, her eyes filled with a pathetic sadness. "I suppose I ought to, after causing you so much embarrassment this afternoon." She stared silently into the cup for a few minutes, as though trying to make up her mind where to begin. When she spoke, it was with a desolation that Adrianna had never before heard from Ruth.

"You and Millie are the only two friends I have, Addy. Real friends, anyway. The only friends I can talk to."

"Then talk to me," Adrianna said softly. "Tell me what's happened to you."

"It's the book."

"The book? Hal's book?"

"My book." Ruth's voice was strained, hoarse. "I wrote it. Put nearly four years of my life, my heart, my soul into it. It was my creation—my child. Not his."

Ruth's anguish was so acute that it was almost a tangible substance hanging over the table. Adrianna thought that if she put out her hand, she might even be able to touch it.

"Then why is Hal listed as the author?"

"Because he stole it from me."

"He stole it? And you let him?"

Ruth nodded dumbly, tears welling in her eyes.

Adrianna choked back the biting words that were on the verge of spilling out, sensing that the last thing Ruth could tolerate at that point was another "doormat" lecture. Instead, Adrianna poured a second cup of coffee, lighted a cigarette, and fixed a calm gaze on Ruth's haunted eyes. "All right, Ruthie, old girl. Begin at the beginning and tell me how you got into this mess."

Ruth straightened up and drew in a long, deep breath, holding it so long that Adrianna was afraid she might pass out. At last she exhaled, slowly, as though letting the air out too quickly would deflate her body like a punctured beach toy.

"I started writing the book nearly four years ago as part of my therapy." She glanced up to catch Adrianna's startled look. "I never told you I was in therapy, did I? Well, I was, for about six months. I also never told you that I spent a year or so in an institution for emotionally disturbed children, did I?"

A fleeting grimace of embarrassment twisted Ruth's mouth. "I was about seven at the time, I think. Sort of a child's version of a nervous breakdown. My parents weren't getting along with each other or with us kids. They fought all the time—literally all the time. Our family was a terrible mess. My brother became a chronic runaway, while I chose another way out—I ran away inside. Retreated into my own little world, where everything was always pleasant, happy, and loving." Ruth braced her arms against the table and plunged on.

"Anyway, the book was about that time in my life—about waking up all alone and scared in a ward full of strange children, of being so afraid that my parents were going to leave me there in that horrible place forever and I'd never see them again. About the orderlies who hit and slapped us if we didn't respond fast enough, and the nurses who were sometimes kind, sometimes sadistically cruel. And the doctors who didn't really seem to care about us at all, but talked in front of us as though we were alien specimens from another planet."

The book took exactly three years and two hundred and twenty-two days to complete—three years and two hundred and twenty-two days of odd, secret hours stolen here and there when Hal was away or dead drunk in front of the television. At least when he was passed out in his chair she knew where he was. The rest of the time she could only guess. Not that she really cared very much anymore. Too many nights crying alone in their bed and too many lipstick-stained collars during their twelve years of marriage had managed to kill whatever traces were left of that grand passion she had once felt for him. And it had been grand once. So grand she'd virtually floated on air for two years, not noticing his straying eyes and his straying hands.

Ruth was typing the last page of the final draft the evening Hal unexpectedly came home, explaining that his "conference" with a new writer had been canceled at the last minute. Translated, that meant his date had either stood him up or walked out on him. Either way, Ruth hadn't expected him back so soon and the manuscript was spread all over the dining-room table where she'd set up her little portable typewriter.

Larkin gave Ruth a quick buss on the back of the neck as she hurriedly gathered up the papers, stuffing them haphazardly into the cardboard box she'd been using to store the manuscript. "What's all this, sweetie?" he asked, idly riffling through the loose sheets spilling out of the box.

"Nothing, Hal. Nothing at all." She grabbed the papers out of his hand and thrust them back into the box. "I'll clear these things away and get you some dinner. Won't be a minute."

"Wait just a damn second there, I want to see what you've been up to. Not writing about me, I hope." He had a firm grip on her wrist, holding her in place against the table while he used his free hand to pick up and scan the pages of her manuscript.

"Did you write this?" he demanded at last, disbelief crinkling the faintly shadowed jowls hanging from his still-handsome, boyish face. "There's some half-decent stuff here."

"Thanks a lot," she answered acidly, pulling loose from his grip. "Forget it, Hal. There's nothing there that would interest either you or World Fashion in the slightest. Not a single catchy phrase about rising and falling hemlines or who's 'making' it with whom in Beverly Hills."

Larkin stood back, arms folded, and watched her pack away the manuscript. A strand of black hair fell rakishly across his forehead, giving him the look of an aging and fleshy Burt Reynolds. Even his carefully practiced stance, with feet set apart, pelvis tilted forward, was calculated to give that impression.

"How long have you been hiding this from me?" he asked at last, deliberately keeping his words low and calm, but with a menacing undertone that chilled Ruth.

"I haven't been hiding anything," she retorted, her face flushing involuntarily. "I just didn't think you were particularly interested in how I spent my spare time."

He ignored her remark and strolled over to the portable bar, where he casually mixed himself a drink, thoughtfully fingering the rim of the heavy tumbler. "What are you going to do with it?"

"Do with it?"

"Don't play games with me, Ruth." His voice grew sharper. "Have you shown this to anyone? An agent? A publisher?"

Ruth put the manuscript away in the bottom drawer of the antique sideboard and moved the typewriter onto a small serving cart stationed under the window. He'd asked the very question she'd been struggling with of late. What should she *do* with the manuscript now that it was finished? Whom should she show it to? The manuscript was good—that much she knew intuitively. She'd spent too many years studying the manuscripts Hal brought home not to recognize a good piece of writing, even if it was her own. But she'd been away from publishing for too long, at Hal's insistence, and she didn't know the right "names" anymore. And the few she had known once were in periodicals, not books. Book publishing was a totally different world, a totally different set of "names." To them she'd be just another unknown hopeful with no published credits to give her manuscript an edge. Over the years she'd tried her hand at writing short stories, submitting them directly to publications that still used fiction, but none had sold.

Larkin quickly downed his drink and went over to the sideboard, pulling out drawers until he found the box she'd stuffed under a pile of linens. "You don't mind if I take this with me tomorrow and give it a thorough read at the office, do you?"

"No, please, Hal. Please don't take it." She rushed at him, stretching for the precious box, but he held it out of reach over his head.

"What are you getting all worked up for?" he asked with injured innocence. "I am an editor, remember. And a damn good one, if I say so myself. Even the best writers need good editing."

Ruth silently conceded defeat and pushed herself away. At least she still had the carbon, she reminded herself as she watched him put her creation away in his briefcase. He hadn't taken the carbon—probably because he hadn't known it was also there in the drawer, jammed into a similar box in the bottom drawer.

Larkin didn't mention the book for three days, but on the fourth he brought the manuscript home with him, at least a photocopied version of it marked up in varying shades of blue and red pencil. "I've made some changes—cut out some of the verbiage and sharpened it up," he curtly announced, all business. "You'll have to rework some of the passages I've marked here in red. The blue passages should be cut out entirely."

After he'd left for the office the following morning, Ruth opened the clean new box that held the photocopied manuscript and pored through the loose sheets, cringing when she came across entire pages crossed out with huge blue X's. Hal's notes, scribbled in the margins, were less than complimentary: "Amateurish phrasing," "Too wordy," "Juvenile," "Trite," "What the hell does this mean?"

Tears flowed down her cheeks and she couldn't stop them. She didn't want to stop them. He had desecrated her manuscript, heartlessly mocking the very core of her soul. His attitude was cold and impersonal, much as it had been when she'd lost the baby nine years ago.

The baby. That was the crux of this, wasn't it? An eight-month-old perfectly formed fetus—a girl—who hadn't survived the long and torturous labor that had reduced Ruth to an exhausted, dazed, empty shell. Sometimes she blamed the doctor for not performing a cesarean that might have saved her baby; other times she blamed herself for failing as a woman, a woman who could give life to another. My God, how she envied Millie those two healthy children of hers! And Hal, totally oblivious of her anguish, had been overheard commenting to one of the more attractive nurses after the delivery that while he felt sorry for his wife, the loss of the baby didn't matter to him one way or the other. Babies, he coolly noted, were nothing more than eating-and-soiling machines that messed up the apartment and got in the way of one's life.

There'd been no more babies after that. No more babies until this book. That was her baby now. The only one she was likely ever to have.

Ruth returned the stiff pages to the box, slammed on the lid, and carried it outside into the long, dim hall-way. Without a second's hesitation she pulled open the door to the garbage chute and dropped the box in, listening as it bounced against the sides of the chute all ten floors down to the basement incinerator. The book was gone, and that was the end of that.

Or what Ruth thought was the end of that. Hal never asked her for the revisions, nor did he mention the manuscript again until one evening about three months later when he burst through the apartment door with an armload of roses and a bottle of champagne. "Stop whatever you're doing in there," he shouted to Ruth in the kitchen. "We're celebrating tonight!"

He thrust the roses into her arms as she pushed through the swinging kitchen door, nearly knocking her backward onto the floor. "What's all this?" she laughed, overwhelmed by his exuberance. "Roses? And champagne?"

"We did it! The book sold!" he crowed triumphantly. "Sold for a hundred and twenty-five thousand dollars!" He waved a check in front of her face, grinning crazily. "For a first novel yet—that's unbelievable! Look, I've got the first half of the advance right here!"

"What?" Ruth felt a little dizzy, a little crazy herself. Her book had sold? "How?" she gasped. "Who bought it?"

"I didn't want to get your hopes up so I didn't tell you, but I took the original copy of the manuscript of *Twin Lives* over to Judd Stassen." He was busy prying out the champagne cork, but stopped long enough to wait for her reaction when he mentioned the top literary agent in the city. "That man has connections everywhere—Simon and Schuster, Alfred Knopf, Little, Brown—you name the house, he's got a contact there!"

Ruth staggered and reached for the back of the faded print sofa, her knees suddenly weak. "You shouldn't have done that, Hal," she managed to whisper as she sank onto the cushions. "I wish you hadn't done that!"

"Why?" he demanded, his face darkening with an angry flush. "I thought you'd be pleased. I thought this is what you wanted!"

How could she explain to Hal that, yes, this is what she wanted, but she had wanted to do it on her own? That she wanted to be the one to shepherd her newborn baby through its infancy and childhood, to see it grow into adulthood under her guidance. Not Hal's. He'd had nothing to do with its conception, its birth. The book was hers, and hers alone. This was her one and only chance to prove that she could actually do something well, and do it right.

Larkin scowled as he turned away and poured more champagne into his glass. "Stupid bitch," he muttered, just loud enough for her to hear.

The realization slowly dawned on Ruth that Larkin was already loaded—half-drunk or high on drugs. Or both. She should have known, as soon as she'd seen his bloodshot eyes, the cocky tilt of his head, that he'd probably been out celebrating most of the afternoon. His moods shifted unpredictably when he was in this condition. One minute he was the essence of charismatic charm, the next cruel and terse, glaring at her as though she were to blame for anything and everything that might be wrong, real or imagined.

Rather than provoke him any further, Ruth silently retreated toward the kitchen. From a corner of her eye she spotted the check lying on the bar where Larkin had laid it down while he was opening the bottle. The sight of the check triggered a rush of questions in her mind. Where was the contract? Why hadn't Hal brought home a contract for her to sign? Certainly no book was ever bought without a contract. And why hadn't the editor assigned to the manuscript been in touch with her about possible revisions, rewrites? Hal seemed to think the manuscript needed a lot of additional work.

Ruth picked up the check and read it. A shock ripped through her like an electric current, causing her hands to shake so violently she could hardly read the print. The check was made out for sixty-two thousand five hundred dollars, all right, but it was made payable to Harold E. Larkin.

"Why . . ." The words stuck in her throat. "Why is your name on this check, Hal? Shouldn't it be made out to me?"

Suddenly Larkin was behind her, his arms wrapped around her and his face nuzzling her hair. "Just a little technicality, sweetie. Don't worry about it. Everything is fine."

She shoved him away, rubbing at the parts of her body where his hands had touched. "Tell me," she insisted. "Tell me how this happened, Hal! Why is your name on this check instead of mine?"

Larkin flashed his most dazzling smile. Also his most dangerous. He advanced toward her again, arms outstretched, an invitation to come and be loved. Once, not so very long ago, such a gesture would have melted away any anger she felt, would have wiped the resentment from her mind. His charm didn't work any longer, she noticed. She was immune at last.

When Ruth didn't move toward him, Larkin dropped his arms and shrugged indifferently. "Stassen thought it would be better this way. That he'd have a better chance of selling it to one of the major houses. You know editors—they rarely pay attention to a first novel, even the greatest first novel ever written, unless they've heard of the author. . . ." His voice trailed off, the explanation unfinished.

Ruth stood squarely in front of her husband, looking him directly in the eye. "Are you telling me you put your name on my book?" she asked quietly.

"It's not the way you think, Ruth. Stassen is right when he says a book isn't salable in today's market unless the author already has a literary reputation. And as an editorial director, I have that reputation. What does it matter whose name appears on the cover—we did it together!"

Her skin felt cold and clammy, her breathing shallow and uneven. Somewhere in the distant recesses of her mind, Ruth feared that she might be going into shock. Moving slowly, her muscles jerking with the effort, she stumbled into the bedroom, turning briefly to stare at Larkin.

"You underhanded, larcenous son of a bitch," she said coldly, without inflection. "I could kill you for this."

Ruth Larkin closed the bedroom door behind her, and for the first time in the twelve years of her married life, deliberately locked her husband out.

5

Adrianna slowly shook her head in amazement. Ruth's story was so unbelievable, and at the same time so typical of her. For as long as Adrianna had known Ruth, she had been a pushover, the perfect patsy. Adrianna had once held out hope that Ruth would wake up one day with a backbone and realize what she'd been doing to herself—and to those few people who'd persevered enough to penetrate her shyness and develop a genuine fondness for her. Now Ruth sat at her kitchen table, haggard and drawn, drained by months of grappling alone with the knowledge that her husband was a bigger louse than even she had suspected. It was one thing for Hal to cheat on their marriage—quite another to cheat Ruth openly, directly, of the only real accomplishment of her life.

Adrianna removed the tortoiseshell combs that held her long auburn hair in a French twist and laid them out neatly, precisely, on the table in front of her. She already knew the answers, but she had to ask the questions, had to offer Ruth the opportunity to put her thoughts and feelings into words. She owed the poor thing that much, at least. If nothing else, it might at least help Ruth to come to grips with her situation.

"Why didn't you tell me all of this sooner?" she asked gently, hoping the question didn't sound accusatory. "I might have been able to help you. You know I would have, don't you?"

Ruth looked at her pleadingly, hands open in a gesture of utter helplessness. "I couldn't, Addy. I couldn't

43

face you—face myself—with what a failure I am." A short, broken sob came from her throat. "You've always been so successful at everything you do. At college you were the most popular girl on campus, president of the sorority, homecoming queen and all that. It all just fell into place for you. Me? I was Adrianna's shadow, a tagalong who was tolerated only because you wanted me there. I wasn't even a failure then. I was just a nothing."

"Honey, that was almost twenty years ago!" Adrianna protested, her accent slipping back into the down-home drawl of her native Georgia, something she rarely allowed to happen in front of others. Unless, of course, it suited her purpose, as it did now.

"Nothing has changed since then, Addy. Don't you see? For years I've tried so hard to prove to everyone, myself included, that I'm no different from you and Millie, that I could be good at something too. You've created a fantastic life for yourself here with John, and Millie is raising two gorgeous children. What did I have, but a husband who tries to bed everything that wears a skirt? After all these years, how could I suddenly come out and openly admit to you that my marriage, my entire life, is nothing but a gigantic fraud? A big, stupid sham?"

"For someone with a documented IQ of 144, you can be incredibly stupid at times," Adrianna sighed. "My life is far from perfect, you know. John has his faults, too, the most annoying one being an overdeveloped sense of dedication. He's dedicated to his work, dedicated to his patients. He even makes love with dedication! Sometimes I wish he would chase a woman or two—it might just make him a little more human."

She leaned forward and lightly touched Ruth's hand, lying with a touching sincerity. "I have never thought of you as a failure, honey. In any conceivable way. Millie and I suspected your marriage wasn't especially happy, but we had no idea it was that bad. Why on earth did you stay with that bastard after you'd found out what he'd done?"

"Where would I go?" Ruth asked simply, running a hand through her short dark hair.

"We were happy once, for a while, at the beginning," she added, her gaze far away in the past. "Sure I knew he had a rotten track record when I married him—two divorces and a string of girlfriends—but I always thought, always hoped, that he'd tire of them someday. And when he did, I'd still be there. And we could go back to the way we were. . . ." She wiped at her brimming eyes, leaving a faint smudge under the right eyebrow.

"And as time went on, and I got older, I began to realize that I'd lost my place in the world. I've been a housewife ever since the baby . . ." She choked on the word. "A housewife for nearly ten years. I'm thirty-nine years old, and I have no real job skills—nothing but a slightly tattered bachelor's degree in English lit and a few years spent in a couple of research departments. What kind of decent-paying job could I possibly get now? How would I support myself? If I divorced Hal there would be no settlement, no alimony. He spends every dollar as fast as he gets it. We have no savings, no property to speak of, that might give me a chance to start over again. Alone."

Ruth grabbed Adrianna's hand and held it hard, so hard Adrianna thought her fingers would be crushed. "Addy, the plain truth is, I'm scared. Scared to go back out in that world by myself. Maybe staying with Hal isn't the best possible solution, but heaven help me, it *is* safe! For both of us." Ruth laughed bitterly. "I know he'd never divorce me. A man like Hal needs a wife in the background in order to worm out of inconvenient entanglements with all those women. That's me, I guess—a household convenience. The ironic part is, I think Hal actually might be fond of me in his own way. As much as he can feel a fondness for anyone other than himself, that is."

The tension between them suddenly evaporated and Ruth released her hand, freeing Adrianna to get up from the table and rinse out the empty coffeepot. She held the pot under the running water longer than necessary, delaying her return to the table and Ruth's tawdry little confession. An idea was beginning to form at the back of her mind, and she needed time to think.

"You must be exhausted, Ruth," she said at last, not yet turning from the sink. "Why don't you go up to bed and get a good night's sleep, and we can go over this again in the morning? Maybe by then we'll both have a fresh perspective."

Adrianna led Ruth into the small elevator that took them up to the fourth floor, where the largest guestroom was kept in readiness in case one of John's out-of-town associates needed overnight accommodations. It was a comfortable, airy room with an elegantly carved canopy bed and working fireplace now cold and empty, shielded by a gleaming brass screen. Adrianna showed Ruth the adjoining bath, and then ran down to her own room on the next floor for a spare nightgown, robe, and slippers. They'd be much too large for Ruth's emaciated frame, but that hardly mattered.

She could hear the bathwater running as she came back up the stairs, although she found Ruth, still fully dressed, sitting immobile on the edge of the bed. Adrianna stepped into the bathroom, turned off the water, and filled a glass from the tap at the sink.

"I've brought you a sleeping pill in case you need it," she said, placing the glass and pill on the nightstand. "Now, go in and take a nice, long soak and then climb into bed. I'll be downstairs in case you want anything." She kissed Ruth lightly on the forehead and turned to go.

"Adrianna?" The voice was a disembodied whisper.

"Yes, honey?"

"Thank you. For everything."

Adrianna looked disinterestedly through the refrigerator before deciding she wasn't hungry. There was too much on her mind to spare much thought for food. Or men, for that matter. Food and men she could have anytime; right now she needed to focus her total concentration on the problems at hand.

She picked up the kitchen extension and punched the buttons with a long red nail, tapping her foot impatiently as she waited for the clicks signaling that the connection had gone through. The receiver at the other end was picked up before the second ring. "Mick," she commanded curtly, "don't wait up any longer for me—I can't come tonight. I'll give you a call in a day or two."

Adrianna hung up before Mick Flanagan could protest. If she'd allowed herself to listen to his intensely sexy voice she might very well have changed her mind about canceling their rendezvous. A mental picture of herself grunting and sweating beneath that two hundred pounds of thrusting, muscled flesh left her weak with desire—and considerably more than a little regretful about her impulsiveness in bringing Ruth home for the night.

Fortunately Flanagan couldn't phone her back because of Adrianna's strict policy of refusing to give her unlisted home phone number to any of her lovers. There'd been a couple of exceptions to that rule, but Mick Flanagan was not one of them. Flanagan was a physically gorgeous specimen of masculinity, but he definitely lacked the finesse required to maintain any semblance of propriety. But then, she reminded herself, it wasn't exactly brain power or good breeding she sought from these encounters.

Adrianna settled down comfortably at the kitchen table to mull over the circumstances in which she and Ruth found themselves. In all of this elaborate town house with its magnificently decorated rooms, including her own elegant study off the bedroom, Adrianna found she did her best thinking in the cheery, brightly lighted kitchen. Possibly it was a throwback to her youth in Savannah, where the kitchen was the center of life and activity. She'd done her homework at the kitchen table, held hands with her first boyfriend at the kitchen table, and had genuinely cried for the last time in her life at the kitchen table. That was the day her father had bullied her into drowning a litter of two-week-old kittens in a bucket of water on the back porch. She'd clenched her teeth and forced herself to do it, pushing six soft, helpless little balls of fur under the water one by one while the mother cat mewed pitifully from inside the latched screen door.

Adrianna consciously sought to dismiss any further memories of cats and kittens. This was no time to become bogged down in sentimentality, not that she was normally prone to lapses of sentimentality. But there was a poignant helplessness about Ruth, she decided, that prompted quick little flashbacks to Pepper, the sleek black cat that had had the misfortune to produce the ill-fated litter. Pepper disappeared after that incident, never again returning to curl up on the foot of Adrianna's bed or brush up against her legs at mealtime. Adrianna had missed the cat for quite some time, but eventually came around to her father's frequently stated point of view that it was a mistake to become too attached to any living creature. Human or beast.

Adrianna shook herself free of these thoughts, located a pad of paper and a pencil near the phone, and prepared to jot down the salient points of her own current situation as they came to mind. John, she estimated, was worth approximately twenty million dollars, while she had slightly less than fifty thousand dollars tucked away in her secret account. Everything—the houses, the cars, even her best jewelry—was held in John's name. Legally she owned nothing but her clothes, furs, and a few pieces of her late mother's silver.

If John died tonight, she would inherit approximately twelve million dollars. Probably closer to eight million, Adrianna calculated, after the state and city taxes were paid, John's son received his share, and all the fees were paid out to the lawyers, the accountants, and the bankers. If, however, John died twelve weeks from now, after setting up the new foundation, she'd be lucky to clear half that amount. Conservatively invested at eight or nine percent, she could realistically expect an after-tax income of less than a quarter of a million dollars a year.

The shock of seeing the figures on paper sent Adrianna bolt upright in her chair. She spent nearly fifty thousand dollars a year now on clothes alone! How on earth would she manage to keep up two houses, the cars, and her art collection on two hundred thousand dollars? It would be absolutely impossible.

A further thought left Adrianna feeling cold and numb. What if John went even further, and gave away more of his estate to this foundation? And more, and more? What was to stop John from getting so caught up in his new role of philanthropic benefactor that he gave away everything he owned?

The possibility wasn't as remote as it might seem. John was almost irrational on the subject of the foundation. He wouldn't listen to a negative word about it— not from her, and not from his financial or legal advisers. The only legal route Adrianna could take to prevent the foundation from ending up with every last cent would be to have John declared mentally incompetent. And that, she knew with a sinking certainty, would be impossible to prove to a court's satisfaction.

Adrianna was no expert on the law, but she'd done enough research before her marriage to know that under New York state law, she, as a wife, had no legal claim on any asset held in her husband's name alone. While he was still alive, that is. Only after her husband is dead can a wife claim an undisputed thirty percent of whatever is left after taxes and other expenses. The key word here, Adrianna decided, was "alive." As long as John was alive, he could spend, gamble, or give away his entire estate and there wasn't a damned thing she could do to stop him.

A very real dread seized Adrianna at the thought of giving up her beautiful home, the designer clothes and jewels, the travel, the men. Especially the men. Her freedom to dally with whomever she pleased whenever she pleased was the only thing that kept her sane. And she was expected to give up all this for the sake of the John G. Farrelly Center for Psychiatric Research? Over her dead body. Or better yet, over John's dead body.

Adrianna struck the table with her fist. There had to be a way, legal or not, to prevent all that money from going to the research center. And she wouldn't rest until she'd found it.

And then there was Ruth. Dear, sensitive, fragile little Ruth. She owed Ruth, owed her a lot more than Ruth would ever know about. All those nights in college when Ruth sat up with her before an exam, cramming her full of that useless trivia she hadn't bothered to study. All those brilliant term papers that Ruth researched so diligently and wrote so well for her. And then there was Ruth herself, the perfect foil, a human backdrop against whom her own personality sparkled and dazzled so spectacularly.

Ruth depended on Hal to protect her from the real world, where she was afraid to compete. So what if Ruth didn't have to compete? What if Ruth had enough money to create her own little cocoon where she could write to her heart's content without fear of Hal's victimization? There must be something left from that $125,000 advance—and surely the royalties, paperback rights, and all the rest of it would add up to a fair amount over the long run. And of course there was always his company-paid life insurance. With Hal out of the way, everything would go to Ruth.

The answer to both their problems was so terribly, incredibly obvious that Adrianna laughed out loud. John and Hal would simply have to die. And soon. Only weeks remained before John signed those papers. And Ruth, trusting little Ruthie, was perilously close to a total breakdown.

But did Ruth, filled with hatred as she was, have the nerve to kill her own husband? Probably not, Adrianna thought. Ruth was remarkably easy to manipulate—Adrianna knew that better than anyone—but this might be stretching even Ruth's gullibility too far. No, Adrianna decided, this piece of manipulation was going to require some assistance. And who was the only other person, besides herself, who could exert a sufficiently strong influence on Ruth?

Millie Phillips, of course.

Adrianna grinned broadly. Now, there was an interesting possibility. One certainly worth exploring more closely.

Adrianna glanced at the wall clock hanging over the

door to the breakfast room. The hour was late, and a phone call might put Millie at risk, but she would have to take that chance. She picked up the phone again and dialed Millie's number in White Plains.

"Hello there," she chirped brightly as Millie's sleepy voice answered. "Can you make arrangements to have someone look after the girls tomorrow while you come into town? Ruth and I have something extremely important to talk to you about. Extremely important."

6

Millie Phillips angrily paced up and down the length of the bedroom, clenching and unclenching her fists, as Ruth once again recounted the events leading up to Hal's sudden rise to literary fame.

"Why didn't you go to the publisher and set him straight right away?" Millie demanded. "Why didn't you tell him you wrote *Twin Lives*—not that sneaky, conniving, low-down son of a bitch!" Millie suddenly broke stride and whirled around to face Ruth, her index finger stabbing the air. "You could still do something about it, you know. Take out a full-page ad in the New York *Times* Book Review and denounce him for what he is. I'd even take up a collection to help you pay for it!"

Ruth, huddled in the middle of the canopy bed, shrank inside Adrianna's overlarge cream satin robe as Millie resumed her restless pacing. "Who would believe me?" Ruth asked in a small voice. "Why should they believe me? Who am I, compared to the editorial director of a big magazine chain like World Fashion? They'd all think I was crazy."

"Forgive me, Ruth Ellen, but there are times I could just wring that wimpy little neck of yours!"

Adrianna, fresh and vibrant in a pale yellow silk blouse and chocolate gabardine slacks, nudged open the bedroom door with her foot while balancing a large silver tray laden with china, food, and the ever-present pot of coffee. "Take it easy, Millie," she said firmly. "I could hear you shouting all the way up in the elevator."

Adrianna had surprised her housekeeper and cleaning lady earlier that morning by giving them an unexpected and unprecedented day off—with pay. Adrianna wanted no one in the house who might accidentally overhear what the three of them discussed in that fourth-floor guestroom.

"Honestly, I just don't understand her at times," Millie continued hotly, addressing Adrianna as though Ruth weren't in the room. "I'd have left that creep in a minute if he'd pulled a stunt like that on me."

Adrianna cocked her head to one side and looked directly at Millie. "Are you sure about that?"

Millie's head snapped back as though Adrianna had slapped her, and she pivoted around to stare out the window overlooking the barren, wintry garden.

Adrianna set the tray down on the foot of the bed and handed Ruth a steaming bowl. "Vegetable soup. I want to see you eat every last bite of it," she ordered. "Coffee, Millie?"

"No," came the curt reply from the window.

Adrianna poured a cup for herself and settled comfortably on the bed, her long legs tucked up underneath her. "It seems to me," she began slowly, "that we're all in the same position, more or less."

Ruth looked up from her soup. "Why do you say that, Addy? You have everything anyone could possibly want—including a husband who absolutely adores you. That alone is more than either Millie or I have."

Adrianna inhaled deeply and looked back and forth between Ruth and Millie. Although Millie was now watching her curiously from across the room, she decided to address herself primarily to Ruth.

"Haven't you ever wondered why John and I don't have any children?" she asked simply.

"I merely assumed you didn't want any."

"Your assumption was wrong. John didn't want any," Adrianna corrected her, putting the emphasis on "John." "He always said one child was enough for him, and he already had that child with his first wife. Of course his son is grown now and off on his own, but even so, John claims he's too old to start over with a whole new family. He doesn't want to be bothered looking after little ones anymore."

"What about you, Addy? Do you want children?"

Adrianna willed her eyes to cloud over, and even managed to produce a small tear that trickled wetly down her cheek. "Desperately, Ruthie. Oh, so desperately. And I had one once. For a little while." She heard a small, gratifying gasp from Ruth; and Millie, she noticed, had moved closer to the bed.

"Do you remember a few years ago when John and I went to Europe for the entire summer? No, of course you wouldn't. There's no reason you should." She paused for dramatic effect.

"We went to Europe so I could have an abortion. John insisted on it." She forced out another tear. "I was so angry and upset at being forced into the abortion that John decided it would be easier on me to have it done abroad. A 'therapeutic change of scene' he called it—as though a change of scene could possibly make up for having my baby taken away like that!"

Adrianna's thoughts turned inward, remembering how John had pleaded and argued during the eight-hour flight over the Atlantic in a futile attempt to change her mind, to convince her to keep the baby, all the time not knowing it wasn't even his. He'd accompanied her only in the hope of talking her out of the abortion. He hadn't succeeded. Nor had he succeeded in counter-manding her order that the surgeon perform a vaginal hysterectomy while he was at it. She certainly had no intention of ever going through another pregnancy again.

"I wanted that baby more than anything else in the world," she lied softly, her hazel eyes focused on Ruth. "But John was furious—almost violent. He threatened to have nothing to do with me or the child. And worse, he said he'd revoke the trust he set up to support my father. Daddy, you know, is in his seventies and very ill. Completely helpless. He's been in a nursing home for ages now, and John pays all the bills. Incredible bills! You wouldn't believe how expensive nursing-home care is these days."

That was close enough to the truth. Ruth and Millie

already knew that Adrianna's father had entered a Savannah retirement home several years ago following the death of her mother. What they didn't know was that Adrianna's father enjoyed far better health than Adrianna had led them to believe. He also paid all his own bills out of a comfortable retirement fund, steadfastly refusing to accept any financial help from John.

"So you see," she added, her voice quavering slightly, "I had no choice. John's attorneys are very, very clever. I might have been able to win some provision for minimal child support if I had filed for a divorce, but John certainly would never have agreed to any provision for my father, much less for me."

Adrianna's performance was undeniably excellent, and she reveled in it. "As long as Daddy is alive, I'll be tied to John for his sake." She bowed her head and her shoulders convulsed. "And the doctors say Daddy could linger on this way for another five or ten years."

"Couldn't you divorce John and start over with someone else? Someone who wants to have children?" Ruth asked.

"Ruthie, look at me!" Adrianna sobbed realistically, her face glistening with a steady flow of tears. "I'll be forty years old in a couple of months—time is running out to have a baby. And divorcing a wealthy man like John isn't something you do overnight. It can take years. Literally years! In the meantime, what do I do about poor Daddy? Let him go on welfare and wind up dying in some filthy public hole somewhere? I couldn't do that to him. I just couldn't!"

The room was unnaturally still, with only the muted sounds of street traffic wafting in through a partially open hall window at the front of the town house. Millie was the first to break the spell cast by Adrianna's performance. "That was very touching, Adrianna, darling. Very, very touching."

"Why do you have to be so cynical?" Ruth asked, glaring at Millie, who stood at the side of the bed coolly appraising Adrianna. "Can't you see how much pain all this is causing her?" Ruth turned back to Adrianna. "I can scarcely believe this of John. He's a doctor, and

doctors are supposed to be so . . . so humane! They're
supposed to preserve life, aren't they? Not destroy it."

"Which only goes to prove that it's a mistake to make
generalizations about anyone. Especially men," Millie
broke in tersely. "I always suspected that under that
genteel, aristocratic veneer, John was a rat like the rest
of his sex."

Adrianna resisted the urge to shout with exultation.
This had been the hardest part—waiting for the signal
that Millie had bought her story. She'd been worried that
Millie, far more perceptive than Ruth, would see through
her version of events for what it was, virtually a
total fabrication built around a few grains of truth. It
was those few grains of truth, Adrianna knew, which
had lent her story its air of credibility.

"All of this is very interesting, of course, and you
have my deepest sympathy, Adrianna, but I don't see
why you think I'm in the same position as you and
Ruth. Considering that I already have two children,
and certainly don't want any more. Especially not with
Ed!"

"Come off it, Millie," Ruth commanded with unusual
sharpness. "We aren't talking about children. We're
talking about husbands. And your Ed certainly doesn't
qualify for anyone's husband-of-the-year award."

"Maybe not, but at least the girls and I have a decent
roof over our heads, clothes on our backs, and food on
the table—which is more than we had five years ago
before I married him," Millie retorted defensively. "That
plumbing-supply business of his has turned out to be a
gold mine. It produces more and more money every
day—more than I ever thought possible from plumbing. And with two kids to put through college in a few
years, that money is going to make quite a difference in
the quality of their educations."

Ruth's eyes widened. "You're staying with Ed, in
spite of all those drunken rages and beatings you've told
us about, just so he'll pay for the girls' college educations? Millie, that's insane!"

"For heaven's sake," Millie sighed in exasperation.
"Ed's no worse than most other husbands. So what if he

drinks too much once in a while and takes it out on me? I can put up with it if it means ensuring my children's futures. And it's not such a terrible bargain, Ruth, when you consider they aren't even Ed's children, and there's no chance their father will ever contribute a nickel to their support, much less their educations."

Millie fingered the frame of a small oil painting propped up in a miniature gilt easel on the chest of drawers. "Look," she said, turning back to face the other two women, "I really don't care to discuss the subject anymore, so why don't we drop it, all right?"

Adrianna studied Millie carefully, noting her restlessness as she wandered about the room, picking up objects and putting them down without really seeing them. There was something in the way Millie moved, in the odd sound of her voice, her defensiveness, that piqued Adrianna's interest. Millie seemed far more reticent and evasive than usual, as though deliberately trying to suppress her normal frankness. The three of them had talked about Ed's abusiveness many times before, so why was Millie unwilling to talk about it now? Before Adrianna had time to speculate any further on the possible reasons for Millie's puzzling behavior, Ruth jumped in and renewed her attack.

"What do you mean your 'bargain' isn't so terrible?" she demanded incredulously. "How long do you think you can go on making up phony 'accident' stories before your precious suburban friends and neighbors start catching on to all your lies? If they haven't already. Really, Millie, how many times can you tell the same people that the bruise on your face was the result of being accidentally hit with a tennis racket during a doubles match, or that you broke your arm—again—slipping on the ice?"

Conflicting emotions played across Millie's face. "What are you trying to do, Ruth?" she cried angrily, leaning over the bed just inches from Ruth and Adrianna. "What are you trying to make me say? That I prostitute myself for the security of my husband's money? All right, maybe I do. But it's no more and no less than what you and Adrianna are doing, is it?"

Millie jerked away from her two old friends and started for the bedroom door, grabbing up her purse along the way. "As for you two," she said, looking back over her shoulder, "I've heard all the 'true confessions' I can stomach for one day." Her hand had scarcely touched the knob when Ruth's cold voice cut through the stillness of the room.

"Hal may have cheated me out of my book," she said with an eerie, icy remoteness, kneeling in the center of the bed. "And John may have cheated Adrianna out of her baby. But Ed is cheating you out of ever so much more. His brutality is making you hard, Mildred Wozackie Palmer Phillips. Hard and tough and bitter. And it's making you ugly inside—so hard and ugly I don't know how you can stand living with yourself."

Millie's defiant facade crumbled, the dark anger in her round blue eyes giving way to fear and shame. "You think you know all about it, don't you?" she whispered hoarsely, holding fiercely onto the door. "But believe me, neither one of you knows one little iota about the kind of hell I live with every day. And you'd better pray to God you never do."

Adrianna shot Ruth a look of warning to be quiet, rose quickly, and went to Millie, tenderly putting an arm around her shoulder. "It seems we're all keeping secrets from each other when maybe we shouldn't be," she crooned softly. "Come back to us, Millie. Please come. We've been friends too many years to fight like this. We have to help each other."

Millie allowed Adrianna to guide her back to the foot of the bed, where she perched uneasily while Adrianna poured her a cup of coffee, liberally lacing it with a shot of brandy from the decanter on the butler's table near the fireplace. So far everything was going according to plan, Adrianna thought with satisfaction. Actually much better than planned. Ruth, apparently without meaning to, had touched a raw nerve in Millie. Now it was up to her to keep Millie talking without pushing her so hard she walked out for good.

"Tell me about this hell Ed is putting you through,"

Adrianna urged. "Are the beatings getting worse? Or is it something else?"

Millie put the coffee cup down on the lacy coverlet, balancing the saucer carefully so the hot liquid wouldn't spill. "I never pretended to you or anyone else that Ed was the ideal husband. He was nice enough when I first met him, and he liked the girls so much." Millie groaned as though in pain and buried her face in her hands. "My God, if I'd only known how much he liked little girls!"

She stopped, as though unwilling to face the pain by putting it into words. Adrianna, sensing that Millie was on the verge of revealing something significant, gently prodded her. "What about the girls, Millie? Tell me about the girls. Is Ed beating them too?"

Millie shook her head, and when she spoke, her voice was so low Adrianna could barely hear her. "Evie. Just Evie. I think he's been . . . with Evie."

The full impact of what Millie was implying crept slowly into Adrianna's consciousness, causing her mouth to open in astonishment. "Are you saying that Ed is having sexual relations with Evelyn?" she asked, stunned. "Are you certain?"

Again Millie shook her head. "No, I'm not certain. I have no proof. But the way Ed looks at her sometimes, especially when he thinks I'm not watching . . . It's so filthy, Addy. Like one of those men who hang around the porno movies in Times Square, leering at the women in the posters. Ed practically drools when he looks at Evie, and he can't keep his hands off her. He's always trying to touch her . . . fondle her!"

"Have you talked to Evie about this?"

"She won't talk to me!" Millie's full despair came to the surface, her voice cracking. "I've approached her several times about it, but she's so damn secretive. So uncommunicative. All she does is hide in her room. I try not to leave them alone in the house together, but sometimes I just can't avoid it. Like on Thursday nights when Deedee has her music lessons, and the teacher is clear across town . . ."

"What about Deedee?" Adrianna probed quickly, keeping up the pressure. "Has Ed gone after Deedee yet?"

Millie's hand shook as she pushed the hair back from her forehead, revealing a small greenish bruise at the hairline. Her upper lip was beaded with perspiration. "I don't think so. Not yet, anyway. But I'm so afraid for her sometimes I think I'll go mad! How in the world am I going to protect her when the time comes? And how will I know when the time has come?"

"And you said I was crazy for staying with Hal," Ruth said with that same odd, cold detachment.

"I did leave Ed. Early last summer after school ended, when I began noticing what was happening to Evie. I took the girls and went to my mother's in Louisiana."

"Why did you go back to him?" The question came from Adrianna.

"He followed us. He told me in no uncertain terms that if I ever left him again, he'd find me wherever I went. He swore he'd kill me—and the girls."

"And you believe him?"

"Yes. I believe him. He's capable of it. Every time I read in the newspapers about some man beating his wife to death, I shudder. That could be me in those stories!"

Adrianna sucked in her breath and waited, but neither of the other women spoke. Millie had unwittingly given her the opening she'd been preparing for. There would never be a better time.

"As I said earlier, we're all pretty much in the same position, aren't we?" She spoke slowly, choosing her words with great care. "We're in the same trap. An economic trap that none of us can break out of. Unless . . ."

Millie, as she suspected, was the first to take the bait. "Unless what, Addy?"

"Unless we destroy them, before they destroy us."

Ruth slowly sank back on the bed, her face ashen. "You mean we ought to kill them?" she whispered. "Murder our own husbands?"

"Of course," Adrianna replied as though it were the most natural suggestion in the world. "Don't you understand, Ruth? It's the only way out for us."

7

Adrianna stretched contentedly in the warm bath-water, luxuriating in the sleek oiled sheen the bubblebath imparted to her skin. She thoroughly enjoyed narcissistic moments such as this, until the fluorescent bulb over the rusting, doorless medicine cabinet dimmed twice, threatening to burn out altogether. She looked at the tacky bare bulb in annoyance. Really, Mick ought to do something about fixing up this disgraceful bathroom if he wanted her to continue her little visits. But then, she remembered, it had been such a struggle to convince him it was necessary to scrub out the tub once in a while. Expecting Mick to undertake a complete redecorating project would be ridiculous.

Men could be so terribly blind to their surroundings, she thought as she listened to Mick moving around in the next room, bumping his massive frame into the furniture as he folded up the sofa bed and clumsily dropped dirty dishes into the sink. She briefly wondered how it was possible for a man with so much grace in bed to be so uncoordinated on his feet.

"Hey, you drown or something in there, sweetheart?" Mick Flanagan poked his large head of black curly hair around the door and grinned. "That looks like fun. Think I'll join you," he said, tugging at the button on his jeans.

Adrianna hurled the wet washcloth at his bare chest and laughed. "You'll do no such thing. Four times in one day is quite enough, thank you. Even for me. Not to mention that I have an important meeting to attend in forty-five minutes."

"So cancel it." Flanagan cheerfully suggested, leaning casually against the bathroom sink, where he had an unobstructed view of her long nude body, clad only in a few dissipating bubbles. "You told me your old man would be out of town for three days. We've still got two left. No point wasting all that time on some stupid meeting."

"If it were any other meeting, I'd probably agree. But this one is different."

Adrianna rose slowly from the water, reveling in Mick's unabashed admiration. She enjoyed displaying her body to those who could appreciate its taut, smooth flesh and flawless skin, and Flanagan was certainly capable of great appreciation. What a pity John wasn't! That man was so preoccupied with his cases, and now with that damn research center, she doubted he'd notice if she walked through the living room stark naked, much less their bedroom.

Mick Flanagan reached over and ran a hand along the skin of her abdomen, letting it drift with the downward curve of her body. "You're one sexy broad, you know that, lady?" he breathed. "I can't seem to get enough of you."

She brushed his hand away and reached for the towel draped across the commode. "I told you I can't stay any longer, much as I would like to. Now, please, get out of the way and let me dress."

Flanagan stepped back and let her go, watching as she smoothly glided into the main room of his grubby little apartment, the towel sweeping along behind her. She stepped over the pile of soiled bedding Flanagan had dumped on the floor and located her clothing neatly hung on the corner rod that served as a closet.

"Sure you can't stay?" Flanagan asked again, eyeing her hungrily as she slipped into her panties and bra. Adrianna smiled, immensely pleased with the power his hunger for her body gave her.

"If you're a very good little boy," she said sweetly,

pulling her skirt over her head, "I might think about coming back soon. Very soon."

"Tomorrow?"

"Possibly. I'll have to let you know."

She hurried through the rest of her dressing, permitted Mick one last deep, passionate kiss, and then she was gone, calling out as she descended the grimy stairway, "And do something about that light in the bathroom, will you?"

Adrianna glanced at her watch in the cab. She had a little time yet—not much, but a little—before she was to meet Ruth and Millie. A week and a half had passed since that heart-to-heart exchange in her fourth-floor guestroom; time enough, Adrianna hoped, for each of them to get used to the idea that the prearranged deaths of their respective husbands was the most sensible solution to their problems. Timing was everything now. Without it, there was no hope of winning their cooperation for what needed to be done.

She still found herself faintly astonished, even ten days later, at how well her hastily contrived plan had worked. That first session had been intended only as an exploratory exercise, an attempt to assess their individual situations and plant the seeds of an idea. Instead she'd struck a hidden wellspring of fear, hate, and impotence. It scarcely seemed possible that these two women, whom she had known so long and so well, could have such tremendous capacities for tolerating, and concealing, the pain they endured daily. Living, as someone once said, their lives of quiet desperation with no one the wiser. And that, Adrianna told herself, was no way to live at all.

The dark, smoky lounge she had chosen for this second meeting was small and discreet, its late-afternoon clientele composed largely of older, well-to-do women seeking a momentary respite from endless days of charity work, art-appreciation seminars, and families that no longer needed or wanted their single-minded devotions. Here they could pass an unhurried hour or two, alone or in small groups, protected by a solicitous management that would, if it became necessary, see to it that the more inebriated ladies arrived safely home at a decorous hour.

To Adrianna's surprise and annoyance, both Ruth and Millie were already seated and well into the first round by the time she arrived. For years she had contrived to be first at their appointed meeting places, to take control of the occasions by selecting their table and sometimes even the menu. For reasons which she couldn't articulate, but merely accepted, Adrianna despised coming in second—or worse, third.

"Isn't this a perfectly charming little place?" Adrianna smiled, careful to keep any trace of vexation out of her voice as she took the chair next to Millie. "Neither of you have been here before, have you?"

Ruth and Millie exchanged glances. "We tried to call you, Addy, but you weren't home," Ruth said, fiddling nervously with the plastic stirrer. "I can't stay long. Hal's publisher is hosting a special dinner in his honor tonight, and I've said I would attend."

"Tell her how he engineered that one," Millie broke in acidly. "Go ahead, tell her. This wonderful man who didn't even miss you the night you spent at Adrianna's because he didn't bother going home himself!"

Ruth ducked her head to avoid Adrianna's eyes. "After I told him I wouldn't be caught dead at that dinner tonight, he phoned his publisher and his agent, Judd Stassen. I've been getting calls from both of their offices for two solid days, particularly the publisher's, telling me that everyone who is anyone in publishing is going to be there tonight, and it would look most peculiar if the wife of their esteemed guest of honor wasn't there."

"So you gave in."

"I'm afraid so, Addy." Ruth looked up brightly. "But I held out for an awfully long time. You would've been proud of me, I think."

"I would have been even more proud if you'd stood your ground altogether," Adrianna remarked simply. "Still, I suppose it's a start." Adrianna shifted her attention to Mille. "And you? How's Ed been behaving?"

Millie shrugged, letting her carefully manicured hands

fall loosely in her lap. "About the same. Well, maybe a little worse. I don't know anymore. Ed had too much to drink the night before last and threw a lamp at me. Fortunately he missed—too drunk to aim straight, I suppose. Anyway, that just seemed to make him angrier and he came at me like a madman. I managed to get away from him and locked myself in the den— barricaded the door with the desk." The mixture of fury and shame on Millie's face was in strong contrast to her flat, almost toneless voice. "That was the closest call yet. His rages are getting progressively more violent. The next time, he might actually succeed in killing me."

"And Evie?"

"Evie," Millie sighed deeply, "is still hiding in her room. Last week I took her with me when I drove Deedee to her music lesson. She was rather sulky at first, you know how kids are, but underneath all the posing I think she was relieved to be out of the house and away from Ed."

"Good. Good."

Adrianna ordered a drink, pulled her cigarettes and lighter from her handbag, and composed her features for business. "Since we apparently don't have much time today"—she glanced at Ruth, who had her gaze fixed on a nearby empty table—"we may as well discuss what we came here to discuss."

"I don't think this is a very good idea, talking about this sort of thing in public," Millie protested. "What if someone should overhear us?"

"They won't hear us. And where else are we going to meet?" Adrianna asked. "It would be stupid to be seen going in and out of each other's homes too often. Besides, in a place like this"—she waved toward the other women occupying tables scattered around the room— "the waiters won't think twice about it. At one time or another almost every woman here has talked about how she'd like to kill her husband, given half a chance."

Ruth shivered in spite of her warm blazer and cashmere sweater. "This whole thing gives me the creeps,

Addy. It really does. There's just something so cold-blooded about it."

"And there was nothing cold-blooded about Hal stealing your book?" Adrianna asked pointedly. "Or the money and the recognition that by rights ought to be yours? Like tonight?" Ruth began to squirm uncomfortably as Adrianna's words struck home. "And what if you write another book, Ruthie? An even better book. Do you really think there's any way that book will be published under your own name as long as Hal is alive? You've already lost one book, Ruth. Are you prepared to lose another? And another?"

"You don't understand," Ruth pleaded, her eyes dark pools of pain. "It's not the idea of Hal's death that particularly disturbs me—I can't think of anyone who probably deserves it more. But, Addy, I just don't think I can kill him." She wadded up the cocktail napkin in a small, tight ball. "No, that's not true. The truth is, I know I can't kill him."

Adrianna stretched her hand across the burnished wood of the lounge table to pat Ruth's arm. "You won't have to, dear."

"I won't?" Ruth looked up with hope.

"Of course not. You won't kill Hal. I will."

There was a stunned silence as both Ruth and Millie stared at her.

"It's really very simple," Adrianna continued calmly, absolutely certain she had their total, undivided attention. "I will kill Hal. Millie will kill John, and you, Ruthie, you will kill Ed."

"Christ!" Millie, who was about to take a sip of her brandy, let the glass slip through her fingers. It hit the table and tilted dangerously before Millie caught it. "Are you serious? Me kill John? I hardly know him!"

"Precisely."

"You're mad, Adrianna. Absolutely mad!" Millie protested, recoiling from her. "Look at us. Take a good look at us." She gestured around the table. "We're not equipped to undertake something like that. We don't know anything about murder, much less how to commit one. And even if we agreed to go along with you, there's no way in hell we could possibly get away with it!"

The waiter materialized at their table with two bowls, one of salted nuts, the other containing pretzel sticks. As soon as he was gone, Adrianna lit another cigarette and serenely contemplated her friends, unperturbed by Millie's objections.

"Most murders are committed in a moment of passion by people who know their victims very well," Adrianna continued, as though Millie hadn't spoken. "There's usually a very obvious motive, no attention to detail, and no advance planning. In spite of that, most murders are never solved! Amazing, isn't it?"

"That may be so," Ruth interjected, "but I agree with Millie. Neither one of us has any experience with death or murder. Wouldn't it be better to hire someone who knows what he's doing?"

"And what do we use for money?" Adrianna asked. "We couldn't possibly raise that much money without our husbands finding out about it. Not to mention that hiring someone would open us up to blackmail later on."

Adrianna watched the smoke from her cigarette curl lazily in the air over their heads. "Given our combined intelligence, it shouldn't be too difficult to come up with a plan that is workable and absolutely foolproof. The first step is making certain that each one of us has an airtight alibi when her husband dies—preferably somewhere out of town and surrounded by people. That being the case, then, the actual murder has to be done by someone else. And since we are all virtual strangers to each other's husbands, there's no way the murders can be traced back to any one of us. If we're careful."

"The three of us—actually commit murder? Three murders, in fact? Adrianna, the whole idea is absurd," Millie said.

"Why?"

"Because . . ." Millie looked at Ruth for help. "Because we just couldn't, that's all!"

"I'll remember you said that when I attend your

funeral service," Adrianna said sourly. "On your head-
stone we can inscribe: 'Here lies Mildred Phillips, the
late battered wife of Edward Phillips. She couldn't, so
he did.' "

Millie turned away, refusing to look at Adrianna.

"It's the truth, Millie. Are you so afraid of the truth?"
Adrianna leaned over the table and put her hand gently
under Millie's chin, turning Millie's head until their
eyes met. "And what about Evelyn and Deedee? What's
going to become of them when Ed finally puts you in
your grave and they take him off to prison? Do you
think Frank Palmer is going to come back from California to take care of his darling daughters? The daughters
he abandoned when he ran off with that woman eight
years ago and hasn't seen since? You told me yourself
he doesn't send them as much as a birthday card."

Millie sat quietly, her emotions betrayed only by the
rapid blinking of her eyes as she fought back the tears.
"I suppose you're right," she conceded reluctantly. "I
just wish there was some other way."

"Well, if you think of one, let me know."

"But why pick me to kill John?" Millie asked, gazing
in Ruth's direction. "Why not let me kill Hal instead?
He's almost as rotten as Ed."

"If you absolutely insist," Adrianna said, her patience
beginning to wear thin, "but I think it would be better
to do it my way. Consider this, Millie: John's death will
be the easiest of the three because it will involve his
plane. The plane is kept in a converted barn at our
place out in Westchester, which is only about fifteen or
twenty miles from your home, right? So it will be a
fairly simple matter for you to run over one afternoon,
do what must be done to the plane, and be home again
before anyone knows you were even gone. For Ruth to
accomplish the same thing would take a lot more time,
effort, and planning." Adrianna paused to give Millie a
chance to absorb the logic of her argument.

"But she'll still have to go out that way in order to kill
Ed," Millie protested.

"True, but Ruth isn't as encumbered as you are,
Millie. She doesn't have to make arrangements for some-

one to look after her children while she disappears for a few hours. You would, though, if you came into the city to kill Hal. Trust me, it's much more practical my way."

Adrianna noticed the glazed expression on Ruth's face. "Are you listening to this, Ruthie? You look like you're miles away."

"I'm listening," Ruth replied softly. "And what you're saying makes a great deal of sense, Addy. But I just don't think I can kill anyone—even a monster like Ed!"

Adrianna swallowed her exasperation and managed, with an effort, to retain her outward composure. "Don't worry yourself, Ruthie," she soothed. "If you can't, then you can't."

Ruth's relief was palpable. "Thank goodness. I don't know what I'd have done if you hadn't said that, Addy. I'm sorry to be such a bother at times."

"You're no bother at all," Adrianna drawled with feigned nonchalance. "Of course, we wouldn't dream of harming a hair on Hal's double-crossing head if you don't reciprocate. Would we, Millie?"

"Absolutely not, if that's the way Ruth wants it."

"Then we have an agreement. Millie will take care of John, and I will take care of Ed." She looked intently at Ruth. "And the only thing you have to do is to keep your mouth shut." Adrianna permitted herself a quick, sarcastic jab. "Do you think you can handle that much at least, Ruthie?"

Ruth nodded mutely, eyes downcast and hands tightly clasped on the table.

"Fine. All right, Millie, let's get down to work on how we're going to gain our freedom."

8

A small furrow of concentration creased Ruth Larkin's brow as she struggled to focus her attention on the head table, where her husband was jovially holding court, eagerly lapping up the words of praise and congratulation being heaped on him by speaker after speaker. Try as she would, however, none of the surrealistic scene seemed to make any sense to Ruth. She felt as if she'd spent the entire evening observing this interminable literary celebration through the wrong end of a clouded telescope.

More than anything else in the world, Ruth wanted only to return to the cozy atmosphere of that murky little lounge where she'd left Adrianna and Millie a few short hours before. Even though she was repelled by the enormity of the deeds they were planning, Ruth found herself desperately needing that closeness, that warmth the three of them drew around each other. And the reality. Only when Adrianna and Millie were near did she feel securely anchored to the real world around her.

She hadn't been anchored to much of anything for the major part of this publisher's dinner, though. In fact most of the evening, including the preceding cocktail party, was just a hazy, indistinct blur to Ruth. Her only memory of the cocktail party was an unsettling impression of having been swallowed up by a sea of strange, unknown faces that were somehow oddly bloated and grotesque, with bulging, critical eyes and large gaping mouths.

Ruth wasn't quite certain what had triggered this retreat back into the familiar, protective mental shell of her early childhood. Perhaps it had been Hal's over-bearing and condescending attitude when he'd arrived home to change into evening clothes and escort her to 21. Or perhaps it was her own sense of guilt at having openly admitted to Adrianna and Millie that she wouldn't mind seeing Hal dead. Whatever the reason, the mental fog was beginning to recede now, leaving her stranded, for the moment at least, in a bewildering and disorienting twilight.

As her awareness slowly intensified, Ruth became conscious of the fact that she'd been placed at a small table far off to one side of the dining room, away from the main gathering clustered in front of the head table. Her dinner plate remained cold and untouched in front of her, although the wineglass showed evidence of use, a half-moon smudge of coral lipstick imprinted on the rim.

"Shouldn't be too much longer now," the man to her left said, leaning close so that his rich, melodious bari-tone wouldn't carry beyond the table. "I think the chairman's finally winding up his speech. He'll be intro-ducing Hal in a moment. A pity he's being so long-winded about it."

Ruth stared uncomprehendingly at this impeccably dressed man with the fastidiously trimmed beard who was speaking to her with such familiarity. They seemed to be alone at the table, two other places set but un-used. Gradually, moment by moment, she began to remember, to sort out the name and the face from that initial confusing swirl of introductions. This man was none other than Judd Stassen, the agent. The agent who'd told Hal that he could sell her book only if Hal Larkin's name was on it in place of hers.

Ruth hadn't the faintest idea how long she'd been sitting next to Stassen, or indeed what conversation, if any, may have passed between them during dinner. But the undeniable recognition of her dinner partner was enough to galvanize her into motion. "I'm sorry, Mr. Stassen," she said stiffly, pushing her chair back from the table. "But I won't be staying for Hal's speech. Please make my excuses to the others."

Stassen put a friendly but restraining hand on her arm. "I know it's been a very long evening and you must be tired, but please don't leave yet, Mrs. Larkin. This won't take much longer, I promise. At least wait for the presentation."

Ruth looked down at the surprisingly strong hand gripping her wrist, then up into the impassive black eyes that gazed through her to the head table beyond. For an instant those unfathomable eyes fastened on hers, and Stassen's face abruptly remolded itself into a benign and kindly smile that indicated he meant her no harm. But Stassen did not relax his grip.

"I understand perfectly what you're going through." His voice was low and unexpectedly gentle. "These award dinners can be terribly tedious, with the same speakers saying the same things over and over again. I suppose boredom is the price that people such as you and I must pay for hobnobbing with the chosen few. But please be patient just a little while longer. This is important to Hal's career . . . and, I hesitate to say, to mine."

Ruth instantly understood that she was trapped in this overheated and overcrowded dining room, trapped by her own weakness in having agreed to attend, and trapped by Stassen's implied insistence that she maintain the appearance of a loving and supportive wife. More than likely, she decided, Hal and Stassen had planned this little scenario well in advance—with Stassen the appointed watchdog to make certain she didn't say the wrong thing to the wrong person about the true authorship of *Twin Lives*. Why else would they be sitting alone at a table set for four, well apart from the rest of the gathering?

"There we are! I told you it wouldn't be long—he's introducing Hal now!"

Ruth looked over to where Hal was rising from his seat and moving toward the podium, hand outstretched to receive a congratulatory shake from the chairman of the board. Hal was grinning broadly, nodding in response to the enthusiastic applause that rolled across the room. As the chairman stepped back to let Hal reach the microphone, he bobbed his head in feigned modesty.

"I can't begin to tell you what it means to me to receive the National Book Critics Circle Award," Larkin boomed into the microphone. "I'm certain all of you have heard it before, so I'll spare you the agony of sitting through it again." He waited for the polite titter of laughter to subside.

"Our distinguished chairman was kind enough to give me the sole credit for winning this award, but in all candor I must share that credit—first with my esteemed publisher, who had the extraordinary courage to back a first novel by a virtually unknown author, and second with my agent, Judd Stassen, who is justifiably famous for his uncanny ability to pick long shots. Judd, I'll be happy to treat you to a day at the track anytime you say!"

Stassen rose in a half-bow, acknowledging the remark with an abbreviated wave of his hand.

"And of course," Hal said laughingly, gesturing in Ruth's direction, "I wouldn't dare go home tonight if I failed to introduce the little woman who helped me so much. Ladies and gentlemen, my wife, Ruth!"

A paralyzing mixture of fear, anger, and humiliation kept Ruth in her seat as Hal impatiently motioned to her to stand up. "Come on, honey," he urged through the microphone. "Let them get a look at you!"

Stassen released the grip on her wrist and placed his hand under her elbow, pushing her up with such unexpected force that Ruth jarred the table, knocking china and glassware to the floor. Muffled laughter came from nearby tables, and Ruth, scarlet with mortification, angrily twisted away as Stassen moved to help her back into the chair.

"I do beg your pardon, Mrs. Larkin," Stassen murmured in acute embarrassment as a team of busboys materialized to clean up the scattered debris. "Sometimes I don't know my own strength. That was extremely clumsy of me. Please accept my heartfelt apologies."

Ruth looked contemptuously at Stassen, but did not reply.

As Hal launched into his prepared remarks, his confident voice rumbling across the room, Stassen self-consciously adjusted his shirt cuffs and reached over to pick up his spilled wineglass, concentrating his attention on the last few drops as though inspecting the dregs of a particularly good vintage.

When the last of the busboys had vanished, Stassen turned toward Ruth, drew in a deep breath, and made a tentative effort to ease the tension between them. "You know, Mrs. Larkin, Hal is an unusually fortunate man," he said, keeping his voice casually neutral. "He has everything—a lovely wife, a prestigious job, and now, a fabulous bestselling novel that's going to make him rich. Who could possibly ask for more?" Stassen paused as though giving Ruth the opportunity to agree. When she did not, he valiantly pressed on, keeping his tone light and conversational in spite of Ruth's stony silence.

"I've known Hal for many, many years. Only slightly, of course, but I do make it a point to meet as many of the top book and magazine editors in town as possible." Stassen nodded somberly, as though imparting a grave secret. "I hope you won't take offense, Mrs. Larkin, but never in a million years would I have guessed that a man like Hal could write with such depth, such sensitivity. It's a truly remarkable achievement, I'd say. One that I'm happy to say I've had a part in."

Ruth's anger gave way to disbelief. Surely this man wasn't making a ghastly sadistic joke at her expense, was he? Certainly he couldn't be that cruel to someone he'd only just met that evening? Particularly the very person he'd helped to rob of this achievement he was now praising so highly? Her eyes darted over to Hal at the podium. Unless, of course, Stassen had been put up to it for some reason she didn't as yet understand.

"From the first moment I read the opening pages of that manuscript, I knew I had to represent this man," Stassen continued, apparently unaware that Ruth's hands had begun to shake uncontrollably under the table. "A talent like that doesn't come along very often. It's a pity he waited so long before putting it to use in a book."

A small moan escaped from Ruth, causing Stassen to suddenly turn and look at her. Really look at her. "Is something wrong, Mrs. Larkin? You're terribly pale."

Ruth turned large tear-filled eyes on Stassen, piercing him with the intense hatred of her stare. "I don't know why you're doing this," she hissed, her voice low and guttural, "unless you get some sort of perverse pleasure out of torturing me. Haven't you and Hal done enough to me already? Why can't you two just leave me alone!"

Stassen jerked back, his eyes skimming helplessly over the crowd as though seeking an explanation for Ruth's outburst from some unknown quarter. Hal was still holding forth at the microphone, and no one else was near, so Stassen settled for a silent contemplation of his hands. From the corner of her eye, however, Ruth could tell that he was watching her warily.

Without warning, Ruth began to gag. She tried in vain to conceal her distress by hunching over the table, fingers pressed tightly over her mouth. Stassen stared at her with alarm, his hands making vague, irregular circles in the air. "Are you ill, Mrs. Larkin?" he asked hesitantly. "Would you like me to find someone to help you to the ladies' room?"

Ruth brusquely waved him off, preferring to remain as still as possible until the nausea subsided. But that wasn't the only reason she was reluctant to leave the table. The violent trembling that had so afflicted her hands a few minutes ago had now spread to her legs, and she didn't dare attempt to stand up just yet. The ceremonies were almost over anyway, and she'd be far less conspicuous sitting quietly at the table waiting for everyone to leave than trying to make a possibly stumbling and ungraceful exit.

"I didn't mean to offend you, Mrs. Larkin," Stassen ventured again, his voice gruff with uncertainty. "Please believe that. It never occurred to me that a mention of your husband's literary genius would upset you so much. Naturally Hal told me how much you'd helped him with the manuscript. The typing and so on . . ."

All at once it became clear, so crystal clear that Ruth wondered how she could have been such an idiot these past few months. Stassen didn't have the slightest inkling that she, and not Hal, had written that book! Everything Hal had told her about the circumstances surrounding the sale of *Twin Lives* had been a lie. Everything. Including that story about Judd Stassen insisting the book needed a "name" author to be salable. The truth was that Stassen had been as much a dupe as she.

The realization left Ruth horrified at her behavior toward this poor man, at her automatic assumption that he and Hal were conspiring together against her. The only thing Judd Stassen was guilty of was trying to be kind to her. And she had been anything but kind in return.

The whole situation was so ludicrous and so humiliating that it pushed Ruth close to the giddy edge of hysteria. Somehow she would have to make amends to Judd Stassen. Mere words seemed so empty, so meaningless, but they were all she had. "I owe you an apology," she told him, her voice breaking. "A very sincere apology for my unspeakable rudeness tonight. Hal's so-called literary genius has made fools out of both of us."

Ruth could see from the expression on Stassen's face that he was totally confused by this sudden change in her mood, and more than a little disturbed by the strangeness of her remark. Not only did she owe him an apology, Ruth decided, she also owed him an explanation. Whether he would believe that explanation was something else.

"Your first impression of Hal was absolutely correct," Ruth continued tightly, struggling to regain control over her quavering voice. "Hal is far too shallow to have written that book. In fact, he didn't write it."

There was a long pause before Stassen asked the question she'd been waiting for. "If Larkin didn't write *Twin Lives,* who did?"

Their eyes locked, and Ruth stared at him earnestly. "Can't you guess? I did. He stole the manuscript from me and took it to you."

Judd Stassen abruptly turned to look at Hal Larkin, who remained behind the lectern receiving handshakes and congratulations from the publisher's staff and guests.

"Yes, yes . . ." Stassen nodded thoughtfully. "I suppose I ought to say I'm terribly shocked and surprised, but in all honesty, I must admit I'm not."

"You really didn't know, then?"

Stassen shook his head and scowled as the milling group surrounding Hal Larkin broke away, only to be replaced by another. "No, not in concrete terms. Just instinct, I suppose. I don't know what else you would call it. After a while a good agent tends to develop a sort of sixth sense about writers. I had a hunch there was more behind this book than Hal was telling me."

Ruth averted her face so Stassen couldn't see the private pain, tinged with triumph, in her eyes.

"But what I don't understand," he continued more gently, "is why you let him take the credit for writing *Twin Lives.* The book is brilliant, truly brilliant. Surely you couldn't have given it up so easily?"

"It's a long story," Ruth said, her composure nearly regained. "Maybe one day I'll tell you about it. I can promise you, though, it won't happen again. Right now I have to make a very important phone call. Do you think you could help me find the telephone?"

Once found, the telephone felt slippery in her damp hand. She misdialed two wrong numbers before Adrianna's silky, reassuring voice answered. "Addy?" Ruth said into the receiver, keeping her voice low so she would not be overheard. "I've changed my mind. I'll do whatever you say."

"Are you certain, Ruthie? Absolutely certain? Once we start, there can be no backing out of the agreement," Adrianna warned.

"Yes, I'm certain. Finally I'm very certain." There was a new note of decisiveness in Ruth's answer. "Just tell me what you want me to do."

9

Hal Larkin hoisted the cheap bathroom glass to his lips and drank greedily, oblivious of the gritty after-taste that scratched the back of his throat.

So far the evening had been spectacular, one of the best in recent memory, and for that he had to thank the exquisite and unbelievably carnal Adrianna Farrelly. And Ruth, of course. Let's not forget Ruth, he re-minded himself. After all, she was the one who'd inad-vertently brought him and Adrianna together, and then so conveniently flown off to Acapulco two days ago for a short vacation. If he were truly lucky, she'd stay in Mexico for a long vacation—say a couple of weeks or more.

Larkin smugly recalled the Saturday afternoon when Adrianna Farrelly joined the endless ranks of women who succumbed so easily to his irresistible sex appeal. It was the day after that publisher's dinner at 21, and he was just getting back to the apartment when he heard the unusual sound of laughter coming from the living room. No one ever came to visit Ruth at home, so he thought at first the unexpected guest had to be someone looking for him, possibly as a result of the ceremonies the previous night. Even so, he was unpre-pared for the sight of the long-limbed, elegant woman reclining languidly on the sofa, her lap filled with a colorful assortment of brochures.

"I do think Las Brisas is the better choice for you, Ruthie," the woman drawled casually, with a slight Southern inflection to her voice. "The service is better

there, and so is the caliber of guests. This other resort"
—she held up one of the folders—"draws a tackier
crowd. Not really the sort of people you'd be comfortable mingling with."

Ruth glanced up and saw Hal standing in the doorway, his puffy and bloodshot eyes fastened hungrily on
Adrianna. "Well, here's the wandering boy at long last,"
she said, making no comment except with her disap-
proving eyes on the rumpled appearance of his dinner
jacket. "Hal, you remember my old college friend
Adrianna Farrelly, don't you?"

"Who could forget the lovely Adrianna?" He grinned,
palming back his disheveled hair. He wished he had
showered and shaved before coming home. But then,
he hadn't expected anyone to be there. No one ever
was, except Ruth. "How long has it been, Adrianna?
Eight, nine years?"

"Something like that," Adrianna agreed, bestowing
one of her tantalizing smiles on him.

"Ruth talks about you all the time—and those theater
lunches you're always having together with what's-her-
name . . . Millie, isn't it?" Larkin prided himself on his
memory for names. Especially women's names. "I've
told Ruth a thousand times we ought to have you and
your husband—John, right? —over some evening for
dinner."

Adrianna gathered up the brochures and stacked them
neatly on the side table at her elbow. "I'm sure we
would love to come. Unfortunately John travels a great
deal in his work, and sometimes it's a little difficult
finding a free evening. But certainly we can work something out."

Larkin picked up the travel brochures and idly flicked
through them, noting that they were all for resorts in
and around Acapulco. "To what do we owe the pleasure
of your visit this afternoon? Are you and Ruth planning
a trip?"

Adrianna's soft laugh was like music, its lilting ca-
dence warm and inviting. "Oh my, yes. But not for
me—just Ruth." She glanced at her friend sitting next
to her and touched her arm protectively. "I've been

trying to persuade Ruth that she really ought to get away from this dreadful weather for a while. She's been looking so thin and pale lately, and a week or so in the sun would do her a world of good—make a whole new woman out of her!"

"I think you're absolutely right."

Ruth shifted uneasily on the sofa, widening the space between Adrianna and herself. "You do?" she asked, sounding faintly surprised that he would agree so readily. "These places are terribly expensive, Hal—especially during the winter season."

Larkin crossed over to the bar and opened a bottle of Scotch, cocking an eyebrow in a questioning look. Both women declined the unspoken offer, and he quickly tossed down a shot, straight. "We can afford it," he said, putting down the shot glass. "Matter of fact, it's the best idea I've heard in a long time. As long as you don't expect me to go with you."

"I hardly expected you to go with me," Ruth answered flatly. "I'm perfectly aware that my wishes or expectations are of little concern to you."

"Still sore about being dragged to that dinner last night, huh?" Hal sneered, his confidence bolstered by the Scotch. He addressed Adrianna directly. "Did she tell you how she ditched me last night? At my own dinner? Last I saw of her, she and my agent were waltzing out the door arm in arm together like long-lost lovers. Left me standing there with egg on my face in front of my publisher and everybody."

"I'm surprised you noticed," Ruth retorted sharply, her eyes flashing. "And yes, Mr. Stassen was kind enough to bring me home. Which is more than you would have done if I'd bothered to wait for you."

Adrianna rose from the sofa, her hands spread in supplication. "Please, I didn't come here to listen to you two fight. Can't we talk about Mexico without this arguing?"

Hal poured another shot of Scotch. "All right, Ruth. How about this trip of yours? Have you decided where and when you want to go?"

Ruth nodded, but let Adrianna speak, watching as

her friend spread out one of the brochures for Hal's inspection. "Las Brisas. Next week, if we can get hotel and airline reservations for her."

"Oh, we'll get her reservations, all right," Hal said with unconcern. "I'll have my secretary work out the travel arrangements on Monday. A place like this won't turn down World Fashion Group. Especially if they think it might lead to a magazine spread." He winked conspiratorially at Adrianna.

"What a marvelous idea!" Adrianna beamed delightedly. "How clever of you to have thought of using the company's connections." Adrianna turned away from Hal and smiled down at Ruth. "Darling, do you think I might have that cup of tea now? Maybe with one of those delightful little grilled cheese sandwiches you do so well? I missed lunch, and all of a sudden I'm simply famished!"

As soon as Ruth was safely out of the room, Adrianna turned back to Hal and gave him the full force of her magnetic charm. "I can see why Ruth has kept us apart all these years," she purred, trailing a long red fingernail down the front of his soiled evening shirt. Goosebumps prickled his flesh at the thought of what that fingernail could do on bare skin. "You are a very, very attractive man."

"And you"—Hal grinned in turn—"are one hell of a sexy lady."

Adrianna inched closer until her breast skimmed Larkin's chest. "Do you really think so?" she breathed, her body sensuously brushing against him.

"Sweetheart, I know so," he said, the familiar pleasurable tension building in his groin. "And believe me, I'm an expert on sexy ladies."

Adrianna suddenly moved a couple of steps away, her back half-turned to him. "You do have a rather notorious reputation," she acknowledged, a small smile curving her lips. "Are you sure you can live up to it?"

Without hesitation he grabbed Adrianna in his arms and smashed his mouth against hers, her sharp intake of breath spurring his hands into a hurried, frenzied exploration of her body under the clinging cashmere dress.

Adrianna elbowed her way free of his embrace and vigorously smoothed down her clothing. "Are you mad, Hal Larkin?" she demanded indignantly. "Here? In your own home, with your wife—and my dear friend—in the next room?"

Larkin's pulse was racing, and he felt hot and uncomfortable in his formal evening clothes. What in hell did she want, anyway? First she asks for it, then she pushes him away. "You tell me where, then," he answered angrily. "Unless, of course, you're one of those women who only like to tease."

Adrianna crossed over to the doorway as though listening for sounds in the kitchen. With a smile that indicated she was satisfied Ruth couldn't hear them, she opened a small leather handbag lying on a nearby table and pulled out a card. "This is my private line at home. Call me when Ruth's travel arrangements are set and we'll make a date." She watched to make sure Larkin had safely pocketed the card. "But remember, I won't meet you until after Ruth has left for Mexico. Is that understood?"

Larkin grinned obscenely and licked his lips. "Whatever you say, Mrs. Farrelly. Whatever you say."

"And now, if you'll excuse me," she said lightly, "I'll go and see if Ruth needs any help in the kitchen."

Making the reservations for Ruth had taken longer than he'd hoped, but now, lying on the bed in the hotel room he rented by the month, Hal Larkin decided the wait had been damn well worth it. Adrianna had been more woman than even he'd anticipated, responding to his overtures with an aggressive, unbridled passion he found both fascinating and, to his own surprise, a little frightening. Not unpleasantly so, though.

They'd made love within minutes of Adrianna's arrival. He almost didn't recognize her at first, dressed as she was in a nondescript coat with a scarf pulled down over a short blond wig, and wearing thick horn-rimmed glasses. He'd been amused at her disguise, and even more amused by her explanation that she didn't want to be spotted by anyone who might mention a chance encounter to John Farrelly. Who from her set of friends would she be likely to meet at the Hotel Crayton?

Adrianna lay now in the curve of his arm, momentarily satiated by their feverish first coupling, her slightly damp auburn hair fanning out across his chest. Next time, he promised himself, they'd take it slow and easy, prolonging the ecstasy he knew they were both capable of achieving.

"Are you awake?" he asked huskily, shifting his arm a bit to ease the pressure of her weight.

"Mmmm. Sort of."

"How about a drink?"

Adrianna pushed herself up into a sitting position and brushed the hair back from her face. He wanted to pull her back down, to feel the warm smoothness of those seductive breasts against his skin, but he also wanted a drink. And at the moment, he wanted a drink more. The two or three he'd downed in order to kill time before Adrianna's arrival were beginning to wear off. It was time for another.

Larkin started to swing a leg off the bed, when Adrianna stopped him with a firm hand on his belly. "Stay there, lover boy," she ordered sweetly. "Make yourself comfortable and I'll get your drink." She glanced curiously around the meagerly furnished room. "Where do you keep it?"

"Bathroom. Ice bucket in the sink, glasses on back of the john."

He dozed lightly as Adrianna busied herself just out of sight in the bathroom, peeling cellophane wrappers off the glasses and clinking ice around in the cheap Styrofoam bucket that came with the room. Pornographic images slid across his semiconscious mind until the piercing squeal of the medicine cabinet's rusty hinges brought him fully awake.

"What are you looking for?" he called sleepily. "The bourbon's there on the floor, next to the tub. Can't miss it."

"I have it," Adrianna answered, her voice faintly echoing in the tiled room. "But I was hoping you might have some mouthwash." There was a small laugh. "Looks like you have an entire drugstore stashed away in here. With everything except mouthwash."

Larkin stretched the kinks out of his arms and legs, his buttocks nearly lifting off the bed. "Should be a bottle of the stuff there somewhere. Try looking under the sink."

Adrianna appeared in the doorway holding only one glass and wearing a skimpy hotel towel wrapped around her middle. It concealed very little. She perched expectantly on the side of the bed while Hal levered himself up on an elbow to drink from the glass she held out to him.

"Where's yours?"

Adrianna's eyes opened wide in mock surprise. "Silly me! I left it in the bathroom!" She ran her hand along his chest, flicking playfully at his nipple. "Never mind, I'll get it later. Go ahead and drink yours," she urged. "I love to watch a real man drink."

Larkin took his cue and downed the bourbon in one long, continuous swallow, not bothering to suppress the resulting belch. He reached out to her, but Adrianna was already up and moving toward the bathroom again.

"Won't be a minute, lover. You rest up all you can, because I have a big surprise in store for you," she said enticingly, this time closing the bathroom door behind her.

Larkin lay back again, pillowing his head on his arms, trying to imagine what Adrianna meant. Most women were pretty transparent, but not this one. This one was definitely different. She was classy on the outside, all right, but underneath that class lurked the soul, and the experience, of a whore. He'd have to be careful with this one, he thought. Given half a chance, a woman like that could chew a man into little pieces and spit him back out before he knew what hit him.

He wished she'd hurry up in there. What in hell could she be doing that would take so long? Larkin was beginning to feel unusually lethargic, the strength sapped from his body as overwhelming fatigue set in. It seemed to take a tremendous effort just to open his eyes and look at his watch, an effort that left him even more tired. A short snooze while she was doing whatever it was she was doing couldn't hurt, he decided. When she was ready, she would just damn well have to wake him up.

Adrianna cracked open the door and peeked into the bedroom, satisfied with the sound of Larkin's deep and regular breathing. He'd fallen asleep far more quickly than she'd expected, but then, she'd done her best to wear him out.

Although she knew it wasn't necessary, Adrianna moved quietly around the room as she gathered up her clothes and searched for hairpins and other items easily overlooked. Nothing of hers must be left in that room, not even something as innocuous as a bobby pin. She dressed quickly and slipped on a pair of thin surgical gloves she'd brought with her, all the while keeping a watchful eye on Larkin's slumbering form. She wasn't certain how long it would take a man of that size to slip into a coma, but she assumed it couldn't be too long.

Adrianna picked up Larkin's glass from the bedside table and carried it into the bathroom, where she dumped out the fragments of ice and washed it carefully with water from the tap. She then partially refilled the glass with bourbon and ice and returned to the bedroom. Gingerly she lifted Larkin's limp hand and pressed his fingers around the glass, finally replacing the drink in its original position on the nightstand.

Next she retrieved the vial of hundred-milligram Seconal she'd found in Larkin's medicine cabinet. The ones Adrianna had mixed into his drink. She'd already flushed the empty red jackets down the toilet and cleaned up any traces that may have spilled, so all that remained was to press his unresponsive fingers around the cleanly wiped sides of the brown plastic bottle. The vial went onto the nightstand next to the drink, and with sudden inspiration she tipped it over so that the scant handful of capsules left inside spilled across the table and onto the floor. To a casual observer it would look as though Larkin had drunkenly knocked the vial over while reaching for the glass.

Adrianna was pleased she hadn't had to use the pills she'd brought with her. Ruth had told her that Larkin kept a remarkable supply of drugs on hand wherever he was, but she couldn't take the chance of not finding something suitably lethal. As it turned out, his medicine cabinet had been crammed with everything from aspirin to a rainbow assortment of barbiturates. She selected the Seconal simply because the bottle contained the most capsules—and because it sported a legitimate pharmacy label bearing Larkin's name.

One last trip around the small room to wipe various surfaces with the towel assured Adrianna that all traces of her presence had been obliterated—right down to the three strands of auburn hair she'd plucked off the pillow next to Larkin's head. She peeled off one glove and touched his forehead lightly, noting that his skin was becoming cold and clammy. That was a good sign. A very good sign.

Confident that she'd done everything humanly possible to ensure that Hal Larkin wouldn't live to see the morning, she put on her coat, stuffed the used towel and the surgical gloves into her large handbag, and headed for the door. Before opening it, however, she turned and blew Larkin a theatrical kiss.

"That, my dear Hal," she whispered, "is good-bye from Ruth. You thieving bastard."

10

Maria Corso knew it wasn't one of her better days even before she unlocked the door to Room 1017. The rank, fetid odor of dried urine and excrement hit her first; then, as her eyes became accustomed to the artificial darkness, she became aware of the unmistakable outline of a body lying on top of the bed. She didn't have to pass the threshold and enter the room to know that the person on the bed was dead, and had been for several hours. The smell of death had been too familiar for too many years for Maria Corso to miss its significance.

Maria groaned inwardly, not out of compassion for the corpse lying alone in the dark, but for herself. Her cleaning schedule was already off by nearly an hour, thanks to a handful of sluggish guests on the ninth floor who couldn't be bothered to get up and out of their rooms before she started her morning rounds. And now she had to find a dead body in the first room she entered on the tenth. This, she told herself, she needed about as much as another varicose vein.

Resentment mingled with resignation as Maria dropped the heavy vacuum cleaner next to the door and crossed the room to pull back the drapes and raise the shades. One window was tightly sealed shut by layers of ancient, flaking paint, but the second window inched up enough to let in a steady draft of fresh cold air. The draft didn't totally eliminate the stench, but it helped.

The unrelenting light of day was not kind to the man on the bed. He was lying on his back, stark naked, with

his legs spread apart. A dark stain spread across the
sheet under his thighs, indicating that at some point,
possibly in the final throes of death, he had voided his
bowels.

The mattress was completely ruined, Maria thought
as she reached for the phone on the nightstand, carefully avoiding the hand dangling over the side of the
bed. At least they couldn't blame this one on her and
deduct another sizable chunk of her paycheck. With
that comforting idea fixed in her mind, she dialed the
front desk and waited through six long rings before the
man on duty answered.

"Call the cops, Henry. We got a dead one up here in
ten-seventeen," she said tiredly. *Dios mío*, but her
legs ached, and it was only ten-thirty. She'd be in
agony by the time she got off work at four, with both
legs swollen to piano size. "That's right, Mr. Larkin's
room. Sure I'll wait for 'em. I ain't going noplace."

She replaced the receiver and looked down again at
the naked man on the bed. Larkin—that was the name
she'd been trying to remember. Mr. Larkin, she decided, was a lot better-looking dead than he had been
alive. Death had erased the telltale signs of dissipation
from his face, smoothing his features into a fresh, boyish
innocence. Even the open, gaping mouth could not
detract from this impression of youthful vulnerability.

Maria crossed herself solemnly and went back to
work, preferring to stay busy until the police sent someone to take charge of the room and its pitiful occupant.
The wait lasted nearly forty-five minutes, by which
time Maria had finished mopping the bathrooom and
was packing Hal Larkin's few belongings in a small
carryall bag she'd found tossed in a corner of the closet.

"What the hell do you think you're doing?" Detective
James Collins demanded from the door. A uniformed
officer stood behind him in the corridor, notebook and
pencil at the ready. "Don't you know no better than to
go messing around with evidence?"

Maria Corso eyed the young detective coolly, noting
his ill-fitting sport coat, loosened tie, and uncombed

hair. "What evidence?" she asked. "This guy's an OD, not a gunshot or knifing."

She stood with arms folded as Collins inspected the corpse, then picked up first the half-empty glass and then the vial from the nightstand, sniffing both. "You report the body?" he asked, keeping his back to her as he walked around the room, opening drawers and peering into the now empty closet.

"Yeah."

"How'd you know he was an OD and not a heart attack or something?"

Maria settled into the one armchair in the room, easing off her worn and tattered shoes. This was obviously going to take a while; no point standing up when she could be sitting down.

"Well, I'll tell you, sonny. I spent eighteen years over at Bellevue cleaning up the emergency room. I probably seen more stiffs in one month than you'll see in the next twenty years. Everything from Sterno to stroke."

"That don't tell me nothing. I want to know how you knew he was an OD."

Maria gave Collins a long-suffering look as she massaged first one leg, then the other, through the opaque support hose. "You weren't listening, sonny," she repeated carefully. "I told you already. I spent eighteen years cleaning up Bellevue."

Collins bent to retrieve a Seconal capsule that had rolled under the bed and dropped it into a plastic evidence bag. "Okay, so you were eighteen years at Bellevue. Big deal. Since that makes you some kind of expert, tell me what the guy swallowed to wind up so dead."

Maria stopped rubbing her legs long enough to point toward the bathroom. "Go look in the medicine cabinet. He got everything in there—uppers, downers, and sideways. Including some junk I ain't never seen before. Don't know what it is."

Collins disappeared into the bathroom and Maria heard the grating squeak of the cabinet door swinging open. He reappeared a few moments later carrying the nearly empty bottle of bourbon she'd stuck inside the leaking ice bucket, intending to throw both out.

"How well you know this guy?" he asked, pointing at Larkin's body with the bottle.

"I seen him around when I was cleaning."

"How long's he been living here?"

"He don't."

Collins put the bottle down on the nightstand next to the glass and empty pharmacy vial. "He don't what?"

"He don't live here," Maria explained patiently. "Only uses the room two, maybe three nights a week. For his girlfriends, you know?"

"You seem to know an awful lot about someone you don't know," Collins remarked evenly. "How'd you know he had girlfriends in here?"

Maria let out a derisive snort. "I saw 'em. Lots of times. None of 'em twice, either. Then there was the bras and pantyhose I'd find under the bed sometimes. Even a girdle once. All different sizes. I'd always put the stuff over on the dresser there, and the next day or the day after, I'd find it again in the wastebasket. Good-quality stuff, too. Never could figure out why he didn't give it back."

Collins pondered this information for a while. "Any of those broads look like a wife?"

"Sure, but not Mr. Larkin's. Weren't no formal introductions, you know?"

Maria broke off as a second uniformed officer came into the room, also carrying a notepad. "Found the manager downstairs. He says the deceased's name is Larkin. Harold E. Larkin. Been renting this room about a year and a half. Turns out he's some kind of big shot. Manager says he wrote a bestseller book, even gave him an autographed copy." The policeman produced a volume from under his arm and held it out to Collins, who compared the picture on the back with the face of the dead man.

"Could be the same guy." Collins placed the book on the dresser next to the bag Maria had been packing with Larkin's possessions. "Did the manager know if he had a job? A family, maybe?"

"His registration card says he works for World Fashion Magazines Group. Secretary's name is Bailey—the switchboard girl says she's not too sure about the first name. Anyways, this Bailey woman calls pretty often to leave messages for Larkin."

Collins nodded to Maria Corso. "You can go. Give your name, address, and phone number to the officer outside so we know where to reach you, okay?"

As Maria picked up the vacuum cleaner and lumbered out of the room, Collins turned back to the officer. "Go find a phone somewhere and tell the coroner's office to send over the meat wagon. I'm going to call this Bailey dame and see if we can get a positive ID on our friend Mr. Larkin here."

Larkin's secretary turned out to be one Margaret Bailey whose crisp efficiency crackled through the telephone lines like static electricity. She accepted the announcement of Larkin's death with a dispassionate quietude that Collins found vaguely unsettling, especially in view of her statement that she'd worked for the man for twelve years. In spite of that long association, however, Margaret Bailey expressed none of the weepy hysterics that Collins had come to expect as a matter of course when delivering bad news to relatives, friends, or co-workers.

"Did Mr. Larkin have a family?" Collins noticed with some annoyance that his own voice was beginning to take on a crisper edge as well, probably in reaction to Margaret Bailey's clipped formality. And he was taking greater care with his grammar, too.

"Yes, he does. Or did," Mrs. Bailey quickly corrected herself. "His present wife is currently visiting Acapulco, and his parents are retired in California. Santa Barbara, I believe."

"Do you know where Mrs. Larkin can be reached?"

"Of course. I made the travel arrangements for her myself. Would you like me to contact her in Mexico?"

Collins carried the phone over to the armchair Maria Corso had recently vacated and sat down. "Yeah. And while you're at it, tell her I'd like to ask her a few questions when she gets back to town. Just a formality, you understand."

"Of course." There was a short pause as Margaret Bailey jotted down his instructions. "Anything else?"

"Yeah." This was the part Collins hated the most—the moment when most of them tended to fall apart. "Would you mind coming over here and identifying the body for us?"

To his astonishment, Margaret Bailey readily agreed. Almost eagerly.

Two days later Ruth Larkin stumbled down the steps of the precinct station in a daze. All the way home on the plane from Mexico, part of her mind had refused to accept the reality of Hal's death, had hoped that Margaret Bailey's terse phone call was the result of an enormous mistake on someone's part. Even while going through customs at Kennedy Airport, Ruth had half-expected Hal to be waiting for her outside the gate. He hadn't been there, of course. Nor had anyone else, for that matter.

Now Detective Collins had laid whatever ambivalent hopes she might have harbored to rest for good. There was no remaining doubt in her mind that Hal Larkin was as dead as a person could get. A lethal combination of drugs and alcohol, Collins had told her. Whether his death was an accident or suicide, they didn't know yet, and probably never would. The final determination was up to the coroner's inquest.

"Speaking personally, rather than officially," the young detective had said, "my guess is that your husband's death was an accident. Happens all the time. A guy has a couple of drinks and decides to boost the effect with a couple of pills. A few more drinks and he forgets he already took some pills, so he takes some more. And so on. Pretty powerful combination, that stuff."

Collins glanced up from the papers on his desk. "On the other hand, the preliminary lab report says there was enough Seconal in him to kill even without the alcohol. That could mean he was either very determined to die, or very stupid. Since we didn't find any suicide note, and his secretary says he was in an unusually good mood the day of his death, I think it's probably safe to say he was very stupid."

Ruth felt her throat constrict as she tried to speak. "Was . . . was anyone with him when he died?"

"How do you mean, 'with him'?"

She bowed her head, unwilling to meet Collins' gaze. "You needn't spare my feelings, Detective. I know all about my husband's extracurricular activities. But I would like to know whether anyone was with him when he died."

Collins shook his head and lowered his eyes to the file on the desk. "We can't say for sure, but I don't think so. No sign of anyone in the room, anyway."

Ruth hadn't realized she was holding her breath until it suddenly came out in a long, low sigh. She couldn't imagine how Adrianna had maneuvered Hal into taking those drugs, but however she'd done it, she'd apparently covered her tracks well. If, in fact, Adrianna had had anything to do with Hal's death. The thought occurred to Ruth that it was entirely possible Hal could have died exactly as this young police detective hypothesized—from a simple accidental, self-administered overdose of drugs and alcohol.

The interview with Collins ended with unexpected abruptness when the detective was called away on another case, and Ruth stood now on the gritty, slush-encrusted pavement outside the police station, uncertain what to do next. There were funeral arrangements to make, people to notify. But what she really wanted to do was talk to Adrianna.

Ruth wondered how Addy would react to being questioned about Hal's death. Would she resent being asked, expecting Ruth to take everything she said and did on faith? Would Adrianna even tell her the truth, or only what she thought Ruth wanted to hear? By the same token, did she, Ruth, really want to know? Yes, Ruth finally decided, shivering with cold, she did want to know. Suddenly it was important, vitally important, to know if Adrianna had killed Hal. If Adrianna was guilty, then Ruth was guilty too. Perhaps even more so. But if

Adrianna was innocent, if he had died from an accidental overdose, then she was free—free of Hal, and free from her part of the agreement.

Ruth walked for four long blocks before she found a pay phone that hadn't been put out of order by vandals. The glass inside the booth was a spiderweb of cracks, but the phone itself remained functional.

"Hello, Farrelly residence."

"May I speak to Mrs. Farrelly, please? This is Ruth Larkin."

"I'm terribly sorry," the housekeeper answered, not sounding sorry at all, "but Mrs. Farrelly is out of town for a few days."

Ruth felt her knees begin to tremble, and she leaned weakly against the side of the booth. "Where," she whispered, "did Adrianna go?"

"Mrs. Farrelly left for Lake Placid this morning."

11

The heavy, snow-laden clouds hung low in the sky as Millie Phillips steered the station wagon along the narrow dirt road that skirted the edges of John Farrelly's Westchester retreat. The earth beneath the wheels was frozen into jagged ruts that bounced the car from one side of the track to the other, while beside her on the front seat, two milk cartons filled with water sloshed dangerously, threatening to spill with each new jolt. As she drew closer to her destination, Millie felt an increasing sense of wonderment at Adrianna's ability to convince people to undertake missions of sheer lunacy. Why else would she, Millie Phillips, an otherwise sane and normal person, be foolish enough to sabotage an airplane in broad daylight when she knew nothing about either sabotage or airplanes?

Millie gently fingered the tender flesh around her right eye, grateful that the swelling seemed to have stopped. A little more and the eye would have closed; then how would she have managed? Driving along this track was difficult enough using two good eyes; with only one, it would have been close to impossible. Yet the bruised flesh did serve as a painful reminder of her ultimate reward for this afternoon's effort: the permanent removal of Ed Phillips from her life and that of her young and far-too-vulnerable daughters. Millie gripped the wheel tightly and silently prayed that when the time came, Ruth would find the courage to do for her what she was doing now for Adrianna.

Last evening had been bad. Not as bad as some of

Ed's previous rampages, but bad enough to convince Millie that Adrianna was absolutely right: these men they'd married, and Ed Phillips in particular, must be destroyed as quickly as possible. There was simply no other alternative.

The evening had begun as so many of them had, with Ed arriving home in a belligerent mood exacerbated by a few drinks at a bar near the office. Millie and the girls tiptoed through the routine of dinner and clearing up, afraid that one wrong word, or even a misinterpreted glance, would set off the volcano of violence they sensed was building up inside Phillips. At moments such as this, Millie had to keep reminding herself that Ed hadn't always been so brutal. In fact, the first few years of their marriage had been pretty good, all things considered. But the pressures and frustrations resulting from his plumbing-supply business had built up to the point where Ed was now losing almost all control of his volatile temper, particularly at home. Although he would never have admitted it, Millie thought that deep inside, Ed Phillips probably knew he wasn't much of a businessman. If the truth were known, he was barely adequate as a plumber. Yet here he was, the proprietor of a highly lucrative wholesale operation that had become successful in spite of his efforts, not because of them.

Millie had hoped that a large dinner, followed by a few cans of beer, would put Ed to sleep in front of the television in the den. She hadn't counted on the phone ringing just as Ed nodded off, bringing him straight out of his chair with a roar of rage that would have frightened the neighbors into phoning the police if there'd been any neighbors close enough to hear. But the houses, set apart on a minimum of two wooded acres, were so isolated that no outsider had ever witnessed the all-too-frequent battles that were waged, as Phillips put it, "to keep you fucking females in line."

Wide-awake now and seething with anger, Phillips prowled the two-story Dutch Colonial house looking for Millie. Millie barely had time to send Evelyn and Deedee down into the basement playroom, with orders to barricade themselves in the laundry room if necessary, before Ed cornered her in the kitchen. Phillips spotted a skillet, filled with detergent and water, soaking in the sink and grabbed the handle, sloshing greasy water over the freshly scrubbed counter and floor.

"Who the fuck was on the phone?" he demanded, coming toward her with the skillet raised over his head. "One of your fancy boyfriends from the tennis club? You dirty little cocksucking whore!"

The skillet crashed into the wall above her head as Millie ducked the blow, escaping under his outstretched arm as he lunged toward her. Fast as she was, though, Phillips was faster and he swung the skillet again, this time catching her in the middle of the back. Millie felt the force of the blow push the air out of her lungs as she went sprawling across the floor. Before she could recover, Phillips had kicked her over onto her back and pulled her up by the front of her blouse.

"No pretty-faced tennis jock is going to look at you twice by the time I get finished with you. But first you're going to clean up that goddamn mess, you hear?" he yelled, pointing at the sudsy water glistening on the floor near the sink. "Now, move it!"

He released her blouse and watched, cradling the dripping skillet, as Millie scrabbled on hands and knees toward the sink, her skirt dragging through the water. She didn't dare stand up to reach the paper towels, so she searched the cabinet under the sink for a new package, which she hurriedly unwrapped, spreading the towels as liberally as she dared. When the last drop of water was sponged off the floor and the sodden towels deposited in the garbage bin, Millie began easing backward toward the door, still on her hands and knees.

"Where do you think you're going, you two-timing bitch?" Phillips grabbed her by the hair, slamming the side of her face into the cabinet door.

Millie fought to free her hair, kicking and biting as best she could while Phillips repeatedly knocked her against the cabinets. The room went dark for a moment, and Millie realized she was losing consciousness.

As the final darkness closed in, Millie caught a fleeting glimpse of Evie opening the basement door.

When Millie came to some time later, Evie was bending over her, applying an ice pack to the side of her face. She didn't know how those little girls had managed to drag her limp body into the family room and lift her up onto the sofa, but they had. Now Deedee silently crouched next to the sofa, stroking her mother's hand, a pile of bloody towels beside her on the floor.

"Mom, can you hear me?" Evie's pinched, anxious face broke her heart, more so than the pain in her own head and body. "Should I call an ambulance?"

Millie probed the side of her face, tracing the cheek and jaw bones with her fingers. Nothing seemed to be broken, thank God, but her lip was split and one tooth felt loose.

"No, no ambulance," she croaked, awkwardly levering herself up into a sitting position. Her ribs ached where Ed had kicked her and her shoulder was bruised and sore, but everything seemed to function as it should. "Where is he?"

"In bed. Asleep."

Millie shivered at the cold, hard expression on Evie's adolescent face. She wouldn't allow herself to think about what Evie must have done to stop Ed and calm him down enough to fall asleep. And Evie wasn't likely to volunteer any information.

She spent the rest of the night there on the couch, and in the morning Ed was his normal taciturn self. He didn't mention the events of the previous evening, and neither did Millie, although the side of her face was a pulpy mass of bruises and her ribs were so sore it hurt just to breathe. She'd looked up the signs of concussion in a first-aid book, and was relieved to discover that she wasn't experiencing any of the major symptoms.

Shortly after Ed left for the office, Adrianna telephoned to inform Millie that today was the day, and so Millie found herself bouncing over a seldom-used access road to seal the fate of John Farrelly, and through him, of Ed Phillips. Of course, as Adrianna had reluctantly conceded, there was no guarantee that putting

water in the plane's gas tanks would work, but it was far
safer than using sugar or some other substance that
might be detected in the event of a post-crash investigation. If the water method didn't work, she added,
they would simply try something else. And keep on
trying until they met with success. Once John Farrelly
was out of the way, Adrianna reminded her, they could
concentrate on Ed Phillips.

The thick stand of trees on either side of the road
suddenly gave way to a clearing, and Millie could see
acre after acre of gently rolling meadow that had once
been tilled farmland. About two hundred yards into the
clearing was an old weather-beaten barn, and beyond
that the main house and accompanying outbuildings.
Adrianna said the only people on the estate were an
elderly couple, the caretakers, who seldom ventured
out of their cottage during the winter months, except to
check on the main house.

Millie slowly nosed the car off the road in among
some trees, hoping she wouldn't get stuck in an unexpected soft spot. Satisfied that the car couldn't be seen
from the main compound, she removed one key from
her key ring and left the others dangling from the
ignition. Moving as quickly as she could, burdened by
the two slippery cartons of water, Millie crossed the
stubbly field toward the side door of the barn.

The lock was new and stiff, but not frozen as Millie
initially feared. After a minute of fiddling, the dead bolt
slid back and Millie stepped into the unexpected warmth
of the barn's interior. As her eyes adjusted to the dim
light inside, Millie was amazed to find that she was in a
large, spotlessly clean room that bore little resemblance
to the inside of any barn she'd ever seen. Farrelly, she
thought, must have spent a fortune renovating the interior of the building. The floor was of smooth, painted
concrete, and the walls paneled in a white stained pine
that gave the vast open space the antiseptic atmosphere
of an operating theater. A workbench and row of built-in
cabinets occupied the rear wall opposite the main double doors, and off to her right a plain board ladder
ascended into an indistinct gloom that Millie assumed

must be the old loft. Somewhere a furnace was apparently at work, filling the building with warm, dry air.

Occupying the center of the floor space was John Farrelly's Beechcraft Bonanza, also white but trimmed in two shades of grayish blue. As Millie inspected the plane, she noted that Adrianna had been right about the easy accessibility of the gas tanks. The wings, particularly toward the fuselage, were only waist-high, and Millie had no trouble locating the small hinged square covers protecting the gas caps. She pried up the first cover easily with a screwdriver she'd carried in her pocket, unscrewed the cap, and poured in the contents of the first carton of water. The faint odor of aviation fuel permeated the air around her, but it would dissipate before Farrelly came to get his plane.

Millie had just unscrewed the cap on the second wing when she heard the sound of voices outside the barn. She couldn't make out the words, but the voices were high-pitched and quavery, most likely belonging to the elderly couple Adrianna had mentioned. Millie slammed the cover back into place on the wing before realizing she still held the gas cap in her hand. This she shoved into her pocket, along with the screwdriver, and raced for the ladder leading to the loft.

Millie climbed frantically, grasping the top rung just as the side door swung outward, letting in a frigid draft of winter air. She flattened herself against the ladder and froze, not daring to move even a finger for fear whoever had come in would spot the movement. Even in that awkward position, however, Millie had a clear view of the scene below, including the two milk cartons, one now empty, that she'd abandoned on the floor under the right wing.

"I tell you I left that wrench in here," the old man was saying as he shuffled across the floor toward the workbench. He was wearing so many layers of clothing that he walked stiff-legged, arms poking rigidly from his sides like an animated scarecrow. A smaller figure, equally well-bundled against the chill afternoon air, trailed behind.

"You're getting senile, Jeremiah," the old woman

shrilled. "I saw that wrench not yesterday up to the garage."

"I looked in the garage. 'Tweren't there."

" 'Tis. You just can't see good enough anymore to look in the proper place."

"Stop your jabbering, woman. I ain't any more blind or senile than you." The old man half-turned to glare at his wife. "Unless you hid it on me. Wouldn't put it past you none."

The old woman grimaced in disgust and headed back toward the door, until something near the plane caught her eye and she changed course in mid-step. Moving with hesitant and arthritic slowness, she stooped under the wing and retrieved the two milk cartons.

"What are these doing in here, Jeremiah?" she demanded querulously. "Dr. Farrelly'll have a fit if you've been leaving garbage around his aeroplane."

"Go to hell, Sadie, I ain't been leaving no garbage anywheres," Jeremiah protested indignantly. He opened the full carton and studied its contents. "No smell. No taste. Looks like water, not milk."

Sadie nodded noncommittally as she squinted at the printing on the cartons. "Don't know the dairy. Not from any market hereabouts," she announced. "Must be he brought 'em up from the city last weekend."

"Put 'em back, then. If Dr. Farrelly left them there, then he must want 'em there."

The old woman bent over and replaced the two cartons under the wing. "Could be you're right. For once." She straightened up with difficulty, holding on to the wing for support. "Now, find that infernal wrench so we can get back to the house."

"You don't have to stay," the old man reminded her irritably.

"And let you wander off to leave the door open again? This time I'm making sure that door's shut good and proper!"

Jeremiah picked up his discarded gloves from the workbench and shuffled toward his wife. "Might as well get along. I told you the wrench weren't in here."

As the door shut behind the elderly couple, Millie

sagged against the ladder, her muscles aching with the sudden release of tension. She waited several minutes in case the bickering pair returned to search again for the wrench, then eased her way back down the ladder. Her hands were shaking so badly that some of the water splashed over the wing as she emptied the second carton into the gas tank, but she found she no longer cared. All she wanted to do was finish up as quickly as possible and get out of there.

The early dusk of midwinter was descending rapidly as Millie departed from the barn and made her way almost casually back across the field to where she'd left the car, the flattened milk cartons tucked under her arm. Now that she'd carried out her part of the agreement, she hardly cared whether anyone saw her or not.

The wintry wind that blew across her battered face no longer filled her with desolation and despair. For the first time in five years, Mildred Phillips actually welcomed the invigorating sting, and its tantalizing promise of eventual widowhood.

12

Adrianna Farrelly glowered darkly as the cab pulled up in front of the Metropolitan Museum of Art, disgorging Ruth Larkin and Millie Phillips in a breathless rush. She waited until the cab picked up another fare and had gone before she left the sheltering warmth of the doorway and strode regally down the wide steps toward the two women.

"I didn't realize how cold it was." Ruth shivered as Adrianna joined them on the sidewalk. "Please, let's go inside before we freeze to death!"

Adrianna pointedly ignored Ruth's pleading, and instead steered them away from the museum and toward the walkway leading into the park. "You think you're cold?" Adrianna asked sarcastically as their boots kicked up frozen gravel along the pavement. "You weren't the one standing out there in the wind waiting for you to show up. I'd just about given up on you two."

"We're not so late, are we?" Ruth protested, her eyes widening at the sharpness of Adrianna's tone. "We didn't mean to be."

"You knew perfectly well that Ruth and I might be a few minutes late," Millie added defensively. "I warned you yesterday on the phone, remember?"

"I remember," Adrianna replied tersely. "But I didn't realize that 'a few minutes' was going to stretch into nearly three-quarters of an hour!"

"We are not three-quarters of an hour late!" Millie objected, her color heightening perceptibly. "Half an hour at the absolute most, and probably closer to only fifteen or twenty minutes."

"I don't think Addy is really upset about our tardiness," Ruth quietly interjected, pulling up the collar of her coat. "Or anything else to do with either of us, for that matter."

Adrianna nodded toward one of the empty benches lining the walkway and led them over, the three women instinctively huddling together for warmth under the weak winter sun. Adrianna, as was her custom, placed herself in the middle.

"Your lateness certainly didn't help," she conceded, somewhat reluctantly, "but you're right, I suppose. It's just that I'm simply worn out from coping with all this publicity over John's disappearance. I never realized how persistent those newspeople can be. They telephone or come to the door at all hours of the day and night, asking the most inane questions. And if that weren't bad enough, I have to sit through endless boring meetings with attorneys, accountants, the university people, and everyone else involved in John's estate. Sometimes I think these people will drive me crazy with all their double-talk!"

The three friends sat without speaking for several minutes, neither Ruth nor Millie willing to agitate Adrianna further by pointing out that she'd brought these problems on herself. As Adrianna's features began to relax and soften with the subsidence of her anger, Ruth delicately broached the subject again.

"It's been over two weeks since John's plane went down in the Adirondacks," she pointed out. "Hasn't the FAA been able to give you any idea when the wreckage might be found?"

Adrianna reached into her handbag for the cigarette case and was mildly surprised to find her hands trembling from the overload of coffee and nicotine she'd been consuming the past few weeks. "All they could say was that the plane might be found today, it might be found when the snow melts in the spring, or it might never be found at all. There's just no way of telling, since they don't know exactly where in those mountains the plane crashed."

"But didn't a forest ranger or someone actually see the plane go down? I thought I read that in one of the newspaper stories about John's disappearance."

"You can't believe everything you read. You of all people should know that, Ruthie." Adrianna ground out the cigarette under the heel of her boot. "A forest ranger saw a fireball or whatever you call it off in the distance, but he couldn't pinpoint the exact location. Not at night, in the mountains. And by the time the search was started at daylight, a new snowstorm had moved in and pretty well covered up everything."

"So what are you going to do now?"

Adrianna gazed out over the gray landscape as though assessing her options. "Nothing, for the moment. At least, that's what the attorneys advise. If the wreckage isn't found after the snow melts in the spring, I'll have to go to court and try to have him declared legally dead so his will can be probated."

Millie, the more pragmatic of the two, immediately understood where Adrianna's fundamental problem lay. "So what are you using for money while all this is going on?" she asked curiously. "Since I assume the executors won't let you touch John's assets until the legalities of his estate are settled."

Adrianna uttered a short sardonic laugh devoid of any real amusement. "Money? Who needs money when you can get credit? You'd be surprised how many people are willing to extend credit to a potentially wealthy widow in anticipation of her inheritance!" She took out another cigarette, changed her mind about smoking it, and put it back in the case. "Don't look so horrified, Ruthie. Certainly you must have encountered the phenomenon by now. At least you were able to produce a body to prove that your husband is dead."

"Thanks to you," Ruth whispered.

"Yes, thanks to me. And I hope you'll remember that when your turn comes to take on Ed." Adrianna shifted her gaze to Millie. "Speaking of which, have you made the necessary arrangements for leaving town yet?"

"As much as I can for the moment." Millie stretched her arm along the back of the bench and was about to explain further when she was cut off in mid-breath.

"Either you have, or you haven't!" Adrianna exploded, only a thin veneer of civility covering her sudden rage. "I can't do everything for you two, you know. You have to help too! This business is taking entirely too long as it is. Now, I want it over with, and over with by next week at the latest! Have I made myself perfectly understood?"

Millie visibly bridled, drawing herself up with great dignity as she gazed directly at Adrianna. "I know you've been having a rough time these last two weeks, Addy," she said stiffly, "but I hardly think that's any reason to take your frustrations out on me after what I've done for you! At the least you could have had the grace to hear me out before jumping down my throat."

"Millie's right," Ruth unexpectedly agreed in a soft voice that trembled with the hurt caused by Adrianna's harshness. "We've done everything you've told us to do, Addy. The fact that John's plane crashed someplace where they can't find it doesn't justify treating us like a couple of recalcitrant servants. I always thought we . . ." Ruth let her words trail off, the thought unfinished.

The beginning of a contrite smile tugged at the resolute set of Adrianna's lips. "I don't know how you do it, Ruthie," she said with considerably more gentleness, ignoring Millie altogether, "but I always seem to end up apologizing to you for something or other. For your sake, then, I'm willing to listen to whatever Millie has to say."

Millie waited until Adrianna finished settling herself more comfortably on the hard bench. "It's very simple, really. Before we left Ruth's apartment this morning, I called my mother in Louisiana. That's why we were so late meeting you at the museum. Ed always checks our phone bills, so I couldn't call her from home, right?"

Adrianna inclined her head slightly in tacit agreement.

"I told her that I desperately needed to come home for a visit with the girls, but that Ed wouldn't let me. She already knows from my weekly letters to her all about Ed's increasing violence toward me, my fears for Evie—everything. Everything, that is, except our plan for taking care of Ed." Millie solemnly clapsed her hands and went on.

"We talked over several possibilities, and finally arranged that when the time is right, I will signal her through Ruthie. Mother will then telephone Ed and tell him that my father has suffered a massive coronary at his hardware store and isn't expected to live. She'll ask him to break the news to me and make arrangements for all of us to fly down for the final good-byes and the funeral."

"Will Ed believe this?"

"Coming from my mother, sounding suitably hysterical, of course he will. She can be an extremely convincing actress when she wants to be. If I told Ed that my father had a heart attack, he'd be calling every hospital in the parish to find out if I was telling the truth. This way he'll be put in the position of having to tell me about my father and he won't think twice about whether or not it's true."

Adrianna nodded thoughtfully while searching for the holes in Millie's plan. "What if Ed decides to go with you?"

"He won't," Millie said with assurance. "He hates illness and hospitals and everything connected with death. He'll stay as far away as he can get."

"That's all very well and good, but what if Ed says you can't go, dying father or no dying father?"

"I don't think he will, for the simple reason that the request comes from a third party—in this case my mother. And as long as he's absolutely certain that we'll come back within a reasonable period of time, he'll probably agree to let us go."

"And how," Adrianna inquired, "are you going to assure him that you'll come back?"

"By making a deal with him," Millie said. "If he agrees to take us to the airport and buy us three round-trip tickets, then I will turn over to him my checkbook and all my credit cards. He knows we can't go very far without money."

"You'd actually travel all the way to Louisiana without access to any money?" Adrianna asked incredulously. "What if something went wrong? Your baggage was lost, or one of the girls became ill? What would you do then?"

"I don't know," Millie replied. "I'll just have to take the chance. There's no other way he'd let me go. I'm certain of it."

They abruptly dropped their discussion as a young couple came in sight along the path, the two so wrapped up in a heated argument that they appeared not to notice the little group of women sitting mutely on a park bench in the middle of a cold winter day. Only random snatches of the argument reached their ears, but the proximity of the quarrelers was sufficient to darken their mood and reduce the three women to a contemplative silence.

Eventually Adrianna rose and brushed the light dusting of snow from the back of her coat. Ruth and Millie followed her lead and also stood up wordlessly, taking up positions on either side as Adrianna once again moved off down the walkway in the direction of the zoo.

"Our plans are coming along rather well," Adrianna said at last, pausing to readjust the scarf at her throat. "Even better than I thought they would. Ruthie, do you want me to show you how to use the gun once more before you go out to Millie's?"

Ruthie looked away and shook her head. Her whispered "No" was barely audible.

"I merely wondered if you had any questions. I'm an old hand with guns, as you know. Daddy taught me to shoot when I could barely walk. And that Beretta I gave you is in perfect condition even though it hasn't been fired much in recent years." Adrianna seemed to drift away from them as she spoke, her eyes slightly unfocused. "I bought that gun just a year or so after John and I were married. John had a patient then who was more violent than most of the others. Every so often he'd escape from the psychiatric ward and call John at home, threatening to kill him. John never took the calls seriously, but I certainly did. I'm perfectly willing to admit I was frightened then—and frightened a few other times by some of his crazy patients."

Adrianna brushed the hair away from her face and looked up through the trees, where the sun was doing its best to break through a thin layer of scudding gray clouds. "John was so angry with me for buying that gun! He threatened to take it right out and toss it in the river because he didn't want firearms of any sort in the house. After a while he relented when he finally understood how much safer I felt having it available, especially when he was out of town." There was a long pause while Adrianna considered her next words, as though the thought had only newly occurred to her.

"It's odd, you know," she said quietly, "but there have been times these past couple of weeks when I've actually missed John. I never thought that was possible—he was such an arrogant, thoughtless, and selfish man at times. Most of the time, really. And yet I find myself thinking of things I must remember to tell him. Isn't that strange?"

Millie's large blue eyes mirrored surprise. "I never realized that John's passing would affect you that much, Addy. Has the possibility occurred to you that John might not be dead after all? Perhaps he survived the crash and found shelter in one of those closed-up summer lodges."

"Christ, I hope not!" Adrianna choked, then found herself laughing for the first time in days. "After all the trouble that sanctimonious old fraud has caused me, the last thing in the world I want is to have him come waltzing down a mountainside some afternoon!"

Adrianna stopped and turned to look for Ruth, who had dropped several paces behind. "You're certainly not contributing very much today, Ruthie. Still worrying about what's going to happen with Ed?"

Ruth bobbed her head, not raising her eyes to meet Adrianna's. "Do I really have to use the gun, Addy?" she asked in a small, stricken voice. "Isn't there some other way? You and Millie didn't have to kill face-to-face. Why do I?"

Adrianna sighed and reached for one of Ruth's gloved hands, alarmed to find that Ruth's arm was practically vibrating with tension. "We've been over this before, Ruthie. There must be no pattern to these deaths. Every one must be different."

Ruth was on the verge of sobbing openly, her eyes filled with fear. "But do I have to shoot him? Couldn't I drain the brake fluid from his car or somehow poison his drinks like you did? I could handle something like that so much better than an outright shooting."

Adrianna and Millie exchanged glances of concern. "We've already had one mechanical failure and one overdose," Adrianna gently explained with all the patience she could muster. "Using either of those methods again could raise suspicions if the authorities ever decided to look too hard at these incidents. No, the gun is best. Afterward you simply drop it into the river. Once it's gone, there is absolutely nothing that can be traced back to any one of us."

"And don't forget the insurance," Millie added, keeping her voice low. "If Ed's death is made to look like out-and-out murder, then the double-indemnity clause in his life-insurance policy automatically goes into effect. Half a million dollars' worth."

Millie reached toward Ruth in a gesture of supplication. "A planned accidental death is entirely too risky, Ruthie. Ed has become so strange and violent these past few years that an insurance investigator just might conclude his death was no accident at all—that he deliberately took his own life and set it up to look like an accident. They'll pay double indemnity for murder, but not for suicide. And with two children to support, I just can't take the chance of something going wrong. I need that money!"

As Millie spoke, Ruth's shoulders sagged in defeat, her last shred of hope gone.

"You have to do it, Ruth. You understand that, don't you?" Adrianna asked.

"Yes, Addy, I understand. I agreed to do whatever you said," she replied softly, a great weariness entering her voice. "And I will. I don't know how, but I will "

"Fine. That's settled then."

Adrianna fondly patted Ruth on the cheek and smiled at Millie. "If you two will excuse me now, I have another appointment with John's lawyers this afternoon."

13

A brief warming spell had turned the snow to slush as Ruth Larkin nervously steered her late husband's Mercedes-Benz into the final surge of evening rush-hour traffic heading north up the East Side Drive out of the city. Ruth didn't like to drive, especially at night, and especially in heavy bumper-to-bumper traffic, which made her even more nervous than usual behind the wheel. And that was without the added stress of Adrianna's Beretta in the handbag on the leather seat beside her, and the knowledge of what she was expected to do with that gun once she reached her destination.

Neither the car's heater pushed all the way to high nor the warm fur of her coat could ward off the cold fear that chilled Ruth to the bone this night. The chills came in waves, her teeth chattering and her shoulders shuddering as she gripped the wheel, her knuckles white under the soft kidskin gloves. There was no way out now. No excuse that Adrianna or Millie would accept if she tried to back out of the agreement at this late date. They would never forgive her. And with Hal gone, she needed Adrianna and Millie more than ever. Without them she was alone, totally alone, in a world that often seemed alien and hostile.

For days Ruth had lived in dread of the long-distance phone call that had finally come that morning. Millie's escape plan had worked out exactly as she'd outlined, and she and the children were now safely at her mother's home in Louisiana. A big family reunion was scheduled for that evening to ensure that everyone knew Millie was back in town—without her husband. Since her family was sizable, there would be plenty of witnesses to verify that she couldn't possibly have had any part in the murder of Ed Phillips.

On one level of her mind, Ruth accepted that Ed Phillips had to die. He was a monster, a monster who would destroy the lives of Millie's two little girls if he weren't stopped. He'd already come dangerously close to destroying Millie on several occasions. But what angered Ruth the most was what Ed Phillips was doing to Millie's little girls. Those children had done nothing to deserve the sort of life they were being forced to live, a life of perpetual fear for themselves and their mother. And all because of one twisted, corrupt man.

Unlike Millie, Ruth had never believed that all men were evil. Some were good, some were bad. Millie in particular, however, always seemed drawn to the bad ones. First that shiftless, irresponsible Frank Palmer had run out on her, leaving her destitute with two small children to house and feed, then Ed Phillips had come along with his phony promises of protecting and cherishing her and the girls forever. Poor Millie, Ruth sighed. Her hatred of men was understandable, if somewhat extreme.

But the necessity for terminating the life of Ed Phillips before he did irreparable harm to Millie and her children still didn't prevent another, larger part of Ruth's mind from recoiling in sheer, stark terror from the repercussions of deliberately committing murder. Even if Ruth was not punished on this earth, murder was still nothing less than a mortal sin, a mortal sin Ruth knew she could never bring herself to confess to another living being, even a faceless priest hidden in the anonymous shadows of a confessional. Ruth had drifted far from the Church during her adult years, but not so far that she didn't dread with all her soul the eternal damnation to which the unabsolved murder of Ed Phillips would condemn her. Ruth Ellen Larkin, who had never before injured another soul, was about to take a human life. And for this she would endure the fires of hell forever. And forever.

Hail Mary, full of grace . . . What should she do, sweet Mother of God? Ruth searched back through her memory, but the familiar comforting words of the rosary eluded her, blotted out by a strange inner feverishness that grew in intensity with each passing mile.

In her mind Ruth could see the flames of hell reaching up into the car, licking at her feet as the rising heat created rivulets of sweat that ran down her face and neck, soaking the collar of her blouse. The transparent flames slowly rose to encircle her, the suffocating heat blistering the skin on her legs and squeezing the air from her lungs. Her eyes ached as she strained to see through the windshield clouded with the acrid black smoke of monstrous fires burning just for her.

Brakes squealed and horns blasted as Ruth wrenched the steering wheel over to the right, crossing two lanes of traffic without warning. An exit sign had suddenly loomed up ahead, glowing eerily through the veiled windshield. She followed the arrows without thinking, without comprehending, believing only that this had to be more than just another exit sign. It had to be a sign from God.

Her panic only increased, though, as the lights and noise of the thruway receded behind, leaving a blank gray stretch of dimly lighted country road ahead that went on and on to nowhere. She was close to giving up all hope of ever finding a safe place to pull off the road when the garish orange and green lights of a small diner winked from the distant darkness, beckoning to her with a neon promise of people and salvation.

Heads swiveled and conversation stopped as Ruth breathlessly pushed through the doorway, curious eyes taking in her expensive fur and the elegant leather handbag she clutched to her chest. She stood gasping for air near the door, bewildered and yet mesmerized by the commonplace scene of people eating their dinners, drinking coffee, smoking cigarettes. She wondered if they could tell, simply by looking at her, how close she'd come to those damning fires? If they could, they didn't seem to care. After a casual inspection of the newcomer, the truckers resumed their usual routines, their easy banterings, as a radio on the counter played a mournful country ballad of love and betrayal.

"Can I help you?"

A tall rawboned woman clad in a once white waitress's uniform was standing in front of Ruth, obviously calculating how much her coat must be worth. Ruth looked at her blankly for a moment, then struggled to pull herself together.

"A phone. Do you have a telephone I can use?"

"Over there, dearie, next to Pac Man on the end." The woman waved toward a bank of five electronic game machines along the far wall. Of the five, only one was being played, and that by a young man so absorbed in the game that he hadn't even looked up to see who had come in. When Ruth hesitated, the waitress gave her a gentle shove. "Don't worry none 'bout Joey. He ain't come up for air since he hit four hundred thousand."

Ruth fumbled through her purse for change, shielding the handbag with her body to prevent anyone from catching a glimpse of the gun nestling on the bottom. She fed the coins into the slot, the answering clinks nearly drowned out by the strident beeps and electronic pongs of the Pac Man game.

The phone rang for what seemed to Ruth an eternity before Adrianna answered, brightly explaining that she'd only just that moment walked in the door and heard the phone. Her tone changed abruptly, however, as it suddenly occurred to her that it was far too early in the evening for Ruth to be calling with a report of success.

"Where are you?" Adrianna demanded with growing anger. "Have you been out to the house yet?"

Ruth huddled against the wall, cradling the receiver against her shoulder. "I don't know where I am, Addy," she whispered, fighting not to cry. "I'm lost. Everything is lost. Please help me, Addy. I don't know what to do. Please don't make me go to hell."

"What?"

"I can't do it. I can't shoot Ed." Her voice rose in

hysteria as the words came tumbling out in a jumbled, disjointed rush. "Please don't make me, Addy. Please!"

There was a long silence from Adrianna's end of the line. "Calm down, Ruthie. Tell me where you are and what's happened to put you in this state."

"I was driving along the thruway thinking about Ed and what was going to happen to me after I shot him, when these flames . . . these flames started coming up through the floor into the car. Murder is a mortal sin, Addy, and I'll burn in those flames if I shoot Ed!"

"Get hold of yourself and stop babbling nonsense, Ruth," Adrianna commanded sternly. "Do you mean your car caught on fire while you were driving?"

"No, Addy, you don't understand!" Ruth was crying openly now, smothering her sobs in the sleeve of her coat. "The car wasn't on fire. I was on fire. The fire was a warning—a warning of what's going to happen if I go through with this tonight. Please, Addy, you have to help me!"

"Of course I'll help you, honey," Adrianna crooned soothingly into the phone. "I just want to make certain I understand this clearly. You're saying that if you go ahead with the agreement and shoot Ed Phillips, you're going to burn up?"

"It was just so awful, Addy. The fire was all around me. I could see the flames—I could feel them burning me!"

"I'm sure you could, honey," Adrianna sighed. "But how do you know those fires weren't burning for something you've already done, rather than something you're going to do? You don't, do you?"

When there was no answer from Ruth, Adrianna plunged on in her cool, controlled voice, hoping it was the correct approach to snap Ruth out of her hysteria.

"Listen to me, Ruthie," she ordered. "There's simply no point in worrying about burning in any fire for killing Ed, when you're going to burn anyway."

"But I won't burn," Ruth protested weakly. "Not if I don't kill Ed."

"Oh yes you will, my darling," Adrianna replied. "You're forgetting Hal. Your own husband was killed with your knowledge, your consent, and your help. That's almost the same as having actually committed the murder yourself, isn't it? Isn't that a mortal sin too?"

Ruth felt sick to her stomach, unaware at first of the insistent tug on her sleeve.

"Hey, lady. That your Mercedes out front?"

Ruth hesitantly looked up to see a burly man standing over her, his bulk emphasized by the layer of sweaters covering his massive frame. "You left your lights on," he was saying, his deep voice sounding far away and muffled. "Christ, it was hot inside that car. You musta had the heater going full blast in there for a real long ways. Gotta watch that sort of thing, lady. Too much heat like that could put you to sleep, make you drive right off the road. Nearly done it myself once or twice."

The receiver slid off her shoulder and dangled loosely from her hand as Adrianna's tinny voice shouted her name. The heater. It was the heater all along. There'd been no flames, no fire. Just her own overwrought imagination playing tricks on her because of a stupid car heater she'd turned on too high to chase away the cold of her fear.

Ruth looked at the phone in her hand, then slowly raised it to her ear again. "It's all right, Addy. I'm here."

Adrianna was openly relieved. "Get back in the car, Ruthie, and go on up to Millie's house. I'll meet you there. Park at the end of the drive and wait for me. Don't do anything until I get there. Can you do that? For me?"

Ruth nodded silently, oblivious of the fact that Adrianna couldn't see her, and hung up the phone. Outside, the night was a little darker, the blinking neon sign no longer a beacon of hope, as a shaken and apprehensive Ruth Larkin once again sat behind the wheel of the Mercedes and headed north for the rolling residential hills of suburban Westchester.

14

Ed Phillips adjusted the volume on the television set in the den and settled back in his reclining chair with a freshly opened can of beer.

At that moment Phillips was preoccupied with the greasy dinner he'd downed at the eatery around the corner from his office several hours earlier. The food still lay heavy and undigested in his stomach, the discomfort unrelieved by the five or six beers he'd drunk since coming home to the darkened, empty house. If that stupid bitch hadn't talked him into letting her fly off to New Orleans with the kids, he'd at least have some decent food in his stomach, and not that grease-coated fiberboard he'd been living on for the past couple of days. Millie wasn't good for much, especially in bed, but she sure was one hell of a first-class cook.

Evie, though, was something else in bed, Phillips thought, only half-watching the basketball game flickering across the TV screen. A nice tender young piece of tail, and a fast learner, too. Not goddamn frigid like her mother. Another couple of years, when her sister Deedee developed some boobs, she'd be ready, too, for his own personal kind of instruction in the finer points of fucking. He rubbed his crotch, grinning at the endless possibilities in store when he finally got between those shapely, downy little legs. Nothing Millie could do to stop him, either, unless she wanted to land back out on the street without a dime. Jesus, that dame was costing him a bundle, what with her fancy tennis club and those two rich bitches in New York who kept taking her into all those ritzy stores where she spent his money like confetti. Here he was, working his butt off to make the kind of dough Millie wanted, and she wouldn't even let him meet those two broads. Probably thought he wasn't good enough for her tight-ass society friends. When she got back, he'd show her who was good enough!

Phillips' eyelids grew heavy as he ruminated about the various ways he'd extract his revenge from Millie once she was within reach of his fists again. He'd do a good job next time, a real good job. The truth was, he should've listened to his good old buddies who tried to tell him five years ago that a broad like that was nothing but trouble.

As Phillips noisily dozed off in his chair in front of the television, the beer can slipping from his grip, Ruth Larkin was less than two hundred yards from the end of his driveway, a shaking hand poised to switch off the Mercedes' headlights as soon as she saw the twin red reflectors marking the entrance. Ruth wasn't certain exactly where the turnoff was, since she'd only been to Millie's house twice, the last time more than two years ago, and both times in the daylight. At night everything looked different. The landmarks she'd used before were obscured now by a darkness so dense that it settled around the car like a shroud.

Ruth passed the reflectors before she realized the significance of the two unblinking red eyes peering out from what seemed to be a solid black wall of shrubbery. She braked quickly, sending the car into a brief sideways skid on the slick pavement, then slowly backed a little ways into the driveway, bringing the car to a stop more off the drive than on.

From her sketchy memory of those previous two visits, Ruth knew there was no way Ed Phillips could see the Mercedes if she parked near the road. The house sat far back on the large country lot in a clearing surrounded by the patchy remnants of an old forest, the trees rendering the house invisible from both the road and the two houses on either side of it. With Millie and the girls out of town, Phillips apparently hadn't seen any reason to turn on the outdoor lights, including the ground-level guidelights evenly spaced along both sides of the twisting gravel drive.

Ruth shut off the engine and sat in the darkness, listening to nothing but her own ragged breathing and an occasional ping from the cooling engine. All Ruth had to do now was wait, wait for Adrianna. Addy would know what to do. Addy always knew what to do. She would be Ruth's salvation now. Her only salvation.

Headlights flashed across the windshield, momentarily catching Ruth's face in the beam, her eyes and mouth gaping holes in a mask of white. The car didn't stop, or even slow, although Ruth was certain the driver must have seen her, must have known that she had no business parked in the bushes at the end of Ed Phillips' driveway. Her heartbeat raced as she waited for the car to return, or worse yet, for the sound of approaching police sirens.

She waited in vain, though, and while she waited, the cold night air slowly seeped back into the car, silently oozing through minute crevices around the doors and windows and creeping up the vents she'd opened to counteract the heater. Ruth hardly noticed the cold at first, even when the vapor of her own breath began to take on substance and swirl around the high arc of the steering wheel. Any minute now and Addy would be there, guiding her and protecting her. And maybe even pulling the trigger for her.

A sudden shiver caught Ruth unaware and she pulled the heavy fur coat tighter around her. Just a little longer and it would all be over, this terrible nightmare which she herself had started. If only she hadn't told Addy and Millie about her book. If only she'd kept her mouth shut about Hal, all these terrible killings wouldn't be happening. But she had told them, and now Hal's blood was on her hands. And possibly even John's. What did it matter if Adrianna had been the one who actually put the Seconal in Hal's drink? Adrianna had only done it for her, because of her. Adrianna was right. Ruth was already a murderer in the sight of God and the Church. Her place in hell was ready and waiting.

Ruth stared into the blackness beyond the windows,

wondering what Hal would think of her if he knew what she had done. Perhaps he did know. Perhaps he was watching her even now, as she sat there in the dark, laughing at her inability to gather enough courage to walk up to that house alone. Ruth could almost hear Hal's low voice rumbling with unconcealed amusement as he pointed out her failings yet again. "You really got yourself cornered this time, didn't you, sweetheart?" he'd chuckle. "You think you're so smart. But this time you've really outsmarted yourself!"

The sound of Hal's imagined voice was so clear and real in the unearthly silence of the car that Ruth covered her ears to block it out. But the biting words went on, mocking her and taunting her.

"Did you really think you could get rid of me that easily, sweetie? You're nothing without me, you know. Not a person, not a woman. Least of all a woman. You couldn't even have a baby right, remember? You messed that up just like you mess up everything."

"Stop it!" Ruth screamed. "Stop it! You're dead, Hal. I know you're dead."

"And now you're going to mess this up too," Hal continued. "But that should come as no surprise. Not to me. And certainly not to you."

"No!" Her voice echoed hollowly inside the car, rippling off the hard glass of the windows and reverberating against the dashboard. "You aren't real. I know you aren't real!"

There was a long, low, disembodied laugh that seemed to emanate from Ruth's own mouth, chilling her very marrow with its sudden maliciousness. She reached inside the handbag on the other seat, feeling the comforting weight of Adrianna's Beretta in her hand.

"You really think Adrianna is going to come and save you this time?" Hal's voice asked inside her head. "Why should she? You're nothing but a pain in the neck to her—a big pain in the neck. You go crying to Adrianna every time some little thing goes wrong, and expect her to make it right for you. Why don't you just get off your cowardly derriere and go do something right yourself for once?"

Ruth looked wildly around the interior of the car, trying to find the source of the voice that was taunting her so. Her finger was on the trigger, ready to take aim and fire.

"Adrianna isn't coming, you know. She isn't going to save you this time," the voice continued, growing stronger. "Go on, little Ruthie. Go on and let's see how much of a real woman you can be!"

Ruth pushed open the door of the Mercedes and ran up the drive, not so much running toward the house as away from the voice and its evil laughter that was both everywhere and nowhere. "Go on, Ruthie. Do it!" Hal's voice chanted. "Do it! Do it!"

The house suddenly loomed ahead as Ruth rounded the final bend of the drive, its dark bulk relieved only by a solitary light glimmering behind one curtained window. Breathless and shivering uncontrollably, Ruth stumbled toward the door and tripped, falling against the smooth painted wood with a strangled cry. Her panic mounting, Ruth fumbled in vain for the bell, and not finding it, jammed the gun into her pocket and began pounding on the door with both fists.

At first Ed Phillips thought the hammering must be coming from the television set, the insistent banging muted by the raucous cheering of the basketball fans. It wasn't until he heard a woman screaming that he came fully awake.

Phillips moved warily toward the foyer, flicking on lights as he went, until the whole front of the house was awash in the artificial glow. Through the windows flanking the door he could see the woman, clad in a dark fur coat, crying hysterically as she glanced back over her shoulder toward the trees. He opened the door only a crack in case it was a trick of some kind, and was surprised by the force with which she hurled herself at the opening and pushed through.

"Help me, please," Ruth cried, clutching desperately at Phillips' shirt. "Help me! He's after me."

Phillips backed away a step, alarmed at her intensity. As she swayed, though, he caught her by the arm and

awkwardly led her into the living room and lowered her
into a chair. Now that he could see her close up in a
better light, he decided she wasn't a half-bad-looking
broad. And expensively dressed, too.

"Sit down and I'll get you a drink," he said almost
kindly. "Then you can tell me what kind of trouble sent
you running to a strange house at this time of night."

"My husband . . ." Ruth managed to gasp, rising
unsteadily from the chair where he'd put her.

"Husband trouble. I should've known. You dames
are all alike, aren't you? Bleed a man for everything
he's got, then put on the big martyr act when he claims
his due," Phillips grunted, opening the wet bar built in
at the end of the living room.

He poured a couple fingers of brandy into the snifter
and turned to find Ruth Larkin standing behind him, a
gun pointed at his head. Strange garbled noises that
sounded like "Do it, Ruthie. Do it!" spilled from the
side of her twisted mouth.

The glass dropped from Ed Phillips' nerveless fingers
just seconds before he saw the white flash erupt from
the gun barrel and felt the impact of the bullet explod-
ing inside his brain.

Ed Phillips died a happy man. In that final split
second, everything he'd always thought about women
was instantly confirmed. Women, he told himself, were
just no fucking good.

15

The unexpected recoil from the Beretta jolted Ruth's arm, shattering the spell that had come over her when Ed Phillips led her into the living room. She stared in horror at the smoking weapon in her hand, too frightened to look directly at the crumpled body at her feet or the spatters of blood and flesh on the wall behind.

"Ruth? Ruth, where are you?" Adrianna's voice called from the doorway. "Are you all right?"

Ruth struggled to answer her, but the words wouldn't come. They stuck in her dry throat, her mouth working silently.

"My God, you shot him! You actually shot him!" Triumph gleamed in Adrianna's eyes as she rushed across the room to gather Ruth in her arms, hugging her tightly. "I knew you could do it."

Adrianna hurriedly pulled Ruth into the foyer and literally pushed her toward the door. "Now, get out of here. Hurry! Get back to the city and throw that gun in the river right away. Tonight."

When Ruth didn't move, Adrianna pushed harder. The lack of focus in Ruth's eyes worried her, but there was no time to do anything about it. There was no telling whether any of the neighbors had heard the shot, and if they had, whether they had called the police. Both of them had to get out of there immediately—Ruth in particular, with the gun. She must get rid of that gun.

"Hurry, Ruthie," Adrianna half-ordered, half-pleaded. "You have to hurry."

Ruth looked at her vaguely, almost as though she wasn't seeing Adrianna at all, but something else. "Hal . . ." Ruth started to say, then stopped.

"Forget about Hal. Forget about everything. Just get in that car and go!"

Ruth obediently turned away and began walking down the drive, her movements jerky and uncoordinated. Adrianna waited impatiently until she was out of sight, then stepped back inside the house just long enough to quickly scan the living room and make certain Ruth had left nothing behind that could be traced to her.

As Adrianna switched off the outside floodlights and closed the front door, Ruth was staggering toward the Mercedes, bewildered to find that it was now parked a little ways behind Adrianna's distinctive white Jaguar. She was only dimly aware of Adrianna having come into the house, of having shouted something at her about the gun and the river. Ruth's head was reeling with a curious detachment that made even the familiar interior of the car seem strange and unreal. But then, everything about this night was strange and unreal. Had she really, truly shot Ed Phillips? Had Hal really come back from the grave to urge her on? To steady her hand as she'd pulled the trigger?

It was becoming so hard to tell anymore what was real and what was not.

The car seemed to steer itself as Ruth drove along the roads of Westchester, passing homes brightly lighted with life and warmth and all the family comings and goings she had yearned for so desperately, but which always seemed to elude her. As she entered the on ramp of the thruway, Ruth scarcely noticed that the car was dangerously gaining speed. Somehow it really didn't seem to matter.

"Jesus Christ, officer, I couldn't stop. I swear I couldn't. She just came shooting out of that ramp like a bat out of hell, right in front of the rig. Never looked at the traffic or nothing."

Peewee Harris shifted his two-hundred-and-forty-pound bulk so he wouldn't directly face the poor chump who'd been driving the big eighteen-wheeler. The guy looked like he was about to cry.

"Is she dead?"

Deputy Sheriff Harris nodded curtly. "Probably. Fire department's on the way to get her out. That car's so bashed in it looks like it's been through a compacter. Couldn't anyone live through something like that."

The driver gazed sorrowfully at the traffic piling up behind the wreck, and the three squad cars with their flashing lights that had converged on the accident scene. In the distance he could hear more sirens approaching. His driving career was over, that was for sure. It ended the moment that Mercedes pulled into the path of his rig. He doubted he'd ever get up the nerve to climb back into a cab again and feel right about it.

Harris saw all of this and more reflected in the man's face as the fire trucks came edging along the shoulder of the road and swung into position around the crushed remains of the Mercedes. There was nothing he could do for this guy anymore. Better to see if he could give the fire-department boys or state troopers a hand.

By the time Harris reached the wreck, the fire department had the door on the driver's side pried off, although the woman was still pinned inside. A paramedic, checking her vital signs, suddenly reached for his equipment bag and loaded a syringe. "Okay, men. She's still alive," he shouted over the commotion going on around them. "But she won't be much longer if you don't step on it and get her out of here."

As the paramedic shifted Ruth's body to straighten her windpipe and ease her breathing, Harris spotted a woman's handbag wedged under her right side. The paramedic followed his glance, then reached around her body to pull it out. As he handed the open bag to Harris, a gun slipped out and clattered to the pavement.

"What the . . ." Harris picked up the weapon and sniffed at it. There was no doubt it'd been fired recently. Very recently.

Ruth's eyelids fluttered briefly, followed by a low, weak moan.

"Lady, can you hear me?"

When she didn't respond, Harris searched through the bag to find her wallet, and hopefully her driver's license. Luckily the license was there, at the top of the plastic card holder. Harris made a mental note of the woman's fashionable city address, then leaned as far into the car as his massive bulk would permit.

"Mrs. Larkin?" he tried again. "Ruth? Can you hear me?"

The paramedic shot Harris a dirty look, but the deputy sheriff persisted, ignoring the fact that he was getting in the man's way. "Come on now, Ruth. Open your eyes and talk to me."

Unintelligible sounds came from her bloody mouth and she groaned again. At last, though, her eyes opened and stayed open. "Help me, Addy. Please help me."

Harris blinked in surprise at the unexpected clarity of her words. "We're trying to help you, Ruth. Just hang in there a little longer, okay?"

"Addy!" The word was almost a scream of pain as Ruth's body jerked and twitched in spasm. "Help me, Addy!"

As the moan subsided, her breathing became increasingly shallow and ragged. Harris wedged himself closer and tried again. "Where'd you get the gun, Ruth? Tell me about the gun."

Ruth's eyes rolled upward as she was hit by another surge of pain. "I killed him, Addy. Just like you told me to. I killed him."

"Okay, Ruth. Daddy's here. Tell Daddy who you killed."

Ruth's response was garbled, the words mashed into unintelligible sounds through her gritted teeth. Beside him, the paramedic was working feverishly to keep Ruth going. "We're losing her," he said to Harris. "You're not going to get much out of her now."

Harris backed out of the car and straightened up. From the corner of his eye, Harris saw a young man clad in clerical garb speaking to one of the state troopers working the traffic detail. Remembering the old and tattered St. Christopher's card he'd found tucked behind Ruth's license, he motioned to the man to come over to the car.

"You a priest?"

"Yes, officer. I was caught up in the traffic jam back there, and thought I might be able to offer some comfort to anyone who may have been injured here."

Harris handed the St. Christopher's card to the priest and stepped back. "She's all yours, Father. Better do your stuff fast. She ain't got much time left. Name's Ruth. Ruth Larkin. Keeps calling for her daddy."

"Thank you, officer. I'll do what I can for her." The priest took Harris' place at the side of the car and reached out to touch Ruth's forehead lightly. His fingers came away covered with blood.

"Ruth? I'm Father O'Brien. Do you want to confess?"

Ruth groaned as his voice reached her, her glazed eyes fixing for a moment on his collar. A small, fleeting smile crossed her face, and her entire body seemed to lose some of its rigidity.

"Forgive me, Father. Please forgive me," she whispered hoarsely. "I killed him."

Ruth's head sagged down onto her chest, but with a supreme effort of will she raised it again, speaking so softly the priest could barely hear her. He heard enough, though, to realize she'd haltingly begun the old Act of Contrition.

"Oh, my God . . . I am heartily sorry for having offended theè, and I detest all my sins because I dread the loss of heaven . . ." As the words drifted beyond comprehensibility, Father O'Brien picked up the litany and gently recited it with her. ". . . and the pains of hell, but most of all I have offended thee, my God, who art all good and deserving of all my love. I firmly resolve with the help of thy grace, to confess my sins, to do penance, and to amend my life. Amen."

As the priest made the sign of the cross over Ruth's mangled body, she sighed once and was gone.

*   *   *

Nearby, concealed in the midst of a small crowd of onlookers kept at bay by the police, Adrianna Farrelly watched as they removed Ruth's limp and bloodied body from the Mercedes, placed it on a stretcher, and covered her face with a sheet.

Adrianna turned her back on the scene as the ambulance slowly pulled away, its siren silenced. Tears of grief cascaded down her cheeks as Adrianna mourned for the first time in nearly thirty years.

II

16

Jack Holland rolled over onto his back and stared glumly at the ceiling. Sleep eluded him, although the big blond beside him was already snoring, her open mouth outlined in unflattering smudges of smeared lipstick.

He tried to remember the woman's name, and realized with annoyance that he couldn't. Maybe she hadn't told him. That was always a possibility. It wouldn't be the first time he'd exchanged formal introductions the morning after instead of the night before. That was one of the advantages—occasionally a disadvantage—of being a confirmed bachelor.

Holland glanced at his watch and grimaced. Not quite eleven yet. No point waiting until morning. He might just as well wake her up now and take her home or back to the bar where he'd met her. He was facing an exceptionally rough day in court tomorrow, and he could use a decent night's sleep without having to exchange pleasantries with a stranger in the morning.

As Holland reached over to shake the woman's shoulder, the shrill ring of the bedside telephone interceded for him, sending the woman bolt upright in bed, her startled eyes wide and alert.

"Sorry about that." He grinned, reaching around behind her to grab the receiver. "I had an extra loud bell put on so I'd be sure not to miss any calls at night. I sleep like the dead."

As the blond eased out of bed, Holland picked up the receiver. "Yeah?"

"Mr. Holland? Deputy Sheriff Harris. Sorry if I woke you."

Holland grunted and shifted the phone over to the other shoulder. "No problem, Harris. What's up?"

"There was kind of a peculiar accident earlier this evening and the commander thought you might want to know about it."

"What kind of accident?"

Harris cleared his throat and began to recite, as though he'd memorized the details. "I was pulled off the road about a mile from the parkway when this car passed me doing about seventy. Before I could pull the driver over, she headed straight onto the parkway right smack in front of a semi. Totaled the car. The driver was a thirty-eight-year-old white female. Dead."

"So? Accidents happen all the time on the parkway." Holland could hear the water running in the shower and he groaned inwardly. A shower was usually a fair indication that a woman planned on sticking around for the rest of the night, whether he wanted her to or not.

"This woman," Harris was explaining carefully, "had a gun. A thirty-two-caliber Beretta. Fired sometime earlier tonight, I'd say. She was pretty incoherent before she died, but she did say something about having killed someone."

"Who?"

"I don't know. She died before she could tell me. All I do know for sure is that she was heading away from White Plains in one hell of a hurry."

"Which leaves us with a confessed murderess who's inconveniently dead, and no victim?"

"Looks that way. Checked out a couple shooting reports that came in tonight, but none involving anything like a Beretta thirty-two."

"ID on the woman?"

"According to the license in her purse, her name was Ruth E. Larkin. There's no answer at the Manhattan address listed on the license, so we haven't got hold of anybody yet for a positive ID."

Holland thought for a moment and jotted the name down on a notepad next to the telephone. "Larkin.

Larkin. That name sounds vaguely familiar. Ring a bell with anyone down there at headquarters?"

"Nope. We're running a check on the gun now, but we haven't gotten a report back yet."

"Okay, Harris. Keep me posted if anything turns up."

Holland was pulling on his pants when the big blond emerged nude from the bathroom, scrubbed clean of her garish makeup and looking not half-bad. Not half-bad at all, he thought admiringly.

The following day was even rougher than Jack Holland had anticipated, starting off badly and going downhill from there. Holland had awakened from a deep, dreamless sleep to find that the big blond, who reluctantly gave her name as Susie, had lifted seventy-five bucks from his wallet and disappeared from the apartment. That was followed by a discouraging six hours in court where a key prosecution witness blew away the major portion of his case by unexpectedly changing his testimony.

By the time Holland returned to his cramped, cluttered office, he was beginning to wonder if he shouldn't have picked an easier route to the governor's mansion. Coping with the headaches of an overworked, understaffed office had been a welcome challenge when he was first elected district attorney ten years ago. Lately, however, it seemed as though most of the challenge was gone and only the headaches remained.

Holland's sour mood didn't lighten until he'd finished the early-evening edition of the newspaper that had been placed, as usual, on his desk. He tore out the page containing the two stories that had caught his attention and picked up the phone, stabbing at the intercom button with his finger. "Did we get a report in yet on that Phillips shooting last night?" he asked, feeling the old familiar surge of excitement roused by the scent of a good case. "Send it in. And while you're at it, find Stein and get her in here, too."

Holland was reading through the Phillips report for the second time when Judith Stein sailed into his office without knocking. He looked up at her gravely, careful to conceal his pleasure at seeing his most capable assistant D.A., and undeniably the most attractive.

Judith Stein was a petite thirty-four-year-old woman with flashing black eyes and a smile that was bright enough to light up Madison Square Garden. She also had a brain that digested and stored information like a computer, and a thinly concealed ambition to occupy his office the minute he decided to move out and up. Holland didn't envy the candidate who dared to oppose her for the job.

"I hear you had a rotten day in court," she said brightly, settling down in the uncomfortable hard visitor's chair at the side of his desk. "At least you can't say I didn't warn you. That jerk had all the makings of a perjurer from the start. The first time I talked to him—"

"Shut up, Stein," Holland interrupted brusquely.

"I was only trying to explain—"

"I know what you were going to explain and I don't want to hear it. Not right now, anyway. Save it for later."

Judith cocked her head quizzically. "Was it that bad?"

"Worse." Holland swung his chair around to stare out the window, his back to Judith. "What are your plans for tonight?"

He could hear Judith getting up from the hard chair and pacing restlessly around the small floor space in front of the desk. Holland never ceased to be amazed that such a small, fragile-looking woman as Judith could contain so much nervous energy.

"Tonight? Let's see. I have the Jackson case coming up for trial in three days, a motion to prepare in the Grunewald case, a stack of files on my desk that I haven't had a chance to look at in weeks . . ." She paused for a quick breath. "Oh, yes. I also have to pick up my cleaning, call my mother, and wash my hair. Does that answer your question?"

Holland swiveled around again and grinned in amusement. "Does eating fit into your schedule anywhere?"

"On my salary, who can afford to eat?" Judith laughed. "It's probably just as well, the way I gain weight. I can't afford to replace all those size three's in my closet with another wardrobe."

"You're eating tonight," Holland said with finality. "Get your coat. I'm buying."

Judith stared at Holland in feigned surprise, a hand theatrically clasped to her bosom. "Six years I've slaved away in this office and you haven't bought me so much as a cup of coffee! Now all of a sudden dinner. What are you trying to do, soften me up so you can fire me over the crepes suzette?"

Holland sighed as he shrugged into his suit coat and tucked the newspaper page into his inner pocket. "Have I mentioned lately that you talk too much, Stein? Now, get your things together. We've got a lot of work to get through this evening."

"Whatever you say, boss. Anything for a free dinner."

The small Italian family restaurant Holland chose was plain but cheerful, with meticulously mended red checkered cloths on the tables and dripping candles stuck into the ubiquitous wine bottles. A young and strikingly curvaceous woman greeted Holland with a welcoming warmth reserved for regular and valued customers, and showed them to a table tucked away in a small alcove off to one side of the main room.

Since it was such an unusual occasion, Judith put up only a halfhearted protest when Holland refilled her glass with Chianti twice before the antipasto arrived. Normally she wouldn't dream of drinking at a business dinner because of alcohol's tendency to loosen her tongue, but she could see no danger in drinking with Jack Holland. As her immediate superior, there were hardly any trade secrets he didn't already know.

They were midway through the most tender scallopini piccata Judith had ever tasted, accompanied by desultory shop talk, when Holland abruptly pulled the torn newspaper page from his pocket. "Have you seen the paper this evening?"

"No. Why?"

He spread the page out in front of her, covering her half-eaten dinner, and pointed at the two articles he'd marked in red pen: "WIDOW OF BEST-SELLING AUTHOR

KILLED IN ACCIDENT," and "LOCAL BUSINESSMAN FOUND
SHOT TO DEATH IN HOME."

"You can't tell by reading those stories, but there's a
connection," Holland said. "A connection that could
blow these two seemingly unrelated incidents wide open
and turn them into one real hot baby of a case."

What Holland didn't add, because Judith already knew,
was that a case loaded with plenty of human drama and
popular appeal could be of immense political benefit to
both of them. A truly spectacular case could not only
help send Holland to the governor's mansion in Albany,
but put Judith in the district attorney's office.

Judith read through both articles slowly, mentally
noting all the pertinent details. "You're right, Jack. I
don't see the connection," she said simply, handing
back the newspaper. "What did the reporters miss?"

Holland grinned and poured them both another glass
of wine. "We haven't told them about the gun yet."

"What gun?"

"A Beretta thirty-two, to be precise. One of the
officers on the accident scene called me last night and
said this Larkin woman had a gun with her. A recently
fired gun. And her dying words were to the effect that
she'd killed someone."

"And you think this someone is the Edward Phillips
from the other story?"

"Could be. We'll know for certain once we have the
ballistics report."

Judith silently thought through the possibilities, trying
to see where Holland was going with his line of reasoning. Convicting a live murderer was one thing, but
there was no political mileage in trying to convict a
dead one. "You think someone else was in on this with
the Larkin woman, then?"

Holland shrugged. "I don't know. Maybe not the
actual shooting. Phillips was found in front of the bar in
his living room, shot once through the head at close
range. From the position of the bottles and a spilled
glass on the floor, the investigators think he was in the
process of pouring a drink—one drink—when he was

killed. Nothing else in the house was disturbed, which probably rules out burglary as a motive."

"So he probably knew the killer and let him or her in."

"Either he knew his killer or he had no reason to be afraid of whoever it was. Particularly if it was a lone woman."

Judith tried, but failed, to suppress a smile. "It always amazes me that so many men refuse to recognize a woman's capacity for murder. Even experienced law-enforcement men who should know better."

Holland ignored Judith's remark. "There has to be a reason that a woman like Ruth Larkin would go up to White Plains and cold-bloodedly shoot a man to death. Could be a tie-in somewhere with the OD death of her husband less than a month ago."

"The newspaper said Phillips is survived by his wife and two stepdaughters. Where were they when he was killed?"

The district attorney shook his head and shrugged. "We don't know. Lieutenant Josephson is trying to track them down."

"Josephson is in charge of the investigation, I gather." Judith watched Holland intently for a reaction, but his bland expression gave nothing away. Judith, however, didn't have any great confidence in Josephson, and guessed Holland probably didn't either. Josephson wasn't necessarily incompetent, but he was young and so far lacking the gut instinct developed by good, experienced detectives who could take the disparate and seemingly contradictory threads of a case and pull them into a solid, logical whole.

Silence hung heavily between them until Judith, annoyed that her remaining veal had grown cold, once again picked up her knife and fork. "So what do you want me to do?" she asked before taking the first bite.

Holland leaned back in his chair and watched her eat. "Bird-dog the investigation. On your own time, of course. Nights, weekends, lunch hours."

Judith groaned openly, thinking of the cases stacked up on her desk. Cases that she was already too busy to get to and which were growing older and staler every day.

"Let Josephson do his job as best he can, but make sure he doesn't overlook anything," Holland continued, oblivious of her pained expression. "You might start by talking to that bookkeeper who found Phillips' body. You know—the woman-to-woman sort of thing. She might come up with something important she didn't tell Josephson."

"I'll do what I can, Jack. But I still don't see the point of all this. If the killer is dead, we have no one to prosecute."

Holland refilled both of their glasses and downed his with relish. "The point, my dear counselor, is that we're looking at a situation with all the earmarks of a real headline-grabber. A famous author—Harold Larkin— is found dead of a drug overdose in a sleazy New York hotel room. A few weeks later his attractive widow guns down a middle-aged owner of a surburban plumbing-supply business. Why?"

Holland raised his hands and ticked off the possibilities on his fingers. "Were Phillips and Ruth Larkin having an affair? Was Phillips trying to blackmail her, or was she trying to blackmail him? Was Phillips somehow connected to Harold Larkin's death and his widow was seeking revenge? Or did she have something to do with Larkin's death and Phillips found out about it? Did Ruth Larkin know ahead of time that Phillips was going to be home alone that night, or was it a prearranged meeting? The possibilities are endlessly fascinating, don't you think?"

"Sure, but—"

Holland waved her off. "Just drink your wine and listen to me a minute. I've got a hunch about this case. I can't explain exactly why, but there's something all wrong about this Phillips murder. I want to know what was behind it—what motivated this Larkin woman to drive all the way up from New York, shoot Phillips, and then deliberately drive in front of a truck on the parkway."

"You think she did that deliberately?"

"Had to. No one in their right mind would enter the parkway doing seventy without even looking to see what was coming at them."

For the second time that evening Holland abruptly changed the subject. "I probably shouldn't tell you this, Stein, but you're the best assistant I've got on staff. Intelligent and ambitious." Holland refolded the page and put it back in his pocket. "So what are you planning to do with your life after putting in your time as district attorney?"

The question took Judith by surprise, causing her to wonder for a moment whether Holland was trying to tease her in a clumsy, offhand way. She had never openly announced her intention to run for D.A., although it was a logical step for someone in her position. After a brief reflection, she decided Holland wasn't trying to make fun of her and seriously wanted to know what her future plans were, although both of them knew she'd never be so foolish as to tell him everything.

"When I was going through law at Harvard on that scholarship, they made it painfully clear that the career options open to women, especially women who were not from wealthy or well-connected families, were terribly limited," Judith answered slowly, carefully weighing her words. "That's one of the reasons I chose the public sector rather than join a private law firm after I got my degree. The opportunities for actually getting somewhere are a lot better." She lowered her eyes so Holland wouldn't see their burning brightness.

"When Sandra Day O'Connor was appointed to the Supreme Court, the law really began to open up for women like me. If she could make it that far, then there was hope that a struggling girl from Flatbush could climb a few rungs higher on the ladder too."

Holland quietly sat across the table from Judith and watched her, his face remaining expressionless as she spoke.

"Of course Justice O'Connor had a lot of help getting to the Supreme Court," Judith continued. "I doubt if a woman ever would have been considered for such an appointment if it hadn't been for the momentum created by the women's-lib movement."

"I had no idea you were a women's liberationist," Holland said, finally showing some surprise.

"I'm not really. At least not in the sense of following the tenets of an organized group. In fact there's a good deal about the lib movement I find offensive, including much of the stridency and the posturing. But I do admire the nerve and the stamina of some of those liberation leaders. If nothing else, they have managed to get across the point that women are people too. People who can accomplish more than just bearing babies. A lot of men try to ignore the fact that women have minds too."

"I hope you don't include me in that group," Holland protested with a laugh. "I've always liked smart women." He waited until the dishes were cleared away from the table and then gazed directly at Judith. "So you're aiming for a seat on the Supreme Court, are you?"

Judith picked up her wineglass and watched the light from the candle flame glow through the deep red liquid. "Not necessarily," she answered at last, not meeting his eyes. "It's a possibility—a remote possibility—but there are other options as well. It's really too soon to say exactly where I'll go from here."

She stole a glance at Holland's face to see if he believed her, but she could read nothing one way or the other in his expression. Holland's inscrutability was one of the factors that made him such a good prosecutor— the defense seldom second-guessed what method of attack he would use in a particular case.

Judith allowed her thoughts to wander freely through her collection of cherished dreams, dreams that were not as unattainable as they had first seemed twelve years earlier when she'd entered law school. She had a long way to go before she reached the U.S. Supreme Court, but that was in her favor too. Judith had studied the ages of the current justices and come to the conclusion that quite a few appointments would be inevitable within the next ten to fifteen years. Some of those appointments were bound to be women, weren't they?

So was there any reason why she shouldn't be one of them?

Jack Holland signaled for the dinner check and then unexpectedly leaned across the table to squeeze one of her diminutive hands. "If you break open the Phillips case," he said with deep seriousness, as though he'd been reading her mind, "and I know you can do it, then nothing will be able to stop you from going right to the top. And believe me, Stein, I'll do everything in my power to help you get there."

17

The Phillips house seemed eerily isolated and almost malevolent as Judith Stein walked quickly around its perimeter, checking the layout of doors and windows. Four days had elapsed since the murder of Ed Phillips, yet the powerful aura of unnatural death still clung to the boxy two-story structure like an invisible pall. The lifeless house was rendered even more depressing by the sight of its once extensive flower beds trampled into unrecognizable clumps of mud by the investigating police officers, and the small mailbox by the front door overflowing with uncollected mail.

Judith had not yet entered the house, preferring to wait for the arrival of Ed Phillips' bookkeeper, Clarice Stuber, who'd originally discovered his body and summoned the police. Miss Stuber had initially resisted Judith's request to meet her at the house, consenting only when Judith strongly hinted that the alternative was a police escort to headquarters.

The sound of wheels on the driveway reached Judith before she actually saw the car, giving her time to compose her features in what she hoped came across as a friendly but authoritative expression. Miss Stuber, she had a feeling, was not going to be particularly cooperative or informative.

The woman who emerged from the inexpensive sedan was an imposing middle-aged figure. She towered over Judith by at least eight inches, her massive frame bearing an equally massive bosom. She wore a sensible tweed coat and felt hat, and carried a plastic shopping bag that Judith was certain contained a pair of "good" office shoes and possibly a meticulously prepared sack lunch.

"Miss Stein? I'd like to get this over with as quickly as possible," the woman announced as she marched purposefully toward the front door. "I have a great deal of work waiting for me at the office."

"I appreciate your coming here so early, and I'll try not to keep you any longer than absolutely necessary," Judith replied smoothly, guiding her away from the door. "Before we go inside, I'd like to ask you a few questions about Mr. Phillips, if you don't mind."

Clarice Stuber looked at her sharply, her mouth set in a grim line. "I've already told the police everything I know. I can't imagine what more I can tell you."

Judith nodded in acknowledgment, saying nothing.

"Really, Miss Stein, I find this most irregular."

"Irregular?" Judith asked. "In what way?"

"Questioning me here. At the house." Miss Stuber's naturally ruddy complexion grew even ruddier. "This is all terribly upsetting for me, you know. Especially since I was the one who found Ed . . . er, Mr. Phillips, that way."

"I understand completely." Judith smiled benignly. "How did you happen to be at the house that day?"

Miss Stuber looked surprised at the question. "Why, it was payroll day! I needed Mr. Phillips' signature on the payroll checks in order to pay the staff. When he didn't come in that morning, I phoned and phoned, never getting an answer. Finally I decided I'd better come over and find out what had happened to him."

"How did you get into the house?"

"With this." She pulled a set of keys from her pocket. "Mr. Phillips always kept spare keys in his office safe. That woman was forever losing hers."

Judith tried to lead Miss Stuber toward a stone bench off to one side of the front garden, but she wouldn't budge from the small portico. "Would you mind telling me who you mean by 'that woman'?"

"His wife, of course," Miss Stuber said, spitting out the words distastefully.

"I see. I gather you don't care very much for Mrs. Phillips?"

The larger woman glared down at Judith as though such a question was highly impertinent. "What I think about Mildred Phillips is none of your business, Miss Stein," she said at last.

"Perhaps, perhaps not," Judith answered evenly. "How long have you worked for Mr. Phillips?"

"Eight, almost nine years now," she answered tersely. "Can we please go inside and get this over with?"

Judith missed nothing as she watched Clarice Stuber unlock the door and lead the way into the foyer. "Why don't you tell me what happened from the time you entered the house?"

Miss Stuber stood in the middle of the foyer and took a deep breath, bracing herself for the ordeal of remembering. But when she spoke, her words came out in a flat, emotionless monotone.

"I rang and rang the doorbell, and when no one came, I unlocked the door and went in. I didn't see him at first because I immediately went upstairs to check the bedroom," she said, nodding toward the stairway. "I was worried that he might have fallen ill during the night and been unable to summon help."

"Did you notice anything out of the ordinary while you were upstairs?"

Miss Stuber snapped out of her reverie and drew herself up to her full height. "I am not accustomed to snooping around my employer's home, Miss Stein," she announced with great dignity. "And I am certainly not familiar enough with the upstairs bedrooms to notice whether anything was 'out of the ordinary' or not!"

Judith suppressed a smile as she casually walked toward the doorway to the living room. "So you returned downstairs and then found Mr. Phillips' body?"

"Not right away." She gestured toward a small hallway leading to the back of the house, and Judith thought she detected the glint of tears beginning to form in Miss Stuber's eyes. "First I went to his den to see if he might be there. But he wasn't. That's when I really started to worry."

"Why was that?"

"The lights were on, and so was the television," she said flatly. "I knew, then, he had to be in the house somewhere. So I turned everything off and went through every room looking for him."

Judith was silent for a moment. Miss Stuber hadn't mentioned the den lights and television to Josephson, or if she had, he hadn't included them in his report. "Were any other lights on when you entered the house?"

"I don't think so," Miss Stuber said thoughtfully. "If there were, I didn't notice them."

The two women walked over to where Clarice Stuber had discovered Ed Phillips' body near the open wet bar. Judith only half-listened to Miss Stuber's recital of the grim details, her attention caught by the tastefully and expensively decorated room. Great care had been paid to each little detail, right down to the artfully arranged objets d'art on the mantel above the natural stone fireplace. Even though teams of investigators and forensic experts had tramped in and out of the room, it still retained a pristine, unused quality, rather, Judith thought, like a professionally decorated model home or a spread in a glossy magazine. Impersonal. That was the description Judith searched her mind for. The room was beautiful, but impersonal, as though no one really lived there. She found herself wondering if the rest of the house was equally impersonal.

As soon as Clarice Stuber stopped talking, Judith once again focused her thoughts on the reason they were there. "Have you spoken with Mrs. Phillips since finding her husband's body?" she asked, keeping her tone disinterestedly neutral.

"Good heavens, no!" Miss Stuber responded sharply.

"Do you know where she is?"

"I neither know, nor am interested in knowing, where Mildred Phillips may be," she said stiffly. "It's my understanding that she and her daughters are off visiting somewhere. Her mother's, I believe Mr. Phillips said."

"And you don't know where that might be?"

"I do not."

Judith nodded her acceptance of Clarice Stuber's statement and stepped closer to the larger woman to peer intently into her face. "Did Mr. Phillips ever mention a Dr. John Farrelly?"

"Farrelly? Never heard of him," she answered, a bit too forcefully. "Mr. Phillips did not believe in going to doctors. He said they were nothing but a bunch of money-hungry bloodsuckers who were more likely to kill you than cure you!"

With that, Clarice Stuber jerked her shoulders back and strode imperiously toward the doorway, pausing only long enough for a parting shot at Judith. "If you have no further questions, Miss Stein, I really must leave. You can reach me at Mr. Phillips' office if you must, although there's nothing more I can tell you."

Judith watched from behind the heavy living-room drapes as Clarice Stuber backed her car around and headed down the driveway with such haste that her wheels kicked up gravel. The interview hadn't gone as smoothly as Judith would have liked, but it had been satisfactory. She found herself impressed by Clarice Stuber's unflagging loyalty to her late employer, although her loyalty appeared to be counterbalanced by an equally strong hostility toward her late employer's wife. It was a curious situation, but one that Judith had come to realize was not all that unusual. What was unusual was that Clarice Stuber made no effort to conceal her animosity toward Mildred Phillips, either in the way she spoke about her or in the frigid glint that came into her eyes whenever Judith mentioned her name.

After a rapid tour of the rest of the Phillips house, Judith remembered the mail piling up in the box outside the door. She brought it in and spread it out on a table in the foyer, scanning the return addresses for anything that might be out of the ordinary. The only piece that caught her eye, however, was a brightly printed postcard addressed to Phillips with a few lines of writing scrawled on the back: "Arrived safely. Father much better. Will call to let you know return flight." It was signed "Millie" and postmarked from Louisiana the day before Ed Phillips was murdered.

Judith smiled broadly as she tucked the postcard into her briefcase. She'd hand it over to Josephson and let him locate the Widow Phillips. She had more important things to do, like clearing her calendar long enough to squeeze in a quick visit to the city, where one of her first stops would be the Park Avenue office of Dr. John Farrelly. Judith very much wanted to know what Ruth Larkin was doing with a gun registered to Dr. Farrelly.

18

Millie Phillips sniffed and dabbed at her eyes with Detective Josephson's handkerchief, then glanced around the squad room to see whether anyone might be watching her. No one was, including the young police officer who'd driven all the way down to John F. Kennedy Airport in his own car to meet her early-morning flight from New Orleans. Despite the crowded confines of Josephson's small compact, the long drive back to White Plains had been conducted in almost unnerving silence, with Josephson volunteering almost no information about the murder of Ed Phillips. The only facts Millie had ascertained so far were that Ed was dead and that Clarice Stuber had found his body.

Millie hadn't even had a chance to see the house yet. Josephson drove her directly to police headquarters, where they now sat facing each other across a gray metal desk with a scratched and battered Formica surface. Using a laborious hunt-and-peck typing style, Josephson filled in the blanks on a receipt for the personal effects that had been removed from Phillips' body—his watch and a handful of coins from his trouser pockets.

"To think that my darling Ed has been gone for nearly a week and I never even knew it! How could such a terrible thing happen, Detective?" she asked in a high, choked voice as he removed the paper from his typewriter and indicated where she should sign her name. "If I hadn't received your phone call yesterday, I still wouldn't know about Ed's murder, would I?"

The young detective loosened his tie and hunched

over the desk to read through the statement, thereby avoiding having to look directly at the attractive widow who sat across from him. Displays of emotion, even well-controlled emotion such as that exhibited by Mildred Phillips, made Martin Josephson distinctly uncomfortable. "I'm afraid the delay in notifying you was unavoidable, Mrs. Phillips. We had a difficult time tracing you to Louisiana. Nobody here seemed to know where you'd gone."

"Yes, I know. You've explained all that, Detective. I'm afraid I did leave rather abruptly. As I told you, my father was suddenly taken ill and my mother needed me at home." She gave a small sob, holding the handkerchief up to her face. "But nearly a whole week! I simply cannot believe it. I really can't, Detective! Ed has been dead for a whole week and I still don't know how or why!"

"All I can tell you right now is that we're working very hard on this case, Mrs. Phillips. I'm not at liberty to tell you any more than that at the moment." Josephson stood up and walked around the desk to Millie's chair.

"Why would anyone want to kill Ed?" Millie asked, shaking her head. "That's what I can't understand. Who could possibly want to kill my husband?"

"That's one of the questions we were hoping you might be able to help us with," Josephson replied stiffly. Millie looked up at him blankly, and then realized he was waiting for her to get up.

"Is it really necessary for me to go to the morgue and identify Ed's body?" she asked plaintively. "You already have Clarice Stuber's identification—certainly that ought to be sufficient."

"Under some circumstances, yes," Josephson said quietly but firmly. "But whenever possible we like to have the next of kin confirm the deceased's identity. I'm sorry to have to put you through this, but you do understand our position, don't you? We have to make absolutely certain there's been no mistake."

*   *   *

Judith Stein was waiting for Millie and Josephson at the entrance to the hospital, having first made certain that the morgue attendant understood that two bodies, not one, would be viewed in a particular sequence. Ordinarily Judith wouldn't have rushed over to the small hospital morgue to witness a simple routine identification, but she had to admit to a strong professional, not to mention personal, curiosity about the woman whose mere name stirred up so much hostility in Clarice Stuber.

What she saw, as Josephson performed the perfunctory introductions, was not very enlightening. Millie struck her as an ordinary well-to-do housewife, dressed well but not lavishly in a camel-hair coat worn over a simply styled wool dress of the same shade. She wore no jewelry other than a single strand of pearls at her throat.

Although Mildred Phillips was at least three to four inches taller than Judith, her blond curls and large blue eyes did give her a certain porcelain-doll prettiness, however. The kind of dainty prettiness that Judith knew could probably drive a woman like Clarice Stuber wild with envy. After all, there was nothing either dainty or pretty about the imposing Miss Stuber. Still, there had to be more behind Clarice Stuber's jealousy than just Mildred Phillips' looks.

As the three of them walked through the long underground tunnels leading to the basement morgue, Millie was surprised to realize that she could detect no particular odor. This absence of any definable odor, combined with her own growing sense of unease, was giving rise to an increasing apprehensiveness about going through with this whole identification process.

Millie's uneasiness stemmed not so much from having to view Ed's dead body—she rather looked forward to that—as from her own ignorance about what may, or may not, have occurred the night Ruth killed him. She'd been phoning both Ruth and Adrianna for days now and getting nowhere. Both of them seemed to have completely disappeared. Ruth didn't answer at her apartment, and Adrianna's housekeeper would only say that she was "out of town" and she didn't know when Mrs. Farrelly would be back. It was possible, Millie supposed, that Adrianna had taken Ruth off somewhere to rest and recuperate, but why hadn't Adrianna let her know in advance where they were going?

Millie also found it somewhat disturbing that this police officer, Josephson, was so evasive about the circumstances surrounding Ed's death. If they had no leads in the case, and she hoped to God they didn't, why couldn't he just come out and tell her so? Were the police too embarrassed to admit they were stumped? Or had something gone wrong?

Judith Stein and Josephson stopped outside a heavy metal door at the end of the tunnel and waited for Millie, who had dropped a few paces behind. The small room they ushered her into was tiled from floor to ceiling in institutional green, with painted green trim now faded and peeling. Through a second door to the right Millie could see into what looked like a dimly lighted operating room dominated by a long, sloping stainless-steel table in the center of the floor. A large white jug marked "formalin" perched precariously close to the edge of a counter under a series of anatomical charts.

The air in the two rooms was chilly, not uncomfortably so, but enough to give Millie the shivers. From somewhere nearby Millie thought she could detect the almost inaudible hum of a refrigeration unit.

"If you're ready, Mrs. Phillips . . . ?" Josephson said, simultaneously nodding to the white-uniformed morgue attendant standing in front of a wall containing what looked like oversized filing-cabinet drawers. The attendant reached down and swung open one of the drawers, pulling out a long stainless-steel shelf that glided forward noisily. On the shelf was a large, indistinct form wrapped in white plastic tied in the middle with a length of string. Attacked to the string was a tag with the name "Phillips" written in block letters and a series of numbers.

As the attendant drew back the plastic sheeting from Ed Phillips' face, Millie let out a startled, strangled gasp. She didn't know exactly what she'd been expecting, but it wasn't this. To her immense shock, Ed's lips had drawn back in a macabre grin of death, as though he was thoroughly enjoying one final joke at Millie's expense. A single bluish-red hole punctured the center of his forehead.

"Is this your husband?" Judith Stein asked gently, standing close to Millie's side. "Is this Edward Phillips?"

Millie jumped at the sound of Judith's voice and quickly turned her back on the body of her husband, mutely nodding her confirmation. She didn't want to see any more. Not now, not ever. She leaned against the cool steel of the drawer cabinets, ignoring the two officials who were watching her so closely. How much easier this would have been, she thought, if the shot had left Ed's face mangled or otherwise unrecognizable. Instead, Millie suspected that the horrible memory of that twisted, leering grin would never entirely leave her—not in the darkness of the nights yet to come, nor in the terror of as-yet-undreamt dreams.

"When can I . . . ?" Millie stopped and cleared her throat. "When can I have the funeral home collect his body?"

Judith motioned to the attendant to close the drawer. "They can come anytime. The medical examiner has authorized the release." She stepped between Millie and the door. "Before you go, however, you might be able to help us with one other matter."

The attendant moved down the bank of drawers and opened another in the row just above. Again a long stainless-steel shelf rolled out into the room, bearing a smaller shapeless form completely encased in white plastic. The tag, however, had been turned so that Millie could not read the name.

"Mrs. Phillips, do you know this woman?"

Millie stepped forward as the attendant undid the string tie above the head and peeled back the plastic. She stared in horror at the small white face, with its fringe of short dark hair plastered in clumps of dried blood against the delicate skull. A jagged, discolored gash ran along the left side of the face from the temple to the base of the jaw.

"No!"

The single word was all Millie Phillips could manage before the room spun out of control and she slumped to the floor, unconscious.

19

"**H**ow could you do that to me?" Millie Phillips raged. "How could you let me walk in there totally unprepared for a shock like that? What a hell of a way to find out that poor Ruthie is dead!"

Adrianna Farrelly sat calmly on the chaise longue and waited while Millie, white-faced with grief and fury, stalked around her cream-and-apricot bedroom.

Minutes after Detective Josephson had dropped her off at the house, Millie began telephoning Adrianna's number at half-hour intervals until finally, at eleven-thirty that evening, Adrianna answered. At six-thirty the following morning, Millie was on her way to the train station to catch the express into the city going directly to the town house, where an unusually terse Adrianna greeted her at the door and led her upstairs to the bedroom, where they would not be overheard by the housekeeper.

"My God, Addy, do you realize what nearly happened in that morgue? If I hadn't blacked out . . ." Millie glared directly at Adrianna. "I was so shocked at seeing Ruth lying there dead that I almost blurted out the whole agreement, Addy! Do you understand? I almost told them everything!"

"What did you tell them after they brought you around?"

"Nothing, no thanks to you. They asked me if I knew her, and I said I'd never seen her before in my life. I didn't know what else to do! That's when they told me she was the one who'd killed Ed. They asked me a lot of questions about Ed—whether he had extramarital affairs and things like that—and all I could do was sit there and shake my head and tell them I knew nothing about anything. They must think I'm a real empty-headed dummy by now!"

Adrianna slowly rose from the chaise and walked over to the ebony luggage rack at the foot of the bed. A suitcase was open on the rack, with a froth of clothes spilling out in colorful piles all over the floor beneath. Adrianna picked a silken chemise out of the suitcase, folded it carefully, and added it to a pile on the bed.

"It's a pity you fainted, but that's something you couldn't control, wasn't it? Still, I suppose it can be explained away easily enough if the matter should come up again. You can simply say that you aren't used to viewing dead bodies, and that the sight of one so badly damaged was more than you could bear."

"That's easy enough for you to say!" Millie angrily protested. "You aren't the one in the middle of this mess, are you?"

Adrianna looked up from her unpacking with mild surprise. "What mess is that, Millie? There is absolutely no way they can connect you with Ed's death. Or even with Ruth, for that matter. Unless you tell them. And I scarcely think you're that stupid, honey."

"So what do I do now? Just sit around and wait to see what kind of stunt those two human bloodhounds pull next?"

"Exactly. This is no time to go off half-cocked and do something silly. The best thing you can do at this point is nothing. Just go on playing the grieving widow and let the investigation run its course. Once the police realize they aren't getting anywhere, the whole incident will be quietly dropped."

Millie perched on the edge of the bed and idly fingered a challis scarf that Adrianna had tossed to one side. "I certainly hope you're right, Addy. If only Ruth hadn't—"

"What's done is done!" Adrianna broke in sharply. "It was an accident. I never meant for Ruthie to die, you know."

"I never thought you did." Millie reacted with equal vehemence. "I was merely going to say that we were so preoccupied with making sure the men were taken care of that we never anticipated anything happening to any of us."

"Poor little Ruthie," Adrianna sighed, sinking down on the bed next to Millie. "If only we'd known how precarious her mental state was, perhaps we could have done something to ease some of the pressure on her. Perhaps we could have come up with another way to take care of Ed, something a little less direct."

"But we didn't know, did we?" Millie quietly agreed. "Ruth was never one to let on when she was in pain. You had to watch for the signs, and we didn't always watch, did we?"

"No. We didn't." Adrianna bowed her head, willing herself not to remember the night Ruth had died, the night she'd phoned in such panic about the imaginary flames in the car, begging and pleading with Adrianna to be released from the agreement. Adrianna had seen the signs of Ruth's deterioration all right, and she had done nothing about it. Or more precisely, she told herself, there was nothing she could have done about it. The plan was already in motion—it was then or never. They might never get such a perfect opportunity again.

"Addy?" Millie whispered, her voice breaking. "I'm going to miss her dreadfully."

Adrianna nodded, her hand covering her mouth. "I know, Millie. I miss her already."

"There's one other thing . . ."

Adrianna glanced over at Millie and then returned to her suitcase, her fingers busily rummaging through a cache of toiletries and cosmetics.

"We can't leave her in that horrible place, Addy. Not wrapped up in a body bag like some derelict they picked up off the streets. She has to have a decent burial, with a proper funeral Mass and all. She would have wanted that." As she spoke, Millie saw a small tear trickle from Adrianna's eye and roll silently down her cheek.

"Don't worry about it, Millie," she said quietly. "It's already been taken care of."

"You have?"

Adrianna gave her a bittersweet smile. "I had my attorneys contact her brother in Chicago. He's a mailman and doesn't have much money, so an 'anonymous' benefactor will pay to have her body shipped home for a full funeral service in the cathedral with flowers and everything. He'll arrive in New York within a few days to claim the body and make the necessary arrangements—with a carte blanche check for whatever expenses are involved."

"Thank goodness. Adrianna, you do think of everything!" Millie suddenly sat up straight as a new thought struck her. "A blank check? Are you out of your mind? A funeral like that could cost a small fortune. Where're you going to get cash to pay for all that?"

Adrianna closed the now empty suitcase and carried it into the adjoining dressing room, where she placed it next to three others exactly like it, only in varying sizes. The dressing room was so large, almost as large as Millie's entire bedroom, that Adrianna had to raise her voice so Millie could hear.

"You surprise me, Millie," she called. "Not once have you asked me where I've been for the past few days. Aren't you even curious?"

Millie rose from the bed and walked over to the window where she could look down on the traffic flowing back and forth in front of the house. She felt much calmer now that the initial shock of seeing Ruth dead in the morgue was beginning to wear off, softened immeasurably by Adrianna's reassurances that Ruth's body would not remain unclaimed and forgotten. She was almost calm enough to think about the funeral arrangements she ought to be making for Ed, and whether or not it would be wise to leave the children with her mother in Louisiana for a while longer, or bring them home to resume their lives. So engrossed was she in these ruminations that she didn't hear Adrianna come up behind her.

"I asked if you weren't curious about where I've been?"

"Good grief, don't startle me like that!" Millie yelped, taking a little step to the side. "Of course I want to know where you've been—and why you didn't let me know Ruth was dead!"

Adrianna stood slightly behind her and gazed out the window over Millie's shoulder. "I don't suppose the newspapers in Louisiana carried the story, but they found what they think is John's plane," she answered with a matter-of-fact serenity that belied her internal excitement.

"When?"

"Oddly enough, the day before Ruth and Ed died. A couple of ski instructors were checking out one of the old trails that's been closed all winter, when they found a piece of metal that looked like it could have come from a plane. The search was reactivated, and two days later they found the fuselage a few hundred yards away buried under several feet of snow. I went up there as soon as I heard what was going on."

"Was John in the plane?"

Adrianna nodded. "There was a body in the plane—although everything was so badly burned they won't be certain it is John until the medical examiner gets the records from his dentist here. But yes, I think it's safe to assume the body is John's."

Millie's face lighted up and she practically danced around Adrianna. "That's wonderful!" she cried. "That will solve so many of your problems with the estate."

Adrianna responded to Millie's enthusiasm with a warm smile. Everything was working out as planned—everything except the death of Ruth, of course. But even that might be for the best in the long run, she thought. Ruth was more at peace in death than she'd ever been in life.

"Have you told the lawyers to start probate yet?"

Before Adrianna could respond that probate could not begin until the identification process was concluded and definite, the phone on the bedside table rang twice, then abruptly stopped. A minute later the housekeeper buzzed the intercom and Adrianna picked up the phone, a puzzled frown creasing her otherwise unlined brow as she listened to the voice at the other end of the line. When the voice had finished she replaced the receiver and turned to face Millie.

"Did you say that woman from the district attorney's office was named Judith Stein?" she asked, her voice very low and wary.

"Yes. Why?"

Adrianna gathered up Millie's coat and handbag from the chair near the door and handed them to her. "That was John's office on the phone. She's just been over there asking questions, and now she's on her way here."

Millie's mouth dropped open as the significance of Adrianna's words sank in.

"Here? But that's impossible! Why on earth is she coming here?"

"I don't know, but you'd better leave. Right now. It wouldn't be wise if you were still here when she arrives."

Millie slipped into her coat and gave Adrianna a quick hug. "I'll call you as soon as I get home, all right? And be careful, Adrianna. Be very, very careful."

Adrianna's mouth was set in a thin, determined line. "I always am, Millie."

20

Judith Stein was certainly not accustomed to being nervous. She'd come a long way in her thirty-four years, beating the odds of near-poverty and the competition of academia to become a respected and reasonably sophisticated member of the legal profession. Yet, standing here outside the Farrellys' front door, Judith felt the palms of her hands growing damp and the minute flutterings of butterflies in her stomach. Such sensations were highly out of character for Judith, except on those exceedingly rare occasions when she found herself in close proximity with great and, to her, almost incomprehensible wealth.

The nearness of money. Scads of it. That was at the root of this unexpected attack of nerves. Judith had recognized the signs immediately. She understood herself well enough to realize that her own lack of financial substance was definitely one of her most vulnerable points. In spite of a keen intelligence which had given her the ability to reason rationally about most things, Judith Stein was not immune to the purely emotional impact of great wealth, and of the power that possessing such wealth implied. And that emotional impact included the very real fear that she would never know what it was like to possess the great quantities of money that people like the Farrellys took for granted.

Judith straightened her back and squared her shoulders. This reaction to money was silly and irrational and she knew it. Knowing it didn't help, of couse, nor did the knowledge that her reaction was not at all unusual.

162

Judith had known any number of people, men and women alike, who could be reduced to quivering imbecility by the presence of someone with great wealth or fame or both. The only way to overcome this senseless feeling of inferiority was by constantly reminding herself that Adrianna Farrelly was no better than herself, and couldn't possibly be any more condescending than some of those rich, pampered featherheads she had encountered from time to time at Harvard. The ones who'd always clucked with sympathy after prying from her the information that her family's sole economic asset consisted of a failing shoe store in Flatbush that barely produced enough revenue to feed and clothe them, much less educate Judith and her younger sisters. And it was always these same girls who ever after maintained a safe distance from her, as though failure could be infectious.

Life wasn't necessarily fair. How many times had her overworked father told her that when she'd come home depressed and discouraged during class breaks? Hundreds, maybe. Perhaps thousands. The social divisions hadn't been so pronounced at Hunter, where she'd done her undergraduate work. But they certainly were at Harvard. Not consciously, perhaps, but those hallowed halls of learning were so strongly imbued with the traditions of the landed gentry that Judith had intuitively known, without needing to be told, that she'd never truly fit in no matter how many grants and fellowships came her way.

Just as she had not quite "fit in" earlier that morning in the tastefully appointed Park Avenue offices of Dr. John G. Farrelly. Farrelly's staff and colleagues had certainly been polite to her, but polite in an overly familiar, patronizing manner that had set Judith's teeth on edge. And now she was about to put herself through this same emotional wringer again, only more so, because this was Farrelly's home turf, his sanctum sanctorum where not even his wealthiest patients would have dared set foot unless their blood was blue enough.

Even with all this foremost in her mind, Judith was totally unprepared for the extraordinarily beautiful woman who opened the door. Her tall, aristocratic bearing was accentuated by the deep royal blue skirt-and-sweater set she wore, as well as the absence of any visible trace of cosmetics on her perfectly molded face.

"Mrs. Farrelly?" Judith asked, acutely conscious of her own tiny stature and awkwardness. "How do you do? I'm Judith Stein. From the district attorney's office in Westchester?"

Adrianna smiled with cool graciousness and stepped back to give Judith room to pass through the open door. "Won't you come in, Miss Stein?"

As Judith followed the elegant Mrs. Farrelly into the spacious living room, she became aware that the "simple" skirt Adrianna wore was constructed, in fact, of such butter-soft suede that it flowed gracefully along the curves of her body like the most delicate of fabrics. And the sweater set, Judith felt certain, had to be of pure, unblended cashmere. She doubted that a strand of polyester had ever touched Adrianna's flawless skin, and she equally doubted that it ever would. By contrast, her own neatly tailored suit of charcoal-gray wool, which had set her back nearly half a month's salary, felt cheap and shabby in spite of its relative newness and expense.

So preoccupied was Judith with inspecting Adrianna's version of the casual "at-home" outfit that she scarcely noticed Adrianna pressing a small buzzer mounted on the wall near the doorway. Within moments there was a discreet knock on the gleaming paneled door and a heavyset middle-aged woman, dressed in a starkly plain black dress, entered bearing a large silver tray laden with a coffeepot, creamer, sugar bowl, and two sets of cups and saucers. Adrianna and Judith sat silently facing each other on the twin love seats as the housekeeper poured out two cups and withdrew as wordlessly as she had come, closing the door securely behind her.

"Now then," Adrianna said calmly, as soon as the housekeeper had gone, "what can I do for you, Miss Stein?"

Judith resisted the temptation to taste the scalding-hot coffee and instead left her cup to cool on the coffee table between them. "I know this is a bad time to come to you with questions about your husband," she started out slowly, "but these questions have a very important bearing on a case I'm working on."

"In Westchester?"

"Yes. In Westchester." Judith took a deep breath, then plunged on, her attack of nerves finally beginning to recede. "I went to your husband's office this morning and they told me about your husband's death. About his plane finally being found and his death confirmed, I mean. I'm so terribly sorry."

"Thank you."

Adrianna, she noticed, sat quietly composed, moving only to sip delicately from the cup she held on her lap.

"If you wouldn't find it too upsetting, Mrs. Farrelly, I would like to ask you some questions about your husband's gun."

"Gun?" Adrianna asked, her eyes widening a fraction. "I wasn't aware that my husband owned a gun."

"Apparently he did. A small handgun—a thirty-two-caliber Beretta. Registered in his name at his office address. His secretary clearly remembers Dr. Farrelly bringing the weapon into the office approximately six or seven years ago and asking her to handle the registration procedure. Apparently she had quite a bit of difficulty with it. In any event, Dr. Farrelly told her you had bought the weapon for personal protection while he was out of town."

Adrianna carefully placed the cup and saucer on the table, opened a small lacquered box nearby, and withdrew a cigarette, which she lighted from a sculptured silver lighter. "I can't imagine why John would tell her a thing like that," she said at last, her voice steady and devoid of emotion, although the smooth skin stretched tight across the high cheekbones had paled. "I've always been opposed to having guns in the house, especially with our excellent security system here. And of course there is always the danger such weapons might fall into the wrong hands, although I'm certain you know more about that than I."

"Did you in fact buy this particular weapon, though? The Beretta?"

"Good heavens, no!" Adrianna replied, her face shaping itself into an expression of indignation. "I don't have the slightest idea of how one would even go about purchasing such a thing!"

Judith repressed a sigh and instead took a small sip of the coffee, determining that it was finally cool enough to drink. She sensed, without being able to express exactly why, that the lovely Mrs. Farrelly was lying through her perfect white teeth.

"Do you know if Dr. Farrelly kept this gun anywhere in the house? His desk perhaps?"

"Not to my knowledge," Adrianna answered, the inscrutable mask once again in place. "If he did, I never saw it. As I've already told you, I wasn't aware that John owned a gun. I can only assume that if he did, he must have kept it at the office."

A telephone rang somewhere at the back of the house, then abruptly stopped. Adrianna Farrelly, however, seemed to take no notice.

"Would the name Edward Phillips have any significance to you?" Judith asked, deciding to try a new tack.

"Phillips? Why, no, I don't think so. Should it?"

"How about Ruth Larkin?" Judith persisted.

Adrianna assumed a thoughtful pose for a moment, then brightened. "Ruth Larkin—that name does sound familiar. Wasn't she in the newspapers for something recently? The exact circumstances escape me, I'm afraid."

Judith watched Adrianna intently, but could detect no meaningful change in her demeanor. "An accident. She was killed in an automobile accident shortly after she shot Edward Phillips to death with your husband's gun."

Adrianna's eyes widened with surprise. "How terrible!" she gasped. "Are you certain? She killed someone with a gun you say belonged to John?"

"Absolutely certain, Mrs. Farrelly. We have the murder weapon and it was definitely registered to your husband."

"This is simply terrible!" Adrianna responded, rising

from the sofa and walking over to the green marble fireplace. "There must be some mistake." She turned to face Judith. "Do you know how this person, this Ruth Larkin, came to have this particular gun?"

"That," said Judith, "is what I am asking you." She would have been inordinately pleased to see a slight crack appear in Adrianna's studied composure, but there was none.

Again the faraway telephone rang. And again it abruptly stopped.

Adrianna returned to the sofa and poured another cup of coffee before sitting down. "I have no idea. Perhaps she was one of John's patients? He was a psychiatrist, you know, and very interested in the workings of the psychopathic criminal mind."

Judith shook her head. "That was one of the first things I checked on at his office this morning. There is no record of Dr. Farrelly ever treating Ruth Larkin. Or her husband, Harold Larkin, for that matter."

"Harold Larkin? The Harold Larkin who wrote that best-selling novel—what was the title, now? A pity, I can't remember. But I do remember it was a wonderful book. I read it only just recently and found it absolutely enthralling. As a matter of fact, I believe we still have the book upstairs in the library. Is that the same person?"

"Yes."

Adrianna sank back against the cushions of the love seat, the slender bejeweled fingers of her right hand pressed to her temple. "Please excuse me, Miss Stein, but this is rather too much for me to take in all at once!"

Judith glanced down at her own ringless hands, then back up at Adrianna. "Did you know Ruth or Harold Larkin, Mrs. Farrelly?"

"Know them?" Adrianna looked puzzled. "I don't think so. It's possible I may have met them—I really can't remember. We, that is John and I, led a rather active social life. We attended many gatherings where it's possible we could have met Mr. or Mrs. Larkin. But as I say, I really can't recall either one of them specifically."

"I see." Judith consulted her watch, and then produced a business card from her handbag. There wasn't any purpose in wasting more time with Adrianna Farrelly. If she knew anything about the gun, and Judith believed it was entirely possible Mrs. Farrelly knew a good deal more than she was telling, she was not about to reveal it to Judith. She'd try one more question, and if that produced nothing, call it quits for the moment.

"What I'm going to ask you may seem insulting, especially in view of your husband's recent death, but please understand I really must ask." Judith leaned forward and gazed directly at Adrianna. "To your knowledge, did Dr. Farrelly have extramarital affairs?"

Adrianna looked startled, then smiled. "Extramarital affairs? Good heavens, no!" Her manner turned instantly serious. "John was the finest husband a woman could have," she explained soberly. "He was a man of very strong moral character who was completely dedicated to his work—and to me. Does that answer your question?"

"Yes, and thank you, Mrs. Farrelly," Judith responded with a small, tight smile while handing over her business card. "If you should happen to remember anything, anything at all about the gun—no matter how trivial it may seem—please give me a call at this number."

"Of course, Miss Stein. I'm so sorry I couldn't have been of more help."

A great sense of release washed over Judith as she departed from Adrianna Farrelly's town house. That woman was cool, she thought. Perhaps just a shade too cool. That gun had been hers all right—Dr. Farrelly's secretary had been absolutely definite on that point, and there was no reason the secretary should lie. But there was every reason Adrianna Farrelly might, especially if she already knew that the gun had been used to commit a murder.

Judith hailed a cab and gave the driver the address of the precinct headquarters she wanted and settled back to mull over what she had learned so far. Or rather, what she hadn't learned.

The interview with Adrianna hadn't been a total loss,

Judith decided, paying no attention to the passing street scenes. If nothing else, it had given her several new angles to explore, including the possibility that Adrianna Farrelly was exactly what she appeared to be—completely innocent of all knowledge about either the gun or the Larkins. If that were so, then Judith would have to look elsewhere for the link between Ruth Larkin and John Farrelly.

The more likely possibility, however, was that Adrianna Farrelly knew all about the existence of the gun. Whether she had been acquainted with either of the Larkins was still undetermined. If she truly hadn't known them, as she claimed, then why, Judith wondered, had she adamantly denied all knowledge of the gun? Wouldn't it have been more logical to admit that the gun was hers, that it was missing, and that she had no idea who had taken it or for what purpose? There was no crime in owning—or even losing—a duly registered handgun.

Unless, of course, John or Adrianna Farrelly had been on fairly familiar terms with Ruth Larkin after all. In that instance she might be trying to protect her husband—or herself—from incrimination by association. Judith doubted the Larkins and the Farrellys moved in the same social circles, but that didn't necessarily preclude an acquaintance. Establishing that such an acquaintance had existed, though, might be difficult, considering that three of the parties implicated were now dead.

And none of this, of course, shed any light on the murder of Edward Phillips. How did Phillips, a Westchester plumbing supplier, fit into the picture? And how did Ruth Larkin get hold of a gun, legally registered to John Farrelly; and having obtained this gun, what had motivated her to shoot Edward Phillips?

Judith felt no closer to resolving the riddle of Phillips' murder when she entered the precinct squad room in search of Detective James Collins, the Manhattan police officer who had initially led the investigation into Harold Larkin's death. The red-haired man who was pointed out to her looked far too young to be on the police force, much less a detective, but Judith had learned the hard way not to draw snap conclusions about anyone's appearance.

"So you're the girl wonder I've been hearing so much about lately!" Collins flashed a lopsided grin as he stretched his hand out toward Judith. "The D.A.'s boys downtown are real impressed with you, you know that?"

Judith found herself returning Collins' infectious smile. "All this from just a few advance phone calls? Maybe I should ask the Manhattan D.A.'s office for help more often." She laughed. "No hard feelings, I hope?"

"Not at all. Fact is, the captain says I should take as much time with you as you need. Sure beats the hell out of answering calls the rest of the day!"

Collins rummaged through the papers on his desk and came up with a manila file that he waved toward Judith. "Made you photocopies of the Larkin case file—my original report, coroner's report, lab report, every piece of paper I could find that relates to the case in any way. What do you want to know first?"

Judith shrugged off her coat, opened a notepad, and uncapped a pen. "Everything you can remember, beginning with the discovery of Harold Larkin's body."

Collins, who'd been thinking through the case ever since he'd heard from the D.A.'s office that Judith was coming in to see him, recited the facts as he recalled them, including the hotel maid's weary insistence that Larkin's demise was nothing more than an accidental OD.

"That's what I thought too, at first," Collins admitted. "I even told Mrs. Larkin as much when she came here. It wasn't until the inquest, when the coroner indicated there was some question about the circumstances surrounding Larkin's death, that we began to look at it in a different light."

"What happened?"

Colllins riffled through the folder until he found a copy of the autopsy report. "I can't give you the verbatim testimony—it's all in the file anyway—but see here under the toxicological examinations where it talks about alcohol content and barbiturate levels and all of that?"

Judith leaned forward to peer over the top of the file. "Yes. Go on."

"Now, this guy, who's already pretty well loaded, supposedly takes a handful of Seconal capsules and washes 'em down with a couple slugs of booze, right? Whether deliberately or not, they couldn't say. For the moment that's beside the point. The fact is that he had sixteen milligrams of secobarbital in his blood—enough to kill him with or without the alcohol. The capsules I recovered from his room were pretty strong, but he'd still have had to take a fair number to get that much secobarbital into his blood system that fast, right?"

"Sounds reasonable," Judith agreed.

Collins flipped back the pages to a paragraph detailing the examination of Larkin's gastrointestinal tract. "You read through all this medical mumbo jumbo they put in here about mucosa and such, and what it boils down to is that his stomach was empty."

"Empty?"

"Yeah. No food. No nothing."

"So Larkin didn't eat dinner that night. So what?"

Collins looked up at her eagerly. "Don't you see? There should have been something in that stomach! At the very least, there should have been some traces of gelatin from that handful of capsules he supposedly swallowed. There wasn't, though. And no needle marks anywhere on the body, either. So how did the Seconal get into him?"

Judith instantly grasped what Collins was trying to tell her. "You think someone deliberately poisoned him, don't you?"

"Damn right that's what I think," Collins agreed, nodding vigorously. "The way I see it, someone emptied those capsules into his booze. He drank the stuff straight, dissolved in alcohol. Real hell of a fast-acting combination there. Probably never even knew what hit him."

Judith took the folder from his hand and glanced through the autopsy report, as well as the report on his only meeting with Ruth Larkin. "I gather you never told Mrs. Larkin about your suspicions?"

"No. I didn't have any suspicions at the time I talked to her. Later on I figured I should wait until I had something stronger to go on. But the couple of leads I had were pretty dead by then, and now so is Mrs. Larkin. All I can do now is just keep the whole thing on the back burner—going back to it when something new hits me."

"Were you able to find out whether anyone else was seen going into Larkin's room the night he died?"

Collins tilted dangerously far back in his chair, arms crossed behind his head. "The night clerk said he thought he remembered seeing a strange woman wearing a head scarf and thick glasses who might've gone up to Larkin's room, but he couldn't be sure. Said she didn't stop at the desk to ask for a room number, so he figured she knew where she was going. Thing of it is, that place has a revolving-door clientele. She could've been going to any one of a half-dozen different rooms that night."

"You think she went to Larkin's room, though."

"Yeah. We did a routine check for prints in the room and didn't find any. I mean we didn't find *any*. The place was wiped clean. Even the glass he drank out of didn't have normal prints on it. And there was no Seconal residue in the dregs, either. Glasses were switched, probably. Somebody had to take care of all that. Then, too," he added, pointing to the folder Judith was holding, "there was the lab report indicating Larkin had had sexual intercourse not too long before his death."

Judith was surprised at the increasing harshness of Collins' tone, as though he was becoming angry all over again that he could have been so easily duped. It happens to the best of us, she wanted to tell him, but wisely decided not to.

"So tell me about Ruth Larkin," she said instead. "What was she like?"

"In pretty bad shape the day I interviewed her. She'd been down in Acapulco on vacation when Larkin died and she couldn't seem to grasp what had happened. Acted kind of spacey, you know? Like she wasn't quite all there." Collins thought back for a minute, remembering the fragile, trembling woman who had sat where Judith Stein sat now. He recalled those limpid dark eyes darting around the room, resting on nothing or no one for long. Deer eyes, he had thought at the time. Frightened, hunted deer eyes.

"Come to think about it, she asked kind of the same question you just did," Collins said thoughtfully.

"What was that?"

"Whether another woman was with Larkin when he died."

Judith raised her eyes from the file and met Collins' gaze. "How long would it take to get a search warrant for Ruth Larkin's apartment?"

The young detective bestowed one of his cheerful grins on her. "I'm way ahead of you, lady. Got one all ready right here. Shall we go?"

21

Mick Flanagan barely ducked in time as the half-full ashtray whistled past his ear, crashing against the far wall and shattering into a thousand sharp fragments. "Hey, what'd you do that for?" he demanded, his injured air making him look more like a little boy falsely accused of raiding the cookie jar than a grown man whose size and fighting ability were already making him something of a minor legend in amateur boxing ranks.

Adrianna Farrelly peeled off the last of her clothing, her panties, and stood at the far side of the unmade sofa bed in naked splendor, the nipples of her breasts taut in the chill of the small, dingy apartment.

"I had to do something to get your attention," she snapped, not bothering to conceal her increasing irritation at his reluctance to come to her. "What do you expect me to do? Force you into bed, or get down on my knees and beg?"

Mick stared in bafflement at Adrianna's hard, glittering eyes. For weeks she hadn't come near him or his apartment, and now she was suddenly, inexplicably back in his life again, hotter and hungrier than he'd ever seen her before. She prowled in front of him like a tigress in heat, ready to rip him apart if he didn't perform to her satisfaction. To his own amazement, he found this raw, unadorned animalism more than just a little frightening.

He moved warily around the bed, uncertain how to react to this new facet of Adrianna's unpredictable personality. He thought he was used to her nearly insatiable demands upon his body, but this development was something entirely different. Something that was dangerously close to becoming predatory on the most basic, elementary level. Something that left Mick Flanagan, in spite of all his vaunted masculinity and overdeveloped physique, completely and totally unnerved.

Adrianna watched with unmasked contempt as Mick sidled farther away from her, his display of weakness feeding the flames of her already murderous rage. A rage aimed not at Mick Flanagan, but at John Farrelly, her late and unlamented husband. That stupid, incompetent, self-righteous son of a bitch had gone and registered her gun! Registered it without telling her!

Even in the aftermath of Ruth's death, Adrianna hadn't been particularly worried about the police finding the gun. Its origins, and actual ownership, were virtually untraceable, since she'd bought it so long ago in a rural Georgia shop where no questions were asked, and no names given. Ordering Ruth to dispose of the weapon in the river was merely a precaution to ensure that it would never be found and used somehow to connect Ruth with the murder of Ed Phillips. Since Ruth had died in the accident, its discovery scarcely seemed to matter.

At least it hadn't mattered until that woman Judith Stein turned up on her doorstep and so sweetly announced that their prize evidence, the murder weapon, was registered in her husband's name! God in heaven, how could that senile old fool have done this to her? He'd known all too well that she hadn't wanted that gun registered. They'd even quarreled about the registration at length after John had relented and agreed she could keep the gun in the house. No wonder he hadn't told her what he'd done! He knew she'd be furious with him. Just how furious she was, he could never have imagined.

The moment she had been sure that Judith Stein was safely gone and on her way in a taxicab, Adrianna also left the house. More precisely, she fled the house with its incessantly ringing telephones and the cloying sym-

pathy of well-wishers who appeared unannounced at
the door. She'd fled in search of release from her raging
white-hot fury and frustration in the only way she knew
how.

Of all the men she'd made love with in the city, she
had pinned her hopes for relief on Mick Flanagan—
Mick of the bulging biceps and trim derriere kept in
peak form with daily workouts at the gym. His staying
power was the best she'd found yet, even if his tech-
nique could use some more refinement. But even Mick
was failing her now, proving himself to be little more
than a sniveling coward when confronted by a woman
with needs and drives more powerful than his own.

As Mick slowly edged away from the foot of the bed,
Adrianna shot him a coyly brittle smile. "What's the
matter, Mickey?" she taunted. "Afraid big, bad Adrianna
might hurt you?"

"C'mon, baby," he pleaded, his hands opening in
supplication, "take it easy, okay? Give me a chance!"

"A chance to do what?" she challenged between
clenched teeth, no longer coy. "It seems to me you've
had every chance in the world and nothing's happened yet. What's your problem? Can't you do it
anymore?"

For an instant Flanagan's eyes flickered toward the
door to the outside corridor, and in that instant Adrianna
hurled herself across the bed at him, wrapping her long
legs around his waist while she pounded his chest and
face with her fists. "You lousy, worthless piece of garbage!" she screamed, hot tears scalding her cheeks.
"You impotent, brainless scum!"

Flanagan staggered under Adrianna's added weight
and slowly sank forward onto the protesting springs of
the sofa bed, pinning down her flailing arms and legs
with the sheer bulk of his body. As Adrianna writhed
beneath him, scratching and clawing his shirt to shreds,
Mick Flanagan felt his own anger, and lust, rising to an
uncontrollable pitch.

"Worthless garbage, huh?" he grunted, freeing a hand
long enough to unbuckle his belt and push down his

pants. "I'll show you who's impotent, you goddamn whoring bitch!"

As Flanagan mounted her with one brutal, vicious thrust, Adrianna Farrelly arched her back and cried out in triumphant passion.

22

The living room of the apartment so recently called home by Hal and Ruth Larkin was comfortable enough, although considerably less lavish than the living room of the Farrellys' town house. A long sofa upholstered in cheerful chintz, a bit threadbare in spots, dominated the smallish room. A matching easy chair had been placed at a right angle toward one end, and behind it, near the archway leading back to the entry hall, stood an open bar displaying an assortment of bottles and glasses.

Judith Stein stood in the center of the room and tried to imagine the sort of people who had lived there. She was having some difficulty inasmuch as the room did not project quite the image she thought it would. Harold Larkin, she knew, had been a big-time magazine editor and a best-selling author, but she would never have guessed it from looking at his home, apart from the fact there were books scattered everywhere. There was little to show that the Larkins ever used their apartment for the sort of glittering, lavish entertaining that Judith assumed Harold Larkin's status in the literary world necessitated. The furniture was well made and no doubt costly, but it was beginning to show distinct signs of wear, and the walls could definitely do with another coat of paint.

The only aspect of the apartment that jibed with Larkin's profession was the bookcases that lined the wall at one end of the living room, the shelves overflowing with a haphazard collection of volumes that looked as though they'd been shoved in any which way. A lone book, a slim volume of poetry, lay open on a sofa cushion next to a carefully folded afghan. Judith picked it up, determined that the printed verses were a little too abstract for her taste, and put it back.

"Find anything interesting?" Detective James Collins asked from the archway.

"No. Have you?"

"Kitchen's pretty bare. Not much food in either the refrigerator or the cupboards, although I suppose a widow living alone wouldn't have any reason to keep the larder full. There were some phone numbers scratched on a pad near the phone. I'll check them out with the telephone company when we get back to the station."

Collins followed Judith's gaze around the living room. "Pretty Spartan in here, isn't it?" he commented. "Not quite what I expected."

"Me neither," Judith agreed. "You want to tackle those books while I have a look around the dining room?"

"Sure. Why not?"

As Collins set to work methodically pulling out and inspecting books, Judith wandered across the hallway to the dining room adjacent to the kitchen. A small electric typewriter had been set up on the table, with a long extension cord snaking across the floor and disappearing under a high antique sideboard. Judith assumed the extension cord was left plugged in permanently, and just kicked out of the way under the sideboard when it wasn't needed.

She rummaged through the two upper drawers of the old sideboard, finding nothing more than the usual assortment of table linens, place mats, and flatware, all with that slightly musty odor that comes from a lack of use and airing. The third and bottom drawer, however, was considerably harder to pull out, owing to its greater weight. Judith managed to get the drawer halfway out before it became resolutely stuck and she had to resort to fishing around inside with her hand.

The drawer, as she quickly discovered, was crammed

to the top with boxes of typing paper, pens, large manila envelopes, and loose sheets that slid around under her fingers. One box in particular seemed to be wedged up toward the back, and Judith figured that was what had caused the drawer to jam. She gave it a couple of whacks with the heel of her palm and it reluctantly came loose, spilling loose papers over the other contents of the drawer. The top sheet slid practically under her nose and she read its three brief lines with mounting interest: "*Twin Lives, My Story*, by Ruth E. Larkin."

"My story," Judith murmured out loud. "How very strange. I thought Harold Larkin was supposed to have written *Twin Lives*."

"You talking to me?" Collins called from the living room.

"No, but come here anyway. There's something I want to show you."

Judith gathered up the loose sheets and put them back into the box in order, with the title page on top. She handed the box to Collins as he crouched beside her. "What do you make of this, Jim?"

"Well, it's a carbon copy, that much I can tell you," he said, flipping through the pages.

"I know that! I meant that first page where it says '*Twin Lives, My Story*, by Ruth E. Larkin.' Wasn't *Twin Lives* Harold Larkin's big bestseller?"

"Yeah. There's at least half a dozen copies of it out in the living room. All of them autographed." Collins gave a little laugh at the eccentricities of authors, then sobered as he realized what Judith was driving at. "You think maybe she wrote it and he copped the glory?" Collins asked.

"Makes a wonderful motive for murder, doesn't it?" Judith smiled. "That and his notorious reputation for the ladies you told me about on the way over. How much more wronged can a wife get?"

Collins sat back on his haunches, thinking. "The problem with that theory, beautiful as it is, is that Ruth Larkin had an airtight alibi for the night old buddy

Harold drank his last. She was thousands of miles away in Acapulco."

"Yes," said Judith slowly. "Just like Mildred Phillips was off in Louisiana the night Ruth Larkin shot Edward Phillips."

"A trade-off?" Collins grinned broadly. "Each kills the other's husband?"

"Stranger things have happened," she answered mildly. "Help me get this drawer up on the table and let's see what other little gems it contains."

For two straight hours Collins and Judith Stein carefully examined the drawer's contents, piece by piece. They opened envelopes, peered at unintelligible notes scrawled in smudged pencil, went through boxes of plain paper sheet by sheet, and even pried off the drawer's brittle old panels to make certain there was no false bottom. In the end, their "to investigate further" pile contained only two items—a somewhat oddly phrased condolence note written on the letterhead of one Judd Stassen, literary agent, and a yellowing standard business envelope with the notation "Last Will and Testament of Ruth E. Larkin. Client Copy."

Judith opened the unsealed flap and withdrew a packet of legal-size papers bound in a stiff blue cover. Across the front someone had scribbled, "Original with attorney." Judith read through the long sheets while Collins impatiently dumped the rest of the papers back into the broken drawer.

"Standard boilerplate," Judith said at last. "Pretty old, too. Leaves everything to her husband, Harold, and if he should predecease her, to her brother, Thomas Wallace, Jr., of Chicago." Judith paused to show Collins an extra sheet that had been attached to the back of the will, along with a small photograph of a radiantly smiling dark-haired woman holding two golden-blond little girls.

"This is a photocopy of a holographic codicil detailing who should be given certain personal items such as particular pieces of jewelry, silver, china, et cetera. I assume she gave the attorney the original copy to file with her will," Judith explained. "As far as I can make out, though, the codicil names only two beneficiaries."

"Who are they?"

"Evelyn Ruth Palmer and Dolores Diane Palmer."

Collins detached the small photograph and carried it over to the light by the window. "I'm pretty sure the woman here is Ruth Larkin. You think the beneficiaries she named are these two little girls?"

"Wouldn't surprise me in the least," Judith said flatly.

Collins looked over at her with interest. "How's that?"

"Those are the names of Mildred Phillips' daughters."

23

"**I** know it's circumstantial, Jack, but it all fits. A Larkin-Phillips conspiracy is the most logical explanation for why every time I turn around I seem to come up against another dead body!"

Judith Stein was so excited she felt like dancing around Jack Holland's desk, and might have done so if there'd been sufficient room in the small office. She'd been so keyed-up since returning from New York that she'd barely slept the night before, and had trouble concentrating on her work while waiting for Holland to return from court. Now that she finally had Holland firmly buttonholed, everything was spilling out in one breathless rush.

"Just think a moment about this hypothetical scenario: Ruth Larkin and Mildred Phillips are friends. For whatever reasons, both of them would like to get rid of their husbands, but divorce isn't a viable solution. So they concoct this plan whereby each does away with the other's husband at a prearranged time when the wife in question has an airtight alibi."

Judith tapped the thick NYPD manila folder she'd placed in front of Holland earlier. "Now, according to Collins' information, Larkin was reputed to be a womanizer, heavy drinker, and occasional drug abuser, so once Ruth Larkin is safely out of town, it's no big problem for Mildred Phillips to arrange to meet Larkin at his hotel room, have sex with him, and then dump a load of Seconal in his drink.

"In the meantime, Ruth Larkin, in exchange for being

rid of Harold Larkin, somehow manages to get hold of a gun belonging to this Dr. Farrelly. How she obtained the gun may be something we'll never know for sure. She could have stolen it or even bought it from someone on the street. What we do know for a fact is that she did have that gun with her when she died, she did drive up to Phillips' home at a time when his wife was out of town, and she did shoot him. That she afterward drove in front of a semi-trailer truck on the parkway was purely accidental, I believe. She was probably distraught and in shock." Judith's voice was beginning to grow hoarse, but the discomfort didn't stop her from going on with her monologue.

"Everything tells me I'm right about this, Jack. It even feels right. The problem is, I just can't prove it yet."

Jack Holland folded his arms on top of the desk and waited patiently as Judith rapidly paced up and down the small floor space between his desk and the door. Six years of experience had taught him not to interrupt when Judith was in the middle of one of her ambulatory speculations. Some of her best theories were developed while she was in motion.

"You know what really bothers me? That apartment. Ruth Larkin's apartment. It was clean as a whistle. Can you believe that?" Judith leaned across Holland's desk, her face close enough for Holland to see the first little lines forming around her eyes. "Collins and I spent hours searching every inch of that place and we didn't turn up one single keepsake. Everyone has keepsakes of one sort or another—everyone, it would appear, except the Larkins. No treasured love letters, no albums of photographs, not even an old Christmas card. Nothing. It was almost as though neither of the Larkins ever existed. If I hadn't found the will and photograph buried under all that manuscript stuff, I would have suspected Collins of taking me to a dummy apartment as some kind of horrendous practical joke."

Judith faced Holland expectantly, waiting for his reaction. "So what do you think?" she demanded. "The facts fit, don't they?"

"Maybe the Larkins didn't have any friends who sent them Christmas cards," Holland observed mildly. "Or wanted their pictures taken."

"Cute, Jack. Real cute." Judith swung away and resumed her restless pacing. "No, she had friends, all right. Friends who got into that apartment before we did and methodically removed every last scrap of potential evidence."

"Mildred Phillips?"

Judith stopped pacing, her back to Holland. "That had occurred to me, but the timing's all wrong. Josephson checked with the police in Louisiana and Mildred Phillips can produce a horde of witnesses who will swear she was there both the night of the shooting and the following week. The town is small enough that practically everyone, including the chief of police, can account for virtually every minute of her time."

"What about this Farrelly woman, then?"

"I don't know. I've been thinking a lot about her lately, and—"

A knock at the door cut Judith off abruptly, and Detective Martin Josephson stuck his head into the room. "You wanted to see me, Mr. Holland?"

"Yes, come in, Josephson," Holland said. "Stein and I are in the middle of going over the Phillips case. Since you're the officer in charge of the investigation, I thought you might like to be here. You got anything new for us?"

The young detective shook his head. "Not much, I'm afraid. I ran a routine check for priors on Phillips and the only thing that came up was a twenty-year-old assault conviction in Alabama. Seems he got drunk one night and beat up some woman. Other than that he was clean." Josephson declined Holland's gesture to be seated, and remained standing by the side of the desk. "One thing's interesting, though."

"What's that, Josephson?"

"Phillips certainly wasn't very popular around here. No real friends, and not too many people who had anything good to say about him, except that bookkeeper of his, Clarice Stuber. The one comment that kept coming up time and again was how could a lady as nice as Mrs. Phillips stand being married to the bum for so long?"

Holland shrugged noncommittally and motioned to Judith. "Apparently she couldn't. Stein thinks that's why he's dead. Stein, why don't you bring Josephson up-to-date on your foray into the city?"

Judith shot Holland a pointed glare that he pretended not to see. He knew perfectly well she disliked having an audience when she was bouncing ideas off him on a purely conjectural basis. But since there was little she could do about Josephson's presence now, Judith swallowed her objections and gave him a sketchy recap of her findings to date.

"Well, Josephson," Holland asked, "do you agree there might be a connection between Mrs. Larkin and Mrs. Phillips?"

Martin Josephson cleared his throat and looked from one to the other before speaking. "It's a plausible theory, sir, if you buy the idea that these two women were capable of pulling it off. I'm not sure I do."

Judith threw up her hands and rolled her eyes in exaggerated disbelief. "And why not, may I ask?"

Josephson fidgeted uncomfortably under Judith's stare. "I don't know, really, except that it would take an awful lot of clever, cold-blooded planning to set up something like Miss Stein is describing. I'm not sure those two ladies had what it takes. At least Mrs. Phillips, anyhow. From the time I've spent with her, I'd say she would have trouble planning tomorrow night's dinner, much less two murders."

Judith noticed with annoyance that a superior smile had spread across Holland's face, and was even more annoyed when he winked broadly at her. "If there is one common error that most men make, even law-enforcement men, it's that they underestimate the intelligence of women," Holland replied evenly, paraphrasing Judith's comment of two weeks earlier. "Especially their criminal intelligence."

"That may be, sir," Josephson said reluctantly, "but the evidence Miss Stein has presented so far strikes me as being pretty flimsy. I don't know how you'd be able to prove in court that these two women were capable of planning and killing each other's husbands, much less that they actually did it."

"Precisely." Holland fiddled with a small bronze paperweight cast in the shape of an American bald eagle. "But I think Stein may be onto something here. If we can establish an irrefutable link between these two women, we'd stand a lot better chance of putting the squeeze on Mildred Phillips."

" 'Putting the squeeze on' sounds like something out of a bad detective novel. Exactly what do you mean by that?" Judith inquired.

"Squeezing a confession out of her, of course." Holland briefly smiled again, more to himself than to either Judith or Josephson. "I can see the headlines now: 'SUBURBAN HOUSEWIFE ADMITS ROLE IN DOUBLE SLAYING CONSPIRACY!' Beautiful, isn't it?"

Judith laughed aloud at Holland's imagery. "Jumping the gun a little, aren't you, Jack? A woman who's smart enough to set up the murder of Harold Larkin to look like an accidental overdose is hardly likely to waltz into your office and freely admit that she knew Ruth Larkin, is she? Especially if she thinks such an admission could make her the prime suspect in the murder of Harold Larkin."

"She might, if she didn't know Larkin's death was under investigation as a probable homicide. And," Holland added with unexpected acerbity, "if you two would do your jobs right in the first place. You already blew one chance to nail Mildred Phillips at the morgue. Don't blow another."

Judith and Josephson were both caught off guard by the startling change in Holland's tone and mood. Judith's face flushed a deep red, while Josephson snapped to rigid attention.

"Now, wait just one minute. There was no way—" Judith started to protest, but Holland silenced her with a quick chopping motion of his hand.

"If you're about to tell me you didn't know about Larkin at the time, save it, Stein. I don't want excuses.

I want action. More to the point, I want a conviction! You two got that? No more kid gloves from now on. We've got to put together a solid case, a really solid case, against Mildred Phillips. None of this half-assed stuff so prevalent around the department lately."

Josephson, still standing at attention, glared at Holland. The cords stood out along his neck, while his fists spasmodically clenched and unclenched at his sides. "With all due respect, sir," he said stiffly, "I would like to remind you that I do not work for the district attorney's office. Chief Ryan is the only one I take orders from concerning the conduct of an active investigation."

Holland reached for the phone. "Whatever you say, Josephson. I'll give the chief a call right now, if that's what you want. And when I do," Holland warned ominously, "you can bet your badge that I'll ask him to make damn sure you're back in uniform jockeying a squad car around town first thing Monday morning."

Josephson took an uncertain step toward Holland's desk. "That won't be necessary, sir," he said, his voice sounding somewhat strangled. "I see your point. Is there any area of this investigation you'd like me to concentrate on in particular?"

Holland slapped the desktop with the palm of his hand. "Yes. Concentrate on the motivation and you'll find the method. Money is usually the motivation in cases like this. Check out Phillips' financial status—his bank account, holdings, et cetera. And don't forget insurance—find out if he had any life insurance, and if so, how much and who the beneficiary is. My guess is you'll find his wife is about to come into one hell of a hunk of money."

Judith stepped forward to retrieve the Larkin case file from Holland's desk. "I don't need a lecture on how to do my job, Jack," she said with strained dignity, her face still an angry crimson. "I've already got the telephone company digging out the billings for both the Larkin and Phillips phone numbers for the past six months, as well as for Phillips' private line at his office. If any one of them telephoned any of the others, we'll know." She paused, waiting to see whether Holland had anything more to say. He didn't.

"I'll also call Louisiana and see if the D.A. down there can send someone out to interview Mildred Phillips' daughters. I'd be willing to bet they knew Ruth Larkin pretty well. At least well enough to be included in her will. Am I forgetting anything?" she added acidly.

Holland grunted and shifted back in his chair. "Farrelly."

"What about Farrelly?"

"While you're burning up the telephone wires, give the FAA a call and see if they have any leads yet on what caused this guy's plane to go down. If there is any suspicion of sabotage, I want to know about it the minute they come up with the first shred of evidence."

"You think we can get Mildred Phillips to confess to that, too?" she asked, sarcasm rasping at her words.

"You just lay the groundwork," Holland said, glowering at the two standing in front of his desk, "and the rest will fall into place. I'm willing to gamble both your jobs that once Mildred Phillips is confronted with the fact that we know about her relationship with Ruth Larkin, she'll give us everything we need to send her to prison for a long, long time."

As Judith and Josephson left Holland's office, Josephson pulled her off to one side of the narrow corridor. "What was that all about?" he angrily demanded, nodding in the direction of Holland's door.

"I wish I knew," Judith answered, certain that she did know. After ten years as district attorney, it was becoming increasingly obvious that Jack Holland had had enough. He wanted out. Out, and up the next rung of the political ladder. And in the doll-like personage of Mildred Phillips, Judith was convinced, Holland could see his ticket to the big time.

Jack Holland looked at the door that had closed behind Judith Stein and Martin Josephson, a slow, satisfied grin spreading over his face. Without a doubt he'd managed to shake up those two so thoroughly they'd be back within a matter of days armed with everything he needed to go before the grand jury and get an indictment.

Mildred Phillips, he thought contentedly, your days of freedom are numbered. Enjoy them while you can.

24

Millie Phillips gripped the arms of the chair until her knuckles turned white and her hands shook with the tension. A look of horror transformed her face from its normal, cheerful openness to a hollow-eyed mask. Three days had elapsed since Judith's stormy meeting in Jack Holland's office, but even if Millie had known what had taken place, which she didn't, she couldn't have been any more devastated than she was at that precise moment.

"I can't believe this! You must have made a mistake. Please, Rod," she asked, her voice rising with hysteria, "please check again."

B. Roderick Howard rose from his deeply cushioned executive chair and crossed around behind Millie, placing a sympathetic hand on her shoulder. "There's no mistake, Millie. I'm sorry."

"But why? I don't understand!"

Howard exhaled loudly and opened a small bar concealed in the base of a bookcase. "You look like you need a drink, Millie. Whiskey and soda all right?"

Millie forced her mouth into a small, tight semblance of a brave smile, then gave up and buried her face in her hands. "Didn't he give you any reason why he would do this to me? Certainly he must have given you a reason!"

"Millie," Howard said patiently, handing her a glass, "I know this has come as a terrible shock, but there's nothing you can do. Take the advice of an old friend and accept the situation as it is. I'll help you in any way

I can. If it's money you need for yourself or the girls, I can probably help you get a second mortgage on the house, or even sell it if you wish. By the way, how are the girls?"

Millie swallowed half the drink and put the glass down on the desk, waiting for the alcohol to take effect and soothe her shattered nerves. "They're all right, Rod, thank you. They're staying with my parents in Louisiana until all this"—she gestured vaguely—"is cleared up. I didn't want them exposed to this dreadful business."

Millie suddenly screwed up her face and her eyes brimmed over with tears. "What am I going to do, Rod?" she wailed. "I was counting on that money for so much! For the girls' educations and everything! And now it's gone. Everything is gone!"

B. Roderick Howard was a large, heavyset man with surprisingly small hands and feet that allowed him to move with a certain easy grace. He also favored light gray suits that, along with his gray eyes and gray hair, enhanced the overall impression of being larger than life. As with most large men, however, Howard could be reduced to a quivering state of acute helplessness by the presence of a weeping woman, especially an attractive woman like Millie Phillips.

He fumbled around in his bottom drawer looking for a box of facial tissues, finding instead only a small travel packet empty except for one crumpled tissue. This he slid across the desk toward Millie, at the same time taking the precaution of offering her his good linen pocket handkerchief as well. "There, there, my dear," he bluffed, not knowing what else to say, "I'm sure everything will be all right for you and the children."

Millie wiped her large blue eyes with the handkerchief and fixed Howard with an accusatory glare. "The least you could have done was to warn me at the time, instead of letting me remain ignorant for two years. And to find out about Ed's treachery like this! Some friend you turned out to be, Roderick Howard."

Howard spread his hands helplessly. "There was nothing I could do, Millie. It was Ed's decision, and as long as he paid the premiums on time, I had no business meddling in his personal affairs. If I'd told you, like you think I should have, that would have been meddling and Ed would have been more than justified in taking his business elsewhere. Be realistic, Millie—I couldn't afford to lose both his corporate and personal business. Not even for friendship's sake."

"Do you realize what your refusal to meddle has cost me, Rod?" Millie shouted, her temper skyrocketing. "Half a million dollars! Half a million dollars that my babies won't have to live on because you were too high and mighty to tell me that Ed had changed the beneficiary on his life-insurance policy!"

"I'm sorry, Millie," he said weakly. "Truly sorry."

"Sorry won't put food on the table or my children through college," Millie retorted hotly, stuffing his handkerchief into her handbag and rising to leave. "When Clarice Stuber comes in to claim the money that rightfully should have been mine, tell her she can fork out the three thousand dollars for Ed's funeral expenses. She can afford it now. I can't." Millie yanked open the door with such force that the hinges squealed in protest. "And while you're at it, you can tell the rich Miss Stuber that I hope she and Ed rot in hell together. That's where they both belong!"

As Millie drove home from Howard's insurance office, her disappointment and bitterness continued to simmer and seethe. Twice she was forced to pull off the road and give in to bouts of racking sobs before she calmed down enough to ease back into traffic. Even so, her whole body trembled with the impact of the blow Roderick Howard had dealt her by revealing that two years ago Ed had changed his life-insurance beneficiary to Clarice Stuber. Two years ago! And Millie had known nothing about it. The bills had come in the mail four times a year as usual, and four times a year she saw the check stub Ed entered in their joint account. How on earth was she to know that Ed had pulled such a sneaky, dirty, low-down trick on her? And why had he done it?

Millie searched her memory, but could think of no

reason in particular why Ed should have turned against her two years ago, no triggering factor that immediately stood out. She'd joined the tennis club about then, but that hadn't seemed to faze Ed at the time. It was only recently that he'd begun making an issue of the time she spent there, accusing her of having affairs with the men she met on the courts. Dear Lord, she'd done many foolish things in her life, but engaging in illicit love affairs was certainly not one of them! Living with Ed was bad enough, but juggling two men at once, one of them a violent, irrational person like Ed, would have been impossible.

The unknown quantity in all of this was Clarice Stuber. Why had Ed named her as beneficiary? It simply didn't make sense. He had plenty of relatives, including a couple of brothers and several nieces and nephews down in Alabama who would have been more logical choices. They were all dirt poor and certainly could have used the money. Why, then, Clarice? Unless he was trying to punish her, his legal wife, for some imagined transgression that she couldn't possibly know anything about.

Of course Clarice Stuber never bothered to conceal the fact that she intensely disliked Millie, and had disliked her from the moment Ed had introduced them at the office just prior to their wedding. Was Clarice in love with Ed? she wondered. Had Clarice been subtly working on him all these years, to poison him against her? To break up their marriage so she could have him and his money? Could that be the reason he had grown so increasingly violent toward her in recent years?

Millie didn't know whether to cry or laugh or do both at the same time. The thought of Clarice Stuber entertaining any sort of romantic notions struck her as being ludicrous to an extreme. The woman had all the charm of an elephant—an ugly, ungainly elephant at that. Who could possibly want to go to bed with her? And she knew Ed well enough to realize that whatever hold Clarice Stuber had had over her husband, sex wasn't it. If nothing else, physically she wasn't the type to turn him on at all. The more Millie thought about it, the more convinced she became that Clarice had been playing a mind game on Ed, a mind game that unwittingly had become deadly.

Be that as it may, Millie decided, Clarice was the winner and she, definitely, the loser. She'd have to think long and hard about the best way to deal with this new and distressing development. The first thing to do was to call Adrianna and lay the whole problem in her lap. If anyone could come up with a workable plan to recoup her losses, Adrianna, with her calculating mind, was certainly the one.

Millie drove into the garage, but rather than entering the house immediately, she sat behind the wheel of her station wagon for a few minutes. A numbness was beginning to steal over her, a mind-deadening numbness brought on by the successive discoveries of Ed's duplicity and Ruth's tragically unnecessary death. Too much was happening too quickly, and all of it bad.

Slowly, wearily, Millie climbed out of the car and entered her home through the breezeway connecting the garage with the kitchen. There was no point in putting it off. Adrianna might as well be apprised of her situation right away. The sooner Adrianna knew, the sooner she could get to work on a way to get Millie out of this mess.

As Millie put her handbag down on the counter next to the coffee maker, the wall phone, a scant two feet away, began to ring.

"Mrs. Phillips? Lieutenant Josephson."

She stifled a groan and did her best to convey a pleasant breathlessness. "Yes, Lieutenant! What can I do for you?"

"There are a few details we're trying to wrap up on your husband's case. Nothing major, you understand," he assured her, "but we do need to talk with you again. Would you be able to come down to headquarters later this afternoon? I assure you this won't take very long."

Millie balled up her fist and slammed it into the wall next to the telephone. "Of course. I want to help the investigation in any way I can. What time should I be there?"

25

Millie Phillips was not unduly alarmed when Detective Josephson first ushered her into a small windowless room at headquarters with the explanation that their conversation would be more private there than in the larger, open squad room. Millie was, however, aware of a marked change in Josephson's attitude toward her since their last meeting. He scarcely looked at her now, and when he spoke to her his words had a clipped, official abruptness that had been absent before. Even so, Millie had little inkling that this interview was anything more than a continuation of the previous question-and-answer sessions which had been easy enough to field.

As Millie and Josephson entered the interrogation room he perfunctorily introduced her to a second officer, Sergeant Marilyn Ruminski, who was already seated at the centrally placed wooden table, a pad and pencil at the ready in front of her. In spite of Sergeant Ruminski's bulky and mannishly tailored uniform, Millie couldn't help but notice that the sergeant was a slender young woman who, if made up properly and dressed more stylishly, would probably be rather pretty.

Millie took the place directly across from Sergeant Ruminski and looked up expectantly as Josephson pulled out the remaining chair, turned it around, and straddled it. "Mrs. Phillips," he began with slow deliberation, "we asked you to come here today because we're still unclear about certain aspects of your husband's murder."

196

"I don't know what more I can tell you, Lieutenant. I wasn't even here when all this happened," Millie said, pursing her lips demurely. "I'm just as confused as you are."

"Maybe. But there are still a few areas we feel you can probably clarify for us."

A small frown creased Millie's brow, narrowing her large eyes. "Detective? I don't understand why all this is necessary. You already know who killed Ed, and you know how she did it. Isn't that enough to close the case?"

Josephson grunted and glanced at Sergeant Ruminski. "In the majority of cases, yes. This one is a little different."

"Different? In what way?" Millie was beginning to develop a sense of unease as Josephson's expression hardened. He leaned toward her, his arms folded along the back of the chair.

"How well did your husband know Ruth Larkin?" he suddenly asked.

Millie's eyes clouded with concern as she glanced back and forth between Josephson and Ruminski. "I've already told you, Detective, I don't know. Ed never mentioned her."

"Doesn't it strike you as odd that this woman, by your account a total stranger, would drive all the way up from New York to shoot your husband for no apparent reason?"

"You are deliberately misunderstanding me, Lieutenant," Millie replied crisply. "I never said she was a total stranger to him. I merely said he had never mentioned knowing her."

"So Ruth Larkin was acquainted with your husband."

"I don't know!" Millie replied in exasperation. "All I can tell you is that he never talked about anyone by that name. But, then, I'm sure he met many people from time to time that he never told me about. Especially women."

Josephson fixed Millie with a long, hard stare. "How about yourself, then? How well did you know Ruth Larkin?"

"Me?" Millie sucked in a sharp breath, her body tensing. "I didn't know her at all!"

"Are you sure?"

"Of course I'm sure!" Millie responded sharply, her voice rising with indignation. "What, for heaven's sake, is going on here? Isn't it bad enough that my husband has been murdered, without having you badger me with idiotic questions about someone I don't even know?"

"Well then," Josephson said, leaning back and stretching his arms, "perhaps you can tell us something about the gun that was used to shoot your husband."

The crafty smirk on Josephson's face triggered a warning bell in Millie's mind. The lieutenant apparently knew something that Millie didn't, which meant she would have to be extremely careful how she responded to his questions. Millie stalled for time by fumbling through her handbag in search of Roderick Howard's borrowed handkerchief.

"The gun, Mrs. Phillips," Josephson prompted.

"I can't tell you anything about the gun, Lieutenant, because I don't know anything!" Millie insisted, gently wiping her eyes with Howard's already mascara-stained handkerchief. "And I don't understand why you're asking me these things!"

"Do you know where the gun came from? Who it belonged to?" Josephson persisted.

"I assume Ruth Larkin."

"Are you certain the gun belonged to Mrs. Larkin?"

"No, I'm not certain!" Millie angrily shot back. "I can only make the assumption that the gun belonged to her. She was the one who used it, wasn't she?"

"Who is Adrianna Farrelly?"

The sudden mention of Adrianna's name, out of the context she'd been expecting, caught Millie off guard, and her normally pink porcelain complexion turned ashen. Adrianna had told her, of course, about the visit from the assistant D.A. and how the authorities had traced the gun back to John, so it was John she'd been expecting Josephson to ask about. Not Adrianna. Was it possible that Adrianna had let slip more to that woman D.A. than she'd intended? As quickly as the thought occurred to her, Millie dismissed it. Adrianna was far too intelligent to tell the authorities anything that might damage her own position. And incriminating Millie would certainly cast a good deal of suspicion on herself in the matter of John's death.

"I have no idea who Adrianna Farrelly is," Millie said at last, almost with relief.

"How about John Farrelly, then?"

"I don't know him either," Millie quickly shot back.

"You don't?"

"No, I don't!" she retorted emphatically, vigorously twisting the handkerchief into knots so Josephson wouldn't see how badly her hands were shaking. Millie fervently wished that Josephson would end this insistent probing that was making her so nervous. Nervous and tired.

"How well did Ruth Larkin know John Farrelly?"

Millie's head shot up and she glared at the police officer. "How in God's name would I know?" she demanded, suddenly furious at Josephson for putting her through this seemingly pointless ordeal. "I've told you everything I can, Lieutenant. What more do you want from me?"

"For openers, I'd like to know exactly how Harold Larkin was murdered," Josephson answered, unexpectedly lowering his voice to a more casual, conversational tone.

"What?" Millie rose so quickly that her chair tumbled over backward, the clatter louder than normal in the small room. "Now, listen here, Lieutenant Josephson, I've had just about enough. I don't understand what you're driving at with these insane questions about people I've never even met, but I do know that I don't have to stay here and take this!"

Millie took two steps toward the door, when Sergeant Ruminski intercepted her and spoke for the first time. "Please be seated, Mrs. Phillips. We have just a few more questions to ask you." The policewoman gripped Millie's hand and firmly guided her back to her place at the table.

"Where were you on the evening of January 13?"

Millie looked wildly around the small, bare room as though looking for somewhere to hide. "At home with my family, naturally. You can ask them. My husband . . ." Millie was stopped by the chilling realization that Ed was no longer there to vouch for her whereabouts at any particular time. She had only the children's word that she was at home, but would they listen to the testimony of children so young?

The implication of Josephson's new line of questioning left Millie speechless with terror. The fact that Josephson had deliberately mentioned Hal Larkin's name, followed by the date of his death, could only mean they had proof that Hal's death wasn't the accident it had been made to look like, and that Josephson seemed to think she might have had something to do with it.

Her suspicions were immediately confirmed by Josephson's next statement. "I don't think you were home at all that night," he commented dispassionately. "I think you were in New York City at the Hotel Crayton drugging Harold Larkin to death."

"No!"

Millie leapt up from her chair again, and this time both Detective Josephson and Sergeant Ruminski were on their feet to prevent her from reaching the door.

"Ruth Larkin murdered your husband, and you murdered hers," Josephson quietly persisted, arms folded across his chest as he stood blocking her way.

"No!" Millie insisted, tears cascading down her face. "I didn't kill Hal. I swear I didn't!"

"Hal?" Josephson repeated, a small smile of triumph curling the corners of his mouth. "Come now, Mrs. Phillips. We have all the evidence we need to prove that you and Ruth Larkin weren't exactly strangers to each other. Judging by the number of telephone calls that were made between your house and hers over the past six months, I'd say you knew Mrs. Larkin rather well. Well enough to call her at least once or twice a week—both before and after the murder of Harold Larkin." Josephson permitted himself a small chuckle. "Not to mention your own daughters, who were more than willing to tell the authorities in Louisiana all about the kindness shown to them by 'Aunt Ruthie.'"

Millie moved away from the two police officers, her back literally to the wall. "I swear I didn't kill Hal," she repeated desperately. "You have to believe me, Lieutenant. I didn't kill him!"

"Who did, then?"

While an internal battle raged over whether or not to tell him, Millie heard herself automatically replying, "I don't know!" She shook her head, struggling to clear away the bewildering fog of confusion and exhaustion that was hampering her ability to think clearly. She'd come perilously close to identifying Adrianna, and that must never happen, she knew. Whatever information they had about her relationship with Ruth had not come from Adrianna, so there was no reason to drag Adrianna into this mess, and every reason not to. Josephson might have his suspicions, but without Millie's cooperation there was nothing he could do about it.

Millie gripped the edge of the table, forcing her mind to assess the situation logically, not emotionally. If she could manage to keep Adrianna's name out of the investigation, Millie was certain that Adrianna would repay her by looking after the welfare of her children. And not only were the children's futures at stake, so was her own. Josephson could not possibly possess any real evidence linking her to Hal Larkin's death, for the simple reason that she hadn't been involved in it. He was obviously bluffing. But if she were foolish enough to implicate Adrianna, it would undoubtedly lead to the revelation of her own role in the destruction of John Farrelly. As long as the police didn't know about her relationship with Adrianna, they couldn't possibly tie Millie to John Farrelly's murder.

"Why did Ruth Larkin murder your husband?" Josephson pressed, standing so close to her their bodies were only inches apart.

"He was beating me up and molesting my daughter," Millie cried. "He threatened to kill me if I tried to leave him!"

Josephson walked around the table and stood behind

Sergeant Ruminski. "So Ruth Larkin shot him for you? And asked for nothing in return?"

"Yes. No." Dismay washed over Millie as she realized that either way she answered, it sounded wrong. "I didn't kill Hal, if that's what you mean," she insisted. "I didn't kill him!"

"Who did?" Josephson asked again.

"I don't know!"

"Where did Ruth Larkin get the gun?"

"I don't know!"

"From John Farrelly?"

Millie lurched toward the table as her legs weakened and gave way. Before she crumpled to the floor, Josephson caught her and lowered her back into the chair.

"Did Ruth Larkin obtain the gun from Dr. Farrelly?" he repeated.

"I don't know," Millie whispered. "I don't know where she got it."

"From Adrianna Farrelly?" Josephson suddenly asked.

Millie shook her head weakly.

"How well do you know Adrianna Farrelly?"

Slowly, with great weariness, Millie raised her head to meet Martin Josephson's gaze. "I do not know her," she answered with finality.

"I see." Josephson once again straddled his chair, his chin resting on the back of his hands. "Do you frequently telephone people you don't know?"

Millie let the question pass without answering.

"But you and Ruth Larkin did plan the murder of your husband, Edward Phillips." His words came as a statement, not a question, and again Millie did not speak.

"Mildred Phillips," Josephson said, reciting with formal deliberation, "you are charged with conspiracy in the murder of your husband, Edward Phillips, and with being an accessory to that crime. You have the right to remain silent. Anything you say can and will be used against you in a court of law. You have the right to an attorney, and to have an attorney present during any questioning. If you cannot afford to hire an attorney, the court will appoint one for you."

Josephson nodded at Sergeant Ruminski, who got up and left the room, and once again turned his attention to Millie. "Do you understand the charges against you, Mrs. Phillips?"

A paralyzing combination of helplessness and exhaustion swept over Millie as she stared down at the scarred surface of the table, wondering how many other people had been trapped as she had been while sitting there. She felt drained and numb from the rapid succession of shocks thrown at her during the course of this seemingly endless day, first by Roderick Howard, and now by Detective Martin Josephson.

"Mrs. Phillips. Do you understand your rights?"

Millie's eyes refused to focus properly, with the result that she wasn't quite certain exactly where Josephson was in the room. "What? Oh. I suppose so," she answered, her voice thick with fatigue. Millie folded her arms on the table and cradled her head, too worn out and sick at heart to even cry.

She had no idea how much time elapsed before Sergeant Ruminski returned and placed a sheaf of papers before her on the table.

"We've prepared a statement for you to sign," Josephson said, lightly touching her shoulder. "Read it over first before you sign."

Millie rubbed her eyes and pushed herself up in the chair, trying to concentrate on what Josephson was telling her.

"If you have any questions, I'll try to answer them," he continued smoothly, his manner unctuously sympathetic.

She took the papers in her shaking hands and tried in vain to read the closely spaced lines of type, but the words danced in a crazy procession that made no sense. Someone, she supposed it was Josephson, placed a pen in her hand and pointed to a line on the last page.

"Your signature goes there, Mrs. Phillips," he said gently.

Millie Phillips scrawled her name across the bottom

of the page, then let the pen slide from her fingers, leaving a long trail of ink across the paper. "I'd like to go home now," she said simply. "Could you please take me home?"

Josephson's smile was deceptively benign. "I'm afraid you won't be going home for quite a long time, Mrs. Phillips," he said, not bothering to conceal his satisfaction at having done his job well.

"Sergeant Ruminski," Josephson curtly ordered, dropping the smile, "book her."

26

Adrianna stood in front of the small bay window surveying the depressingly barren landscape that rolled away from the small rise where the two-hundred-year-old farmhouse hulked large and lonely, little shielded from the winds of the dying winter by an encircling shrine of naked trees. Although the snow was melted and gone now, the Westchester countryside remained frozen and forlorn, unwarmed by the watery sun that sent feeble rays skimming over the bristly stubble of the fallow pastures.

She'd almost forgotten how much she hated that house and the fourteen acres of empty fields and woods that surrounded it. John had taken tremendous pride in the old farm, of course. Particularly its history, which he had assiduously traced as far back into colonial times as the records would allow. He'd spent every free weekend roaming the fields, returning to the house at dusk with interminable tales of how he had startled a pheasant or spotted an unsuspecting fox. Mercifully, Adrianna thought, the number of free weekends that John had in which to indulge himself in such boring pastimes had become increasingly rare over the last few years of his life.

Once John's estate was settled and the property legally became hers, Adrianna planned on wasting no time in selling it. The attorneys had warned her that it might take a year or two to wind up all the legal ends because of the complexities involved in settling such a large estate, but that was all right with Adrianna. The immediate danger posed by the creation of the John G. Farrelly Research Center was over now, the court had allocated her a generous portion of the estate's income for her living expenses, and she could afford to be patient. The bulk of the estate would come to her in due course, as she'd always planned it should.

Besides, the farm gave her the perfect excuse to spend time in Westchester, where she could keep a closer watch on Millie's case. Adrianna had been appalled to learn of Millie's arrest, and even more appalled to learn that Millie had had to rely on a public defender appointed by the court to represent her at the arraignment. Adrianna hadn't dared go near either Millie or the attorney, so obtaining precise details of the case had been difficult at best. Within moments, however, all that would be remedied.

Adrianna watched through the window as a long, sleek car pulled up in front of the house and a portly man with an unruly mane of silver-white hair emerged from the rear. He glanced at the house quizzically, said something to the chauffeur, then made his way toward the door with arthritic slowness, aided by an unadorned, highly polished black cane. Sadie, the caretaker's wife, seemed to take forever in answering the insistent buzz of the doorbell, but eventually she appeared in the doorway of the small front study.

"A gentleman to see you, ma'am. Says his name is Carroll Westman."

"Show him in, Sadie. And please see that we aren't disturbed."

Westman emerged from behind Sadie and stood just inside the door, eyes blinking rapidly as he tried to adjust to the dusky half-light in the room. Adrianna, as planned, had the advantage on him, standing as she did in the bay window with the weak sunlight behind her. She knew her face was in shadow, and all Westman could make out was a tall, slender silhouette. She, on the other hand, had a clear view of Westman's features and could study him in detail.

Westman, she noticed, was considerably shorter than she'd expected, and had a softly round, slightly jowly face that bore an expression of benign jollity which contrasted sharply with the intelligent glint of his cold gray eyes.

"Thank you for agreeing to come all the way up here to see me," Adrianna said, extending her hand in greeting. "I trust you had a pleasant drive?"

"Quite pleasant," Westman responded in a deep, plummy voice, stepping forward to take her outstretched hand. "I must confess I didn't see much of the scenery, though. I'm afraid I dozed off in the car."

Adrianna motioned Westman toward a pair of richly upholstered leather wing chairs set in front of the study's small brick fireplace. "Would you care for some tea or coffee, Mr. Westman? Or perhaps something stronger?"

Westman propped his cane against the wall next to the gleaming set of brass fireplace tools and settled into one of the chairs with a slight grunt of discomfort. "Coffee would be fine," he said, craning to catch a clear view of Adrianna's face as she moved away from the bay window toward the door to issue instructions to Sadie.

Adrianna, however, deliberately kept her head turned away, for no other reason than that she found herself enjoying the theatrical overtones of the scene. And she could sense that Westman was intrigued by the air of mystery she was creating, and that could be essential to gaining his help. Carroll Westman, she'd been warned, had a reputation for refusing to take on even extraordinarily wealthy clients if their cases struck him as being somewhat less than intellectually stimulating.

They exchanged pleasantries about the weather and other innocuous subjects, with Adrianna remaining standing in the shadows all the while, until Sadie had brought the coffee and departed. Only then did Adrianna step into the dim pool of light cast by the fire and take the empty chair next to Westman.

"My attorneys tell me you are one of the five top criminal lawyers in the country. Is that an accurate assessment, Mr. Westman?" Adrianna asked softly.

"I believe so, yes. Of course there are those who might dispute the qualifications of the other four."

Adrianna smiled and sipped her coffee. "I'm pleased

you don't indulge in false protestations of modesty. I don't believe in doing so either."

Westman shifted painfully in his chair before taking up his own cup, dropping in three spoonfuls of sugar and stirring the brew with methodical thoroughness.

"I must admit to being a little curious as to why you apparently feel you need an attorney who specializes in criminal law, Mrs. Farrelly." His eyes narrowed as he watched her critically. "Have you committed a crime?"

Adrianna's laugh was low and amused. "Perhaps. But that is not why I asked you here today." She replaced the cup on the small side table next to the chair. "To answer your question, Mr. Westman, I am not seeking your services for myself."

"Who, then, may I ask?"

Adrianna pressed her fingers together in a prayerful pose, hands pressed to her chin just below her perfectly sculptured mouth. "Before I tell you that," she answered carefully, "let me ask you one question."

"Certainly."

"Would it matter a great deal to you whether the individual in question was guilty or not?"

Now it was Carroll Westman's turn to laugh.

"My dear lady, there are some people who estimate that a full ninety-seven percent of my clients are guilty. Guilt or innocence is a matter for a jury to decide, not the attorney. Speaking only for myself, however, I will say I find very little challenge in defending the innocent!"

"Excellent." Adrianna rose and went over to the desk, where she picked up a manila folder. She handed the folder to him and switched on a reading light next to his chair. "The woman I want you to defend is in serious trouble. According to the newspapers, she admitted her guilt to the police two weeks ago today."

Westman shrugged and waited for Adrianna to continue.

"I had a clipping service send me a collection of newspaper articles about the case in order to give you some of the background. Not everything is there, of course, but I can perhaps fill in some of the details for you."

Adrianna calmly drank her coffee while Westman donned his reading glasses and scanned the clippings, pausing now and then to read a paragraph more closely. At last he closed the folder and peered at her over the top of his glasses.

"I gather this Mildred Phillips is to be my client?"

"Yes."

"At present her attorney is a public defender. That generally means she has no assets of any substance."

"That is correct."

"To represent someone in this sort of position can be extremely costly," he pointed out somberly. "It's been my experience that a case such as this, properly pursued through the various levels of the court system, can easily run into six figures."

Adrianna again walked over to the desk, this time sitting down and opening the top drawer. "How much of a retainer do you require, Mr. Westman?" she asked mildly. "Would fifty thousand dollars be sufficient?"

Westman held up his hand to stop her from writing the check and shook his head. "You misunderstand me, Mrs. Farrelly. I haven't yet agreed to take the case. There's a great deal more I need to know first."

"Of course. Where would you like me to begin?"

Speaking with deceptive softness, Adrianna recounted the increasingly vicious beatings Ed Phillips had meted out to Millie, as well as Millie's suspicions that he was molesting Evie. This she followed with the story of Hal and Ruth Larkin. The two tales were essentially correct, as far as they went. Adrianna, of course, did not include any references to her own involvement in the course of events, nor the steps Millie had taken to rid Adrianna of Dr. John G. Farrelly and his Foundation for Psychiatric Research.

Carroll Westman sat silently staring into the fire for several minutes after Adrianna finished, eventually raising his coolly appraising eyes to Adrianna. "You seem to know a great deal about these two ladies," he said quietly.

Adrianna nodded in acknowledgment, assuming the statement required no response.

"May I ask how you came by all this intimate information?"

She met his gaze levelly. "The three of us have been close friends for twenty years. Since we were in college together."

"I see. Are the police aware of your relationship with Mrs. Phillips? Or Mrs. Larkin?"

"No. At least not to my knowledge. I assume if Millie had told them anything, they would have been to see me by now. They haven't."

"Could you hand me my cane, please? I really must move around a bit to relieve the stiffness of this infernal arthritis." Westman grimaced as he struggled out from the depths of the wing chair, his face smoothing out as Adrianna placed the sleek cane in his hand. He took a couple of hobbling steps around the chair and then turned back to see where she was.

"This gun . . ." he said, watching her face intently for a reaction. "Exactly how did Ruth Larkin obtain your husband's gun?"

A tiny smile played at the corners of Adrianna's mouth. "For argument's sake, let's say I gave it to her," she replied calmly.

Westman chuckled knowingly. "I thought as much." He moved haltingly toward the bay window, where he stood staring out at the gray fields as Adrianna had done a couple of hours earlier. "For argument's sake, then, I would have two clients to defend. The one the authorities know about, and the one they don't."

"Does that disturb you?"

Another low chuckle of amusement emanated from the silver-haired man. "Hardly, my dear. Such a situation is far more common than you might think." Westman eased his aching joints down onto the window seat, letting the pale sunlight do its best to warm his head and back.

"What you have told me so far has been extremely interesting," he said, nodding in approval. "But I think it would be advisable, my dear lady, if you now told me the full story of what really happened."

27

Judith Stein marched into Jack Holland's office and stood expectantly in front of the desk. When he showed no immediate sign of wrapping up his telephone conversation and giving her his undivided attention, she began gesturing at him to hurry up.

Holland, however, refused to be rushed. While Judith paced around the small office sighing in exaggerated exasperation, hands outstretched in supplication to the unseen sky, Holland leisurely reclined in his chair and put his feet up on the desk, the phone cradled against his left shoulder.

Judith was on the verge of marching out as abruptly as she had marched in when Holland's conversation, which he seemed to take perverse delight in protracting as long as possible, eventually came to an end. "What's the problem now, Stein?" he asked with an undertone of amusement.

Judith Stein leaned against the corner of his desk, staring at a spot over his head. "Mildred Phillips was bailed out of jail half an hour ago," she announced flatly.

Holland sat up, all trace of amusement gone from his face. "I was afraid that would happen when Judge Kripkin went against our recommendations and set a bail figure. Who put up the money for her?"

Now it was Judith's turn to smirk. "Her new attorney, apparently. At least his name is on the receipt. A gentleman by the name of Carroll C. Westman."

"*The* Carroll Westman?"

"The one and the only." Judith lowered her eyes to meet Holland's. "This case becomes more interesting by the minute, doesn't it, Jack?"

Holland let out a long, low whistle, picked out a newly sharpened pencil from the supply in his drawer, and made a note of Westman's name on the yellow legal pad in front of him. "I thought Westman was involved with a big case out on the West Coast. I wonder what he's doing here?" Holland looked up at Judith. "And more to the point, who's paying him? From what I've heard about Carroll Westman, he gave up taking charity cases twenty-five years ago after hitting the big-bucks level. And you can bet your sweet aspidistra that bond he posted wasn't his money, either."

"Hiring a man like Westman would cost a bundle of money, wouldn't it?" Judith asked rhetorically, immediately answering her own question. "A real big bundle."

"Upward of a couple hundred thousand, I would guess. It all depends."

Judith smiled in amazement, shaking her head. "Can you imagine making two hundred thousand dollars for handling just one case, Jack? Just one lousy little case? What I could do with that kind of money!"

Holland grimaced and tried to stretch the kinks out of his back. A rare weekend game of racquetball had left every muscle in his body, from the neck on down, sore and aching. "I've got to admit that private practice begins to look pretty good after a few years of this, Stein. But don't let the glitter fool you. This," he said, gesturing around the office, "is the only way to get anywhere in the world that counts—politics."

"I know," Judith sighed. "I keep telling myself that. One of these days I might even begin believing it."

"Take the advice of someone who knows. You've picked the only path to real power."

Jack Holland took up the pencil again and began doodling on the legal pad. "As long as we're on the subject, you'd better bring me up-to-date on everything that's happening in the Phillips case. If we're going up against a defense attorney like Carroll Westman, we'll need every piece of hard evidence we can get our hands on."

Judith folded her arms and stood deep in thought for a few moments. "Well," she said at last, her voice unusually quiet, "the strongest piece of evidence we have at the moment, of course, is that statement she made to Josephson admitting she and Ruth Larkin planned the murder of Edward Phillips. The corroborating evidence is weaker than I would like—I doubt it could stand alone. But as long as we have her statement to work with, we shouldn't have any trouble getting an indictment and making a second-degree-murder charge stick."

Holland nodded, then pointed at Judith with the pencil. "You've gone over everything with Josephson again, haven't you? To make sure there were no holes in the procedure? Nothing that Westman can use against us?"

"Of course," Judith replied indignantly. "Josephson and that sergeant—Sergeant Ruminski—are both prepared to swear in court that Mildred Phillips was read her rights before, during, and after questioning. They've assured me there's absolutely no doubt in their minds that Phillips knew exactly what she was doing when she signed that statement admitting she was an accomplice to her husband's murder."

"Good. Now, what about that other matter—that author's murder?"

"Harold Larkin? No progress there, I'm afraid. At least nothing solid we can turn over to the Manhattan D.A."

Holland slammed his open palm flat on the desktop. "What in hell have you been doing all this time, Stein? You know how important it is to nail Phillips on that one too! Jesus, if we hand Manhattan an airtight case on Mildred Phillips, they'll have to give us the credit— national credit, too. Larkin was a well-known writer, Stein. No way they could bury a case like that."

Judith's eyes flashed as she angrily stared Holland down. "I can't create evidence out of thin air!" she retorted hotly. "For two weeks we've been questioning

Mildred Phillips and getting nowhere. All she does is repeat that she knows nothing about the Larkin murder and had nothing to do with it. And you know what, Jack? I almost believe her!"

"You're not paid to believe the defendants, Stein," Holland shouted. "You're paid to see that they're put behind bars where they belong. If she won't confess to murdering Larkin, then Manhattan will have to go after her with circumstantial evidence."

"There is no circumstantial evidence strong enough to seek an indictment!" Judith cried in frustration. "That's what I keep trying to tell you, Jack. Not one iota. We even had them bring the hotel night clerk up for a lineup and he couldn't identify Mildred Phillips as the woman he saw entering the lobby that night. Without a witness or at least one piece of physical evidence—even a partial fingerprint would do—nobody can prove she was ever in that hotel room. The only thing in our favor is that Phillips can't produce a solid alibi for the night Larkin died. That might be enough to convince you that she's guilty, but it certainly won't be enough to convince a jury!"

"Whose side are you on anyway?" Holland glared. "We've got a woman who's confessed she set up the murder of her own husband. You think a jury can't make the connection between a woman who would go that far and one who is also capable of committing outright murder? Especially as part of a package conspiracy?"

"Not beyond a reasonable doubt!" Judith insisted, grasping the edge of Holland's desk. "You're the one who's always harping on the point that a jury must be convinced beyond a reasonable doubt. The Larkin thing is riddled with reasonable doubt, Jack."

"Not if we can get Manhattan to present the evidence in the right way, it isn't. You keep forgetting, my dear young counselor," Holland hissed, "that even the weakest evidence gains weight if there's enough of it. By the time we get through with that Phillips woman, she'll make Lucretia Borgia look like a saint."

Judith's eyes narrowed at the menacing undertone to

Holland's voice. "What sort of evidence are you talking about, Jack? When you get down to it, all we really have is the testimony of people like Clarice Stuber. And that woman's jealousy is so patently obvious that she'd probably stir up more sympathy for Phillips than anything else."

"They can handle that all right by getting Stuber to tone down some of the venom while she's on the stand. Plus we can line up a psychiatrist or two that Manhattan can call in as expert witnesses to testify about the psychological makeup of a person who would arrange the murder of her husband."

"First, though, we have to convince a jury up here that she was capable of arranging her husband's murder," Judith reminded him. "Without that, the whole Larkin case falls apart. We have to do our own worrying about Clarice Stuber, particularly the fact that she was the one who wound up with all of Ed Phillips' insurance money. The defense is bound to play that aspect to the hilt, Jack, and in the process raise a whole lot of doubt in the jurors' minds."

Jack Holland suddenly grinned. "Where's that remarkable brain of yours these days, Stein? Don't you see? The insurance angle gives us a perfect motive either way."

A puzzled frown crossed Judith's face as she tried to follow Holland's line of reasoning. "A motive either way?"

"Exactly!" A feverish gleam glittered in Holland's eyes. "On the one hand, if Phillips thought she was still the beneficiary, half a million dollars makes an excellent motive for murdering her husband. On the other hand, being replaced by Clarice Stuber as beneficiary makes for an equally good motive for revenge. See? It works out beautifully no matter which way the defense tries to go!"

"But that insurance agent, Roderick Howard, insists that Phillips didn't know her husband had switched beneficiaries. He said she became hysterical when he had to tell her."

"Stein, Stein, Stein . . ." Holland shook his head

sadly. "I just told you how that's all to our advantage. If the defense claims she didn't know about the switch, then the anticipation of getting half a million dollars in insurance money remains a powerful motive. If they contend that she did know, then we fall back on the revenge aspect."

Judith stood in front of Holland's bookcase and thoughtfully ran her finger along the spines of the leatherbound volumes. "Okay, I agree the complicity charge is falling into place," she said slowly. "We stand a good-to-excellent chance of getting a conviction on that. But I'm still doubtful about bringing in the Manhattan D.A.'s office yet and trying to get her charged with felony murder in the death of Harold Larkin." Judith chose her words carefully. "Jack, I just don't think there's enough to go to trial with. They might be willing to chance it against that incredibly stupid public defender Phillips started out with, but not against a seasoned, savvy defense attorney like Carroll Westman. Never."

"Look, Stein," Holland said, rising fom the chair to stretch his back. "Once we've got a conviction on the Phillips murder, the Larkin case will be a snap. We concentrate on the conspiracy first, and the other will follow in due course. Trust me—Manhattan will eat it up."

Judith glanced at him over her shoulder. "There's one other thing that really bothers me about all of this . . ." she said, her voice dropping uncertainly.

"What?"

"I don't know yet exactly how the Farrellys fit into the picture. Adrianna Farrelly, in particular. There's something about that woman that disturbs me—and that gun she claims to know nothing about. I'm positive she's mixed up in this somehow."

Holland walked around to the front of the desk, shoved over a pile of papers, and sat on the corner. "Has the FAA issued a report yet on her husband's plane crash?"

"Their findings are inconclusive," Judith said with a little sigh. "They can only guess that the crash was caused more by pilot error than mechanical failure. The fire destroyed most of the fuselage, including all the instruments, so they pieced together what they could and found no proof of what they call 'power, structural, or control malfunction.' Nor did the autopsy on Farrelly's remains turn up anything suspicious in the way of drugs or alcohol."

Holland grunted. "What'd they say about possible sabotage?"

"I asked about that, naturally. The investigator I spoke with said sabotage is not impossible—apparently he's run into that sort of thing on a few occasions—but without physical evidence, unprovable. No one dumped sugar in the gas tanks or anything obvious like that. And if the fuel had been deliberately watered down, the crash and fire eliminated any chance of detecting that."

"I see." Holland frowned as he stared down at the threadbare carpeting in front of the desk. "What else?"

Judith Stein ceased her casual inspection of Holland's collection of lawbooks and turned to face her boss, stunned by the sudden realization of how hard and callous this job seemed to be making him. The thought fleetingly crossed her mind that if ten years as district attorney could do that to Jack Holland, what would it do to her? And did she really want that prospect for her future? Was the attainment of political success, and everything it entailed, really worth it? Probably, she decided, although she knew she'd be giving the subject more consideration in the days and weeks to come.

"We have the log of the Phillips home telephone calls," Judith answered, brushing away the distressing mental image of herself as a hard-bitten old crone ten years down the line. "Mildred Phillips certainly made a lot of phone calls to the Farrelly residence in New York—both before and after the death of Dr. John Farrelly."

Judith Stein walked toward the door to the outer office. "Not only do I think that Adrianna Farrelly is involved in this Phillips-Larkin business, Jack, I'd also be willing to bet that Adrianna Farrelly had more than a little something to do with her own husband's death as well, and is now putting up the money to finance Mildred Phillips' defense."

She paused at the door, one hand on the knob. "I don't know how she's involved in all of this yet. But I will someday. I will."

28

The squat Dutch Colonial home of Millie Phillips took on the atmosphere of a besieged encampment over the following weeks. Private security guards, hired by Carroll C. Westman at Adrianna's expense, patrolled the perimeter of the two-acre property to chase away curiosity seekers and journalists bent on obtaining an "exclusive" interview with the woman branded by the newspapers as the "Black Widow of Westchester."

The residents of the normally sedate upper-middle-class suburban neighborhood initially reacted to all of this with moralistic outrage tinged with an element of fear at having an accused murderess in their midst. But eventually, as the novelty began to wear off, they came to accept the guards and procession of strange cars in and out of the Phillips driveway as a normal part of the daily routine.

The woman inside the house, however, was scarcely recognizable as the same Millie Phillips who, just a few short months ago, had breathlessly bounced into Leonardo's for a lunch and theater date with her two oldest and dearest friends. She'd grown gaunt and hollow-eyed, more a prisoner in her own home than she'd been behind the bars of the cramped communal jail cell she'd occupied for two weeks until she was released on bail. While her cellmates were hardly the sort of women Millie would have normally sought for friends, a couple of the older ones had taken her under their protection and provided her with a small measure of reserved sympathy and support that she'd found oddly touching under the circumstances.

Even though Millie had traded in the standard-issue jail garb of sweatshirt and coarse cotton trousers for her own wardrobe of trim gabardine slacks and soft wool sweaters, the change of clothes and surroundings only served to aggravate the energy-sapping isolation and depression that dogged her every waking moment, a depression that deepened a little more each evening as she placed the ritual telephone call to Louisiana to speak with her daughters.

Except for those few brief minutes every evening, Millie found herself completely cut off from everything and everyone that mattered to her, including Adrianna. During his brief introductory visit to her in the women's section of the jail, Carroll Westman had made it quite clear that while Adrianna was willing to pay for Millie's legal expenses, all contact between them had to cease until the case was settled in or out of court.

"You mean I can't even talk to her on the phone?" Millie had asked in dismay, eyeing this strange man with a degree of misgiving. Millie, badly frightened by the mysterious workings of the legal system that enmeshed her, was reluctant at first to accept that anyone, even an attorney of Carroll Westman's caliber, could truly help her now. She had been praying that Adrianna would find some way to get her out of this mess, but in her wildest dreams she'd never expected Adrianna to go out and hire one of the foremost trial lawyers in the country. Now, sitting across the table from this man who exuded confidence even in the dirty, dingy interview room they'd been assigned, Millie felt the first dim glimmerings of hope, glimmerings that would eventually lead to an emotional roller-coaster of unprecedented heights and depths.

"Especially not on the telephone," Westman emphasized, frowning darkly. "Phone calls are not as private as you may think. And"—he paused for dramatic effect—"phone calls mean records. And records of calls can be used in several potentially harmful ways against you. Do you understand?"

Millie's face grew deathly white at the implication of Westman's words. "Do you mean they"—she waved her hand vaguely toward the door—"may know about every telephone conversation I've ever had?"

The silver-haired man smiled his uniquely contradictory smile—benign yet cold. "In a manner of speaking, yes. At least the ones you initiated on your home phone. I assume by now the prosecutor has obtained your telephone records from the telephone company and has checked out those numbers that appear most frequently."

"Including Addy's." Millie's voice was scarcely more than a whisper.

"Yes. Including Mrs. Farrelly's."

"But I swore I didn't know Adrianna. Now they'll be able to prove that I do!"

Westman patted her arm comfortingly. "Not necessarily. All they can prove is that a phone call, or phone calls, were made from your home to hers. They can't prove that you actually placed those calls yourself, or that she received them. It's a fine distinction, but it could be an important one."

"So what do I do now?"

"Absolutely nothing, for the moment. And that includes no more phone calls or statements. If anyone from the district attorney's office attempts to question you about anything, anything at all, you must insist that I, or a member of my staff, be present. Otherwise say nothing. Do I make myself perfectly clear?"

"Mr. Westman, I'll do whatever you say."

Carroll Westman smiled again. "I rather thought you might."

Shortly after that interview, Westman escorted a jubilant Millie from the jail back to her home. And that, she discovered, was just the beginning of her real incarceration. For hours at a stretch over the following weeks, Westman grilled Millie about every aspect of her life, from the day she first met Adrianna and Ruth, through the terrible events of that black, black day when Roderick Howard revealed that she wouldn't receive Ed's insurance money and Detective Josephson maneuvered her into confessing her part in Ed's murder.

Westman forced her to go over and over that distressing session with Josephson so often that Millie frequently found herself waking up in the middle of the night screaming in protest. She knew she'd acted stupidly in signing that statement. She'd known that much without Westman having to tell her, and to his credit he never once threw it back at her. He took the attitude that what was done was done, and they would simply have to find a way to undo the damage. So he poked and prodded, questioned and interrogated, until Millie feared her mind would become as unhinged as Ruth's.

God, how she missed Ruthie! She missed Ruth's gentleness, her compassion, and her acceptance of Millie and Adrianna in spite of their shortcomings and quirks. They hadn't always been kind to Ruth, but Ruth had been unfailingly kind to both of them. In retrospect Millie realized that Ruthie, more so than Adrianna, had been the one to take care of her after Frank Palmer had walked out on her and the girls. Day or night, it hadn't mattered what the time, Ruth had responded to her anguished phone calls and listened with endless patience as Millie unburdened all of her anger, grief, and frustration. Adrianna had loaned her small sums of money to tide her over, but Ruthie had given her generous amounts of love and sympathy.

Now Millie stood alone in the gleaming white prison that was her own kitchen, and thought of how the three of them had been welded together by the interwoven events of their individual lives. Alone they occasionally floundered, but together they balanced each other. Ruth's quiet warmth had done much to mellow Adrianna's brittle coldness, and Adrianna's superior intellect had tempered Millie's emotionalism. Millie's zestful extroversion, in turn, had sometimes goaded Ruth out of her self-effacing shyness.

That was the way it had been for twenty years, and never would be again. Ruthie was gone; the circle broken.

As Millie mechanically filled the coffeepot in anticipation of Westman's next scheduled visit, she wondered whether she and Adrianna would be able to continue on together, without Ruthie's mediating influence. Then, with a clarity she'd never before experienced, Millie understood the parallels in the isolation shared by Adrianna and herself. Curious she hadn't noticed until now, but then she'd never been one for introspection, nor had she ever had so much empty time in which to do nothing but think.

Her own isolation, she sensed, was basically physical. She still had the love of her children and parents, although she was separated from them by distance and events, shut away inside a house with guards at the door who, she suspected, had orders to keep her in as well as keep strangers out. But Adrianna—Adrianna was enduring a more permanent sort of isolation. For all of her jet-set tendencies and rotating lovers, Adrianna was undeniably isolated emotionally. Whether that was by choice or by accident, Millie couldn't say, but the net result was that she, Mildred Wozackie Palmer Phillips, remained the only person alive whom Adrianna trusted enough to see the real woman beneath the carefully constructed facade of her public personality.

So it was with a small measure of relief that Millie finished loading the tea cart with their lunch and freshly brewed coffee and pushed it out to the bright plant-filled sunroom at the back of the house to await Westman's arrival. Adrianna, she was now convinced, would do everything in her considerable power to prevent Millie from going to prison. She needed Millie as much as Millie needed her. In some ways, perhaps, Adrianna needed Millie more.

As soon as Millie heard the tires of Westman's car crunching on the gravel drive outside, she poured two cups of coffee, liberally lacing Westman's with sugar the way he liked it. Presently she heard his peculiarly gaited shuffle in the hallway, the click of the closet door as he deposited his overcoat and hat, and at last the tap of his cane reaching the flagstone floor of the sunroom.

"My dear Millie, you look absolutely delightful this afternoon!" he said cheerfully, patting her cheek with a paternal affection. "Too thin, though. Much too thin.

You really must eat and keep up your strength, you know. Can't have you wasting away to a shadow."

Westman lowered himself with some difficulty into one of the wicker chairs placed in the pool of sunlight. He took his time selecting from the plate of sandwiches Millie had prepared, tasted one delicately, and sipped from his coffee cup. "Your family is well, I trust? The children are reasonably adjusted to living in Louisiana?"

The welcoming smile faded from Millie's face and she cast her eyes down. "They're all right. As well as can be expected under the circumstances. Except . . ."

"Except what, my dear?"

"Every night Evie and Deedee ask me when they can come home." Millie looked out through the large expanse of glass just as one of the security guards turned the corner of the house and disappeared into a line of trees bordering the rear of the property. "My parents have put them in school there so they won't fall too far behind in their classwork, but they miss me. They miss being with their mother. And I don't know what to tell them anymore."

Westman ignored the partially eaten sandwich on his plate and produced a cigar from an inner coat pocket. With more ceremony than Millie thought was absolutely necessary, he clipped off one end and proceeded to light it, taking long, deep drags that filled the small room with a thin haze of faintly acrid smoke.

"Well now," he said at last, placing the smoldering cigar in an ashtray Millie had thoughtfully provided, "I know the law must seem to move at a terribly slow pace. However, I think I can safely say that at last we may be getting somewhere."

Millie brightened immediately. "Really? Is something happening? Please tell me what's happening—"

Westman held up a silencing hand. "Let's not get carried away, Millie," he cautioned somberly "This isn't over yet. Not by a long shot. And I cannot guarantee that what I have put into motion will work."

Millie nodded vigorously, pursing her mouth to signal that she was doing her best to stifle her impatience. By now she knew Westman well enough to understand that he would not be hurried. He would tell her what he wanted her to know in his own way, in his own time. On several occasions in the past weeks he had lectured her on the necessity for developing patience. Once within the jaws of the court system, he explained, a snail's pace could be considered excellent progress.

"To be more specific," Westman continued, pausing between words to retrieve the cigar and blow a series of smoke rings, "we have obtained a court date."

Millie felt her body grow rigid with dread, her heart pounding so hard she feared it might burst through her rib cage. "So soon?" she croaked, her mouth dry.

Westman glanced at her with solicitude. "Two court dates, I should have said. The first is for a hearing on a pretrial motion I filed a few days ago. The outcome of that hearing will determine whether the case does, indeed, go to trial on the second date."

Millie looked at Westman with confusion. "I don't understand, Mr. Westman. How can there be no trial? Unless you think I ought to plead guilty?"

Carroll Westman laughed softly. "Mrs. Farrelly would be most put out if I advised you to plead guilty, don't you think?" He took another sip of coffee, then re-lighted the cigar that had gone out. "No, you won't plead guilty, my dear. Rest assured on that."

"But how are you going to prevent the trial?" Millie persisted, still perplexed.

"By eliminating the prosecution's single most damaging bit of evidence," Westman explained, speaking carefully, as though to a very young child. "We will simply ask the court to quash—by that I mean suppress—your entire confession. Without that, the prosecution has no provable case."

"Can that really be done?" Millie asked in wonderment.

"We'll see, my dear. We'll see. A great deal will depend on the strength of character of those two police officers who interrogated you. But one week from to-day, we'll know whether it can be done or not."

29

Millie Phillips huddled miserably in the corner of Carroll Westman's car, valiantly trying not to lose the few bites of toast and orange juice he'd forced her to eat before they set out for court.

She'd spent most of the night in the bathroom alternating between bouts of the dry heaves and hyperventilating. Irene Atchinson, Westman's longtime "secretary/companion," who had consented to watch over Millie in the days immediately preceding the hearing, grew so alarmed that at one point, around four A.M., she'd seriously contemplated telephoning Westman and warning him that he might have to seek a continuance. Eventually, though, Millie managed to keep down a Valium long enough to gain some benefit from its tranquilizing effects. She even dozed fitfully for a couple hours or so before Irene reluctantly awakened her to say it was time to begin getting dressed. So, clad in her favorite cream wool suit, now a size too large on her shrunken body, Millie had stepped out into the balmy air of the early-spring morning for the drive to court.

But with most of her concentration focused inward, seeking the strength she would need to face the day ahead, Millie saw little of the budding spring unfolding around her, or the small crowd of onlookers who gathered on the courthouse steps and whispered among themselves as the sleek black car disgorged its passengers. Flanked by Carroll Westman on one side and Irene Atchinson on the other, Millie was quickly and silently propelled up the steps, into an elevator, and then down a long, echoing corridor filled with unknown people, some of whom stared at her with open hostility. A camera flash suddenly went off in front of her eyes and Millie, blinded for a couple of seconds, whirled around in panic until Westman put a steadying arm around her shoulders.

Inside the courtroom Millie and Westman took their places at one of the two long tables set just in front of the railing, with Irene Atchinson taking up her customary position in the first row of seats directly behind. While Westman unloaded the contents of his briefcase, neatly stacking the papers in precise individual piles, Millie stole a glance at the table across the way and was startled when the woman she recognized as Judith Stein returned her look with a brief nod and a tiny smile that Millie couldn't recognize as either encouraging or menacing.

She found Judith Stein's unexpected gesture so disconcerting that it was a few moments before Millie realized Carroll Westman was speaking to her. "The judge will be coming in any moment now," Westman was saying, his hand placed comfortingly on her arm. "Do you think you're going to be all right?"

Millie nodded, not trusting her voice enough to speak.

"Very good. But if, at any time, you think you're going to become ill, let me know at once." Westman momentarily paused as the judge appeared in the doorway. "I know I've told you this before, but I want to caution you again. No matter what is said about you by a witness on the stand, you are not to respond in any way. Is that clear, Millie? I want no hysterics from you. Nothing that could possibly prejudice our case."

Millie nodded again in acknowledgment, unable to meet the steady gaze of Westman's cold gray eyes, then rose to her feet with Westman and the others as Judge Hubert Kripkin entered the crowded courtroom. She could feel the ripple of tense excitement that flowed through both participants and spectators as the black-robed judge stepped up behind the high bench and officially opened the suppression hearing in the case of the People of the State of New York against Mildred Phillips, defendant.

"Mr. Westman," Judge Kripkin queried in stern, stentorian tones, "is the defendant, Mildred Phillips, present in the courtroom?"

"Yes, your Honor, she is."

The judge's eyes swiveled to Millie with a stare almost as cold as Carroll Westman's. "Please step forward, Mrs. Phillips," he commanded.

Millie stumbled as she rounded the corner of the table, but caught the edge and quickly regained her balance. Standing with as much dignity as she could muster under the circumstances, with Westman slightly behind her, Millie faced the bench.

"You are the defendant known as Mildred Phillips?"

Millie's response was so soft that Judge Kripkin leaned across the desk, a hand cupped behind his ear. "Speak up, Mrs. Phillips. The court reporter cannot record what she cannot hear!"

"Yes, your Honor," Millie replied again, this time too loudly. A small titter swept through the spectators.

The judge settled back in his chair. "That's better. Now, Mrs. Phillips, are you under any medication today?"

Millie vaguely remembered the Valium she'd swallowed in the early hours of the morning, but decided that probably wasn't what the judge meant by medication. "No, sir," she answered a bit uncertainly.

"Do you understand the nature of the charges against you?"

She half-turned to look questioningly at Westman, who indicated she should answer yes.

As Judge Kripkin's deep voice monotonously droned on in a lengthy and involved recital of the murder and conspiracy charges, Millie surreptitiously inspected her surroundings, deciding that the indirect lighting and wood paneling, with its mellow patina of age, made the courtroom seem far less frightening than she had anticipated. The room was designed with a certain stiff formality, but not the oppressive sterility she thought it would have.

"Mr. Holland, are you prepared to proceed?"

A tall, imposing man stood up behind the other table, dwarfing the diminutive Judith Stein. "The People are ready, your Honor."

Millie returned to her seat, but soon ceased to listen as Westman and the tall man, identified by the court as District Attorney Jack Holland, conversed with the judge about various legal technicalities. They spoke in a mysterious jargon that made about as much sense to Millie as a discussion of nuclear physics, and seemed to her equally as irrelevant. Eventually, though, Carroll Westman took up his cane again and sauntered back to the table as casually as his arthritic hips would allow.

Jack Holland stood in the center of the open space in front of the bench. "The People will call Detective Martin Josephson to the stand, your Honor."

As Josephson entered the courtroom, wearing a creased sports jacket and overly narrow tie, a sudden chill caused Millie to shudder visibly. She quickly looked away as Josephson passed close by the table.

Once Josephson was sworn in and Holland began his questioning, Millie was astounded to realize that Josephson's version of events the day she signed the incriminating statement bore very little resemblance to what she remembered as having actually happened. It wasn't that the police officer lied exactly, but the way he phrased his answers gave the impression that Millie had understood at the time that she was under suspicion as an accomplice in her husband's murder. Several times she attempted whispered protests to Carrol Westman, only to have him harshly cut her off while he concentrated on the testimony.

After what seemed like an eternity, but in reality was only little more than an hour, she heard Jack Holland tell the court that he had no more questions at that time. Beside her, Carroll Westman rose creakily to his feet and shuffled forward, apparently in so much pain that she wondered how he managed to stand up at all.

"Mr. Josephson," Westman began in a deceptively thin, tremulous voice, "how long have you been a detective?"

Josephson shifted uncomfortably in his seat. "A year and a half. Thereabouts."

"And before that?"

"Four years in uniform."

"So you are a police officer of some experience, then? Not what I believe they call a 'rookie'?"

Josephson looked down, as though modesty prevented him from truthfully answering the question. "I guess you could say that."

Westman leaned his weight heavily against the rail of the witness box. "When did you first meet Mildred Phillips?"

"When I picked her up at the airport. JFK."

"Isn't that a little unusual, Mr. Josephson? Picking up a murder victim's relative at the airport? Or was she a suspect from the beginning?"

"No, sir."

Westman partly turned to face the spectators. They could see his flinty grin, but Josephson couldn't. "No? It's not unusual to pick up relatives at the airport?"

Josephson hunched over as though trying to make himself smaller. "She wasn't a suspect at that time," he mumbled.

"Was she a suspect when you escorted her to the morgue to view the bodies of Edward Phillips and Ruth Larkin?"

"No, sir. That was the same day."

"How about when you talked to her three days later at headquarters?"

"No."

"The following week?"

"No."

"Well, then, Mr. Josephson"—Carroll Westman's tone strengthened, taking on an edge of exasperation—"can you tell me exactly when Mrs. Phillips did become a suspect in this case?"

"After we examined her telephone records and found a significant number of calls had been made to Ruth Larkin's residence prior to the night of the shooting. This struck us as being odd, because she had denied knowing Ruth Larkin."

"Did it occur to you that the murdered man, Edward Phillips, might conceivably have made those phone calls?"

Josephson looked up at the ceiling. "At first, yes, but the pattern didn't fit. Most of the calls were made during the daytime, when Phillips would have been at his office. And the Larkin number didn't show up on any of the records for his office phone system."

Westman watched Josephson closely, his eyes steady and unblinking. "So you automatically assumed that Mrs. Phillips was making those calls. What happened then?"

"I called her back in for further questioning." Josephson seemed to regain confidence as he moved back into familiar territory. He, Holland, and Judith Stein had gone over and over his testimony so many times in the past week that he could have recited the answers in his sleep.

"When you telephoned Mrs. Phillips that last time, exactly what did you say to her?"

"I don't remember the exact words, but it was something to the effect that I had some more questions to ask her and would she please come down to headquarters."

"Mmmmm." Westman pushed himself up from the witness-box railing and limped a few paces away. "Was it, perhaps, to the effect that there were a few minor points you wanted to clear up, and that the interview wouldn't take long?"

Josephson paused. "I don't remember using those words," he said at last. "But I suppose I could have."

"When you telephoned Mrs. Phillips that last time, I am correct in assuming she was then a suspect?"

"Yes."

"Did you suggest to her at that time she might consider bringing an attorney with her?"

There was an even longer pause as Josephson sank lower in his chair. "I might have. I don't remember."

"My, my," Westman replied, almost genially. "As you demonstrated in your responses to Mr. Holland, you are able to remember the entire interrogation in minute detail, yet you can't remember a simple telephone conversation a mere hour before?" Westman locked eyes with Josephson. "I suggest you deliberately did not make mention of the need for an attorney, Mr. Josephson, because you did not yet want Mrs. Phillips to know she was a suspect!"

"Objection!" Holland was on his feet. "Mr. Westman is drawing conclusions on behalf of the witness."

Judge Hubert Kripkin glared across the bench at Carroll Westman. "Sustained."

Westman acknowledged the rebuke and returned to Josephson. "When Mrs. Phillips arrived at headquarters some time later, did you immediately advise her that under the Miranda ruling she was entitled to have an attorney present?"

"Not at that time, no."

"When, exactly," Westman pressed, "did you advise her of her right to legal counsel?"

"During the interrogation," Josephson replied sullenly.

"During the interrogation," Westman echoed. "At the beginning of the interrogation? In the middle, perhaps? Or was it closer to the end? Say, just before you had her sign the statement?"

"It was sometime during the interrogation," Josephson insisted. "I don't remember exactly when I read her her rights, but I know I did it! I read them at least twice—including the time just before she signed the statement."

Westman's face hardened. "At any time during this interrogation, either before or after you informed her of her rights, did Mrs. Phillips ask to see an attorney?"

"No, she did not," Josephson replied emphatically.

"Didn't that strike you as being a little peculiar?" The silver-haired attorney lowered his voice to a more conversational level. "Here you've testified that Mrs. Phillips was fully informed of her right to consult an attorney, and to have an attorney present during questioning, yet she never asked for one. Why is that, do you think?"

"I have no idea, sir."

"Did Mrs. Phillips strike you as being a stupid woman, Mr. Josephson? Incapable of understanding her rights under the law?"

"No, sir."

"When you informed Mrs. Phillips of her rights the first time, what did she say, Mr. Josephson?"

"Say?"

"Yes. How did she respond? What were her words?"

Josephson squirmed on his chair and rubbed his chin. "I don't recall that she said anything."

"Is that usual? Don't you generally ask suspects whether or not they understand what you've just told them?"

Josephson sank lower, a hand partially covering his mouth. "She may have said something. I don't remember."

Westman softly chuckled at this response. "Since you seem to be having so much trouble with your memory this morning, Mr. Josephson, perhaps we should go on to another subject before you forget that as well."

Jack Holland shot to his feet again. "Your Honor, Mr. Westman is insulting the witness!"

Judge Kripkin nodded curtly to Holland and then addressed Carroll Westman directly. "I would like to remind you, Mr. Westman, that this is only a preliminary hearing. There is no jury present, only myself. And I am not particularly impressed by the badgering of witnesses."

The courtly defense attorney bowed his head in obeisance and slowly limped back to the witness box, where he leaned his upper body heavily against the railing.

"If you would be so kind, sir," Westman said with exaggerated politeness, "could we return to the subject of the telephone records? Did you happen to mention these telephone-company records during the interrogation of Mrs. Phillips?"

Josephson flashed Westman a quick contemptuous grin. "Yes, I did. When I told the defendant that we knew about her numerous telephone calls to the Larkin woman, she admitted she had been acquainted with the deceased, and had planned the murder of Ed Phillips with her."

"Mrs. Phillips freely admitted complicity? Just like that?" Westman inquired with surprise, snapping his fingers. "How did she admit this complicity, Mr. Josephson? With what words, precisely, did she phrase this admission?"

Confusion flickered across Josephson's face as he searched his memory for an answer. He hadn't been asked that particular question during the rehearsals and he wasn't ready for it. "I don't recall her exact words," he said slowly. "Something to the effect that her husband used to beat her up a lot."

Westman shifted his upper body closer to Josephson, his legs thrust out at an awkward angle. "That's very interesting, if I do say so. I have here a copy of the statement we were given, which your district attorney has thoughtfully entered as 'Exhibit A.' Do you recognize this as being a copy of the statement Mrs. Phillips signed?" Josephson glanced through the sheaf of papers Westman produced from his pocket. "It looks like it, yes."

"Good. Well, according to this statement, Mrs. Phillips allegedly said, and I quote: 'I entered into an agreement with Mrs. Ruth Larkin whereby she agreed to shoot and kill my husband.' Unquote." Westman fixed Josephson with a hard, cold stare. "Is that what she really said, Mr. Josephson? Were those her precise words?"

The police office shrugged, the short sleeves of his sport coat riding up well past his shirt cuffs. "Something like that, I guess."

"You guess?" Westman exploded, his entire body suddenly quivering with barely suppressed rage. "Do you mean you can't tell me with any more certainty than that?" He uttered a short, sharp laugh that sounded more like a bark. "Those were your words, weren't they, Mr. Josephson? I suggest to you that the defendent, Mildred Phillips, never said anything even remotely like that!"

He stabbed a finger toward Josephson's chest. "The wording was yours, all yours, wasn't it? When she started telling you about the physical abuse her husband inflicted on her, you took that as an admission of guilt and had your words written into the statement as though they had come from her. Then you took advantage of the fact that by then Mrs. Phillips was exhausted, confused, upset, and without counsel to coerce her into signing a statement that is patently false!"

The courtroom was unnaturally quiet as everyone waited for Josephson's response. At last, in a voice that was scarcely audible, Josephson croaked, "I never forced her to sign it. She signed of her own free will."

Carroll Westman pushed himself away from the witness-box railing as though unwilling to remain near anyone so repugnant and limped over to stand in front of the judge's bench. "I have no more questions for Mr. Josephson at this time, your Honor."

Judge Hubert Kripkin grunted and picked up his gavel, cradling it in his left hand. "Will you want to call Mr. Josephson back to the stand later, Mr. Westman?"

"I should like to reserve that option, your Honor, if he can keep himself available."

The judge nodded curtly. "Any further questions, Mr. Holland?"

Jack Holland, gray-faced and visibly shaken, remained seated. "No, your Honor. Not at this time."

Judge Kripkin drew back the sleeve of his robe and consulted his watch. "It's nearly noon, gentlemen. We'll break for lunch and resume at two o'clock."

30

Judith Stein spread a dab more horseradish on what was supposed to have been a hot roast-beef sandwich, taking painstaking care with the simple operation in order to avoid having to look at Jack Holland.

"That goddamn son of a bitch," Holland muttered between clenched teeth. "I'll get that son of a bitch if it's the last goddamn thing I ever do! How could that half-wit have been so goddamn stupid?"

Judith replaced the top half of the bun, then carefully cut the sandwich in two, using the dull knife as a miniature saw so the juices wouldn't squirt all over the sides of the flimsy paper plate and onto Holland's desk. She winced as the enraged district attorney slammed his fist into the wall next to the bookcase, rattling the collage of framed university degrees and elaborately scripted honors that he had collected over the years.

"He made us look like incompetent morons—do you know that, Stein? Morons! Months of work reduced to a pile of crap."

Judith moved a stack of files, widening the small space at the side of Holland's desk that she was using for her lunch. With great deliberation she unwrapped the kosher dill that had come with the now lukewarm roast-beef sandwich and placed it, too, on the plate. "Are you going to eat your lunch, Jack?" she asked mildly, still not looking up. "It's getting cold."

"Lunch? Who the hell can eat lunch at a time like this?" Holland stared down at her, bitterness etched into the lines around his mouth. "What is it with you,

Stein? You got ice water in your veins today? We've got a case that's going down the tubes and you're sitting there like this is some hoity-toity tea party!"

Judith sighed and dropped her hands to her lap. She wasn't hungry either, and Holland wasn't doing much to improve her appetite. Curious, this reversal of their roles. She was the one who would normally be ranting and raving around the office while Holland sat impassively behind the desk. Strange how the more the pressure built up inside Holland, the calmer she became.

There was no point, she decided, in trying to tell Holland that it was his own overriding need to see justice served that was largely responsible for this turn of events. If he hadn't pushed Josephson, and herself for that matter, so hard for a fast conviction, Josephson might not have felt the need to take such an irresponsible chance on trapping Mildred Phillips. But any comment along those lines would serve only to provoke another tirade, and she was growing weary of Holland's increasingly acrimonious outbursts.

Judith rewrapped the sandwich, paper plate and all, and put it back in the white paper sack in which it had come from the delicatessen. She finished off her coffee, tossed the Styrofoam cup and the bag in the wastebasket, and stood up.

"Where do you think you're going?" Holland demanded harshly.

She smoothed down her skirt and collected her handbag and briefcase. "To find Sergeant Ruminski," she answered simply, walking out the door before Jack Holland could respond.

Only a few minutes remained before the hearing was scheduled to reconvene when Judith finally tracked down Marilyn Ruminski in the ladies' washroom around the corner from the courtroom. She checked the stalls to make sure they were alone, then confronted the young policewoman in front of the washbasins.

"Why did you and Josephson lie to us about Mildred Phillips' statement?" Judith asked bluntly. "And the fact that she hadn't been read her rights until the interrogation was nearly over?"

Marilyn's mouth opened in surprise, but no sound came out. She had not been present in the courtroom, and Josephson had followed the judge's instructions for once and not discussed his testimony with her.

"Do you realize what you and Martin Josephson have done?" Judith asked again, keeping her voice low and firm. "You two have handed us a classic case of police entrapment. A woman guilty of murder will probably get off with nothing worse than a couple of weeks already spent in jail because you two tried to pull a fast one."

The policewoman, her mouth still working, sagged against the Formica counter. "But he told me . . ." she protested weakly.

"Told you what? That he'd get you kicked off the police force if you didn't go along with that cock-and-bull story about the interrogation being on the up-and-up?" Judith snorted. "I think you can begin counting your days left on the force anyway."

A small, shaky hand came up as though to fend Judith off. "He swore to me that he'd read her the Miranda warning before he brought her into the interrogation room! He said it wouldn't make any difference whether I heard him say it or not."

"So you went ahead and typed it on the statement, right? Along with that bit about confessing to complicity. Just the way he told you to?"

The young woman hung her head without answering.

"And you never once questioned the legality of what you were doing?" Judith pressed. "You never once questioned the wisdom of withholding vital information from the district attorney's office?"

"But he promised me . . ." Marilyn cried, tears springing to her eyes. "He said no one would ever know!"

"On the contrary, Marilyn," Judith replied tersely. "It would appear that everyone knew except Mr. Holland and myself! Now, pull yourself together and get ready to go in there when you're called."

"But how do I testify, Miss Stein?" she asked plaintively. "What do I tell them?"

Judith turned on the cold-water tap, dampened a

paper towel, and handed it to the young, frightened policewoman. "Just answer the questions truthfully, Marilyn. That's all we ever expected of you in the first place."

31

From Sergeant Ruminski's point of view, her time on the witness stand was mercifully brief. From Millie Phillips' viewpoint, however, the minutes spent listening to the policewoman's nasal, toneless recital were more like endless hours of unbearable suspense.

In response to Holland's terse questions, the policewoman reluctantly admitted that she had typed out Millie's statement according to specific instructions issued by Lieutenant Martin Josephson. The statement, she confirmed, did not reflect a precise presentation of the events as they had occurred during the interrogation.

"Mr. Westman, do you have any questions for the witness?" Judge Kripkin asked, pointedly staring at the distinguished attorney.

"I don't think that will be necessary, your Honor," Westman replied, a half-smile playing across his mouth. "Mr. Holland appears to have covered all the pertinent areas."

As soon as Judge Kripkin spoke the formal words of dismissal to the uniformed female officer, Millie became aware of a change in the courtroom atmosphere. It was the defense's turn to present its case, and every person in the room was waiting to see whether Carroll Westman would put Mildred Phillips on the stand.

Millie had protested vehemently, almost hysterically, when Westman first told her she would have to testify, whether she liked the idea or not. He'd ignored her every protest, patiently explaining that if the case did go to a full jury trial, the prosecution could seriously damage her position by making an issue out of the fact that she hadn't testified during the hearing. Millie didn't quite understand how that could be, but faced with the sheer power of Westman's implacable insistence, she seemed to have no choice other than to accept the inevitable.

Up to the moment Judge Kripkin instructed her to take the stand, Millie clung to the thin hope that her testimony wouldn't be needed, especially after Westman's skillful cross-examination of Martin Josephson had produced the desired results. Ignorant as she was about most legal procedures, Millie was quick enough to realize that once she was in that witness box, what she said, and how she said it, would strongly influence the judge's decision. And the judge's decision, in turn, would ultimately determine whether or not she stood trial as an accomplice to Ed's murder. Her entire future depended on convincing the judge to quash that confession. Yet she'd seen Carroll Westman make mincemeat out of Josephson's testimony. There was no guarantee that Jack Holland wouldn't do the same to hers.

Summoning whatever reserves of mental and emotional strength she had left, Millie entered the witness box and placed her hand on the Bible held out by the clerk, her voice quivering slightly as she solemnly swore to tell the truth to the best of her ability. The problem was, as Westman had demonstrated over the past weeks, that truth had many facets, and Millie couldn't always discern which facet would be the most effective.

Westman eased into the direct examination gently, leading Millie through a series of seemingly innocuous questions about her background, her home, and her family. As her responses grew stronger, more confident, Westman gradually moved into the more difficult questions.

"Millie," he asked with quiet sympathy, "when did you first learn of the death of your husband?"

"The night Detective Josephson called me at my parents' home. He told me Ed had been shot to death five days earlier."

"Did he tell you who killed Ed?"

"No."

"You returned home the following day, correct?"

"Yes." Millie tightly clenched her fists in her lap, anticipating the drift of Westman's questions.

"Was that also the day Mr. Josephson took you down to the morgue to identify your husband's body?"

"Yes."

"While you were at the morgue, were you shown a body other than your husband's?"

Tears flooded Millie's eyes at the unwanted memory of Ruth's battered and bloody face shrouded by the plastic body bag. "Yes," she whispered.

"Who was that second person, Millie?"

"Ruth Larkin," she answered simply.

Westman moved closer to the railing of the witness box, almost touching her. "You knew Ruth Larkin, didn't you? You recognized her?"

She lowered her eyes. "Yes."

"What happened then?"

When Millie raised them again to look at Westman, her large eyes were filled with tears and pain. "It was just too much of a shock all at once—having to identify Ed's body and then finding out that Ruth was dead. I'm afraid I fainted."

Westman glanced at Judge Kripkin out of the corner of his eye to make certain the jurist's full attention was directed at Millie, who was silently, but openly, weeping. "You say you fainted. But when you recovered consciousness, you denied knowing Ruth Larkin, did you not?"

"Yes, I did."

"Would you please tell the court why you denied knowing Ruth Larkin?"

Millie's hands fluttered open in a gesture of helplessness, one hand rising to her cheek to brush away the tears. "I'm not sure, really. Part of it was shock because I hadn't known she was dead, and part of it was fear, I think. I was upset and frightened—frightened that if they knew Ruth and I had been longtime friends, they might think I'd had something to do with that horrible thing she did . . . shooting my husband."

"So you lied?" Westman queried gently.

"Yes."

"Do you know why Ruth Larkin would want to shoot your husband?"

Jack Holland rose from his seat and advanced toward the bench. "Objection, your Honor. Counsel is asking the witness to surmise a motive for the deceased."

Westman stepped back from the witness box and addressed the judge. "Your Honor, I feel this question has a strong bearing on my client's actions, and reactions, to the events surrounding her husband's murder."

"Objection noted," Kripkin responded crisply. "However, I will allow the witness to answer."

Millie imagined she could hear Westman give a small sigh of relief as he repeated the question for her benefit. "Millie? Why did Ruth Larkin shoot your husband?"

"I can't say for certain, but just a few weeks before, her own husband, Hal Larkin, died of an accidental drug overdose," Millie replied slowly, weighing her words. "Ruth began acting very strangely after Hal's death, very withdrawn. I tried my best to help her, but there didn't seem to be anything I could do or say to reach her. She just got worse and worse."

Millie turned slightly and gazed earnestly at the judge, addressing him as though he were the only person in the courtroom. "For some time, several years in fact, my husband, Ed, had acted violently toward me. He beat me on many occasions. That was bad enough, but then he started in on my older daughter, Evelyn. Molesting her, I mean, not beating her. When Ruth found out what he was doing to Evelyn, she became even more upset. She'd always been extremely close to my children, more like a second mother than a friend, really. And she simply couldn't accept that Ed might be hurting one of them."

"Did Mrs. Larkin encourage you to take the children and leave your husband?" Westman asked, still keeping an eye on Judge Kripkin.

"Several times. I was afraid to, though. I tried that once and he followed us and threatened to kill me if I did it again." Millie suddenly stopped, realizing that she was beginning to speak too fast, her words running together. She looked nervously at Carroll Westman, who smiled encouragingly.

"Was Mrs. Larkin aware that you were taking the children to Louisiana to visit your family?"

"Yes." Millie nodded. "It was kind of a sudden, spur-of-the-moment trip. My father became ill and Ed agreed to let us go see him. The day we left I phoned Ruth to tell her I wouldn't be able to keep our luncheon date in the city the following day."

Westman straightened up and frowned thoughtfully. "So Mrs. Larkin was aware that you and the children were going to be out of town and that your husband was remaining home alone?"

"Yes."

"Did Mrs. Larkin ever threaten to kill your husband?"

Millie bowed her head for a moment, then raised it to look at Westman. "I never took her seriously. It was just talk. You know the way people say 'I could kill him for that'? Well, that was the sort of thing she said sometimes. I didn't think it meant anything. I certainly never expected her to go out and actually do it!"

And that, she told herself silently, was the truth. Down deep inside, she really hadn't expected Ruth to go through with the plan. How Ruth had ever gotten up enough nerve to shoot Ed in the face remained a complete mystery to Millie.

"Millie," Westman asked, carefully enunciating each word, "did you ask Ruth Larkin to kill your husband?"

Millie Phillips fixed a clear, steady gaze on Judge Kripkin. "No, sir. I did not."

And that was also the truth. Millie felt confident she could pass a lie-detector test on that one if she ever had to. Adrianna, not Millie, had decided that Ruth should kill Ed, and how she should do it. Millie had had no real say in that part of the agreement.

"I have no more questions at this time, your Honor."

As Carroll Westman painfully shuffled back to his seat at the defense table, Jack Holland slowly approached Millie, walked past the witness box, then turned suddenly to confront her face-to-face.

"Mrs. Phillips," he asked tersely, "your husband had a life-insurance policy, did he not?"

"I believe so, yes."

"I'd say you know so," he retorted dryly. "What was the value of that insurance policy?"

Millie was silent for a moment, as though trying to recall. "I believe it was two hundred and fifty thousand dollars."

"With a double-indemnity clause? Doubling that amount in the event of unnatural death?"

"I believe so, yes."

Holland restlessly paced up and down in front of the witness box. "When Ed Phillips took out that policy, whom did he name as beneficiary?"

"Me," Millie answered quietly.

The district attorney practically gloated as he passed in front of Millie. "Half a million dollars is a lot of money, isn't it?"

"Yes."

"You've already testified about the beatings your husband gave you, so I can safely assume that yours wasn't a particularly happy marriage?"

Millie stared helplessly at Carroll Westman, but he merely gestured at her to answer the question. "No," she said at last.

"At the time of Ed Phillips' death, were you aware that you were no longer your husband's beneficiary?"

"No."

"Who was?"

Millie sucked in her breath, then let it out slowly. "The insurance agent told me Ed had named his bookkeeper, Clarice Stuber."

"Did your husband and Miss Stuber have a close working relationship, Mrs. Phillips?"

"I have no idea," Millie answered irritably.

Holland turned and walked away from Millie. "Edward Phillips was not the father of your children, was he?"

"No. I was married previously and divorced."

"Did Edward Phillips legally adopt your children after your marriage?"

"No."

"What was your financial condition after your husband's death, Mrs. Phillips? Good, fair, poor?"

Millie stared at the hands in her lap. "Poor."

Holland returned to the witness box and rested his arm on the railing. "Would you mind elaborating on that, Mrs. Phillips? Exactly how poor?"

Carroll Westman raised his hand in objection, catching the judge's attention. "Your Honor, I fail to see what this line of questioning has to do with the issue at hand—the suppression of Mrs. Phillips' statement."

Jack Holland approached the bench, his hands open in explanation. "If you will bear with me, your Honor, I will demonstrate the point of all of this in a moment."

Judge Kripkin nodded. "All right, Mr. Holland. I will permit the witness to explain her financial situation. Go ahead, Mrs. Phillips."

She again looked to Westman for help, but saw him give a little shrug of resignation. "After Ed's death, I found I was virtually broke. We'd been living up to the limit of his income, and in a few instances beyond it," she said with a small tremor in her voice. "We had first and second mortgages on the house, heavy installment loans on the cars, and practically no savings at all. What little there was, I have sent to my mother to help care for the children. The bank is in the process of foreclosing on the rest."

Holland was almost beginning to look pleased. "So in essence, Mrs. Phillips, if your husband had decided to leave you, say, for Miss Stuber, you could have expected very little in the way of a divorce settlement, and absolutely nothing for child support. Am I correct?"

Millie refused to meet Holland's gaze. Instead, she kept her eyes fixed on her hands, twisting the simple gold wedding band she still wore. "I suppose so, but the question never came up. He never said anything about leaving me, for Miss Stuber or anyone else."

"By the same token, if you had wanted to leave your husband, you still wouldn't have received anything. Is that correct? Your husband's only major financial asset was that insurance policy, was it not? With its attractive half-million-dollar double-indemnity clause?"

"Your Honor, I really must protest this line of questioning. Mr. Holland's insinuations are outrageous!" The arthritic attorney had levered himself to his feet and was starting toward the bench when Holland shot him a triumphant grin and backed away from the witness box.

"I don't think Mrs. Phillips has to answer that if she doesn't want to, your Honor," Holland replied smoothly. "I think we can all guess what the answer is."

"Mr. Holland!" Judge Kripkin warned sharply, glaring down at him from the bench, "this is a courtroom, not a barroom." He turned to the court reporter and ordered her to strike the district attorney's last comment from the record. "You may proceed, Mr. Holland," he said, "if you can do so with some decorum."

Jack Holland signaled his assent and strode back to where Judith Stein sat silently at the prosecution's table. He picked up a sheaf of papers and returned to where Millie sat nervously pulling her wedding ring off and on.

"Mrs. Phillips, I believe you have already identified Exhibit A as being your statement. Would you please do so again with this copy?" He handed her the papers and waited until she'd finished going through them.

"Yes, this is the statement."

Holland rocked back and forth on the balls of his feet, his hands clasped behind his back. "Mr. Westman has made an issue of the fact that you were not represented by an attorney when you gave that statement." He stopped rocking and stared at Millie. "Mrs. Phillips, do you ever watch television?"

Millie's eyes widened in surprise. "Television?"

"Yes, do you watch television?"

"Sometimes."

Holland smiled at her reassuringly. "At the risk of sounding facetious and angering the court, do you ever watch cops-and-robbers shows on television?"

Millie nodded hesitantly, not certain what Holland was driving at. "I suppose so."

"Then you have probably heard, more than once, the

famous Miranda warning that all police officers are now required to read? The one that goes: 'You have the right to remain silent. Anything you say can and will be held against you in a court of law. You have the right to an attorney and have your attorney present during questioning. If you cannot afford an attorney, one will be appointed for you by the court.'" Holland paused. "Does that refresh your memory, Mrs. Phillips?"

Millie again looked beseechingly at Westman, but to no avail. "Yes, I've heard that," she said in a voice that was scarcely more than a whisper.

"So you were aware that you had the right to ask for an attorney, then?"

Millie's eyes locked with Holland's. "No, I wasn't," she corrected him.

Now it was Holland's turn to react with surprise. "You weren't? But you've just admitted you've heard the warning a number of times on television!"

"That's true," she replied evenly. "But on those shows, the police only read those rights to people when they're arresting them."

"So?"

"Detective Josephson never told me I was under arrest. So how was I to know I needed an attorney?"

The courtroom exploded into laughter as Jack Holland angrily stalked back to his seat, flinging the papers across the table. "I have no further questions, your Honor," he said stiffly.

The judge, vainly trying to suppress his own smile of amusement, looked toward Carroll Westman. The courtly attorney returned his look with a broad grin, then stood up behind the table. "I have no further questions for Mrs. Phillips," he said genially, "but I would like to recall Mr. Josephson, if I might."

A glowering Martin Josephson returned to the stand, sitting hunched over and sullen on the hard chair. He refused to acknowledge Westman's shuffling approach until the defense attorney was just inches away.

"Mr. Josephson," he began casually, "we've heard quite a bit of testimony today indicating that the . . . er, procedure you used to obtain this statement from

Mrs. Phillips was not quite what you would call ortho-dox. What we have not yet discussed, however, was Mrs. Phillips' state of mind during the interrogation." Westman braced himself against the railing, easing the weight on one leg. "Mr. Josephson, how did Mrs. Phillips act during the interrogation? Did she seem to com-prehend what was going on?"

Josephson shifted around on the chair, unable to find a comfortable position. "I would say so, yes. She seemed all right to me."

Westman rubbed his chin with his free hand. "She seemed all right, you say? Then let me ask you this: after the interrogation had ended and she had signed the statement, what did Mildred Phillips say? Didn't she ask you a question at that point?"

Josephson ducked his head, keeping his eyes down. "She said she was tired," he answered reluctantly. "Then she asked me to take her home."

Westman straightened up and moved back a step from the witness box. "Is that the sort of response you would normally expect from a person who has just confessed to complicity in the murder of her husband?"

Josephson shook his head slowly. "No."

"Mr. Josephson," Westman said sternly, his strong voice ringing through the courtroom, "did Mrs. Phillips, at any time during that interrogation, in fact state that she and Ruth Larkin together planned the murder of Ed Phillips?"

The young officer, his police career in ruins, sank even lower. "Not in so many words," he mumbled.

"In any words at all?" Westman pressed.

"No."

"I have no further questions, your Honor," Westman responded, turning his back on Martin Josephson.

The judge, with even more solemnity than he usually demonstrated, announced a brief recess and abruptly disappeared through the door behind the bench. When he just as abruptly reappeared twenty-five agonizing minutes later, he carried a single sheet of paper in his hand.

"The court has duly considered the testimony heard

here today," he intoned slowly, precisely enunciating each syllable, "and has reached a decision. A decision which, in light of the many recent court rulings regarding the conduct of law-enforcement officers, should have not been necessary."

Kripkin paused and peered over the top of the paper, then resumed. "The court holds that the written statement signed by the defendant, Mildred Phillips, is inadmissible, and accordingly suppressed."

As the courtroom erupted into pandemonium, a tall woman clad in a nondescript coat, head scarf, and thick horn-rimmed glasses slipped from a back-row seat and, unobserved by anyone except the bailiff, squeezed out through the heavy double doors.

32

Judith Stein unaccountably found herself standing at the top of the courthouse steps, next to Carroll Westman, as a jubilant and radiant Mildred Phillips walked alone through the crowd of newsmen and well-wishers toward the dark blue limousine waiting at the curb.

"Don't feel too badly, my dear," Westman said, placing a friendly hand on her shoulder. "You did a splendid job on the background work. I was most impressed. But even the best of us loses a case occasionally."

Judith started in surprise and turned to face the rotund gentleman who was hardly much taller than she. The assistant district attorney hadn't known that Westman was even aware of her presence in the courtroom, much less her contributions in putting the Phillips case together.

"It was an interesting experience, don't you think?" Westman continued smoothly. "The sort of case we dedicated attorneys-at-law just hate to give up on."

"Oh, I'm not giving up," Judith replied serenely, watching as Millie Phillips worked her way closer to the waiting limousine. "Someday, somehow, I will know the full story of what really happened to Edward Phillips. And to Harold Larkin and John Farrelly. You can be sure of that."

There was almost a thaw in Westman's wintry gray eyes. "I do believe you will, my dear. I do believe you will!"

As the rear door of the limousine opened and Millie

Phillips started to climb in, Judith caught a brief glimpse of Adrianna Farrelly leaning forward, stretching out an elegant white hand to aid her.

"And if I were Mildred Phillips," Judith added quietly, "I would spend the remaining days of my life looking over my shoulder and wondering when Adrianna Farrelly was going to plunge the fatal knife between my ribs."

Carroll C. Westman threw back his head and laughed, a long, loud laugh of genuine pleasure. Then, with an old-fashioned gallantry he hadn't used since his youth, he twirled his cane, offered the young woman his arm, and escorted her down the broad courthouse steps.

About the Authors

Sarah L. McMurry is a professional journalist who has worked as a writer/reporter for United Press International and CBS Radio. She is currently associate editor of three medical magazines.

Francesco P. Lualdi is a publishing veteran who got his start at *Look* magazine and Dell Publications, and was publisher of Popular Library for 15 years. At present he is Editorial Director of Rhodes Geographic Library, Inc.

GIRLS IN HIGH PLACES

A NOVEL BY
Sugar Rautbord
and
Elizabeth Nickles

*A glitzy, fast-paced novel of high-finance,
high-society, and high-infidelity . . .*

In this dizzying woman's-eye-view of love and
luxury at the top—by two authors who've been
there—three of the world's brightest, most
glamorous women hitch their wildest ambitions and
fiery passions to one very attractive rising star—
dazzlingly rich CEO Graham Donaldson. And
although the fallout from corporate intrigue, a
kidnapping, and plain old raw treachery sometimes
collides with their meteoric success, Catherine,
Eve, and Bambi agree that while power and money
may not buy happiness, it can come oh so close. . . .

Coming in January
From NAL Hardcover Books